2 95

BY ALL WE HOLD DEAR

SUSAN EVANS McCLOUD

BY ALL WE HOLD DEAR

A N O V E L

BOOKCRAFT
Salt Lake City, Utah

Copyright © 1983 by Bookcraft, Inc.

Library of Congress Catalog Card Number: 83-72681
ISBN O-88494-507-3

2 3 4 5 6 7 8 9 10   89 88 87 86 85

Lithographed in the United States of America
PUBLISHERS PRESS
Salt Lake City, Utah

This one is for Heather Brittan,
who has suffered long in her exile—
standing against the "cold, dark world"
alone.

Acknowledgments

I would like to extend grateful acknowledgment to Harlow Smoot, Gregory Seal, and Jack Johnson for their special help and support in preparation of this manuscript. Thanks also to Grant Kinick, whose contributions to this project were unique.

I owe a special debt to the captain and crew of the *Mississippi Queen* and to the people of Natchez and Rosedown, who carried the spirit of antebellum Dixie into today so that I, and I hope my readers, might breathe of its fragrance and be enriched by its pathos and beauty.

_Prologue

James Ellis closed the door to his study and turned the key. He needed to be alone for a few moments—collect his thoughts, get a hold on himself. He had served as stake president for a year and a half now and been bishop twice before. He was used to sending boys off on missions. But never a boy of his own. Until now.

Jamie was his only son and he had come later, after five daughters—beautiful daughters. He fancied himself a natural father for girls. He had always been at ease around women, relished their company, known how to humor their whims. So he'd thought perhaps there was no son in the offing. And yet he had wanted someone to bear his name—someone to pass his priesthood on to.

And the son had come: one boy, all his eggs in one basket. James Gordon Ellis, Jr.: honor student, track star, German scholar, bagpipe player, and history buff—a sensitive boy and a natural leader; James Gordon Ellis: deacon, teacher, priest—now elder in the Melchizedek Priesthood, and missionary.

James himself had never served a mission. When he was nineteen he had known nothing about the Mormons. At twenty-four, in his last year at George Washington Law School, he had made a discovery that changed his life: One of his classmates, a young man he quite admired, whose company he enjoyed, was a Latter-day Saint. Once the discovery was made he asked curious questions, innocent questions. . . . He smiled, remembering—though, actually, those early memories were quite painful.

He walked over to one of the shelves and reached a little to pull down a small, slender volume, very old. He sat in his favorite chair and opened the book. The leather creaked in protest under his hand. Gingerly he smoothed the yellowed pages.

How many times through the years, he thought, *have I done this? Opened this little volume in search of answers, and found only silence. The silence of age and time.*

He drew out the faded daguerreotype. The worn features looked out at him: the full, provocative smile, the lovely Grecian nose, the high delicate cheekbones, masses of dark silken curls, and those wonderful eyes that gazed into his, seeming both sad and dreamy, but harboring something deeper that made them alive, a mirror to the lost girl who had lived behind them. As a young man he'd imagined himself half in love with this woman, though in fact she was his great-great-grandmother.

He turned the picture over. On the back in fine writing, faded but still discernible, were the words:

Angeline Gordon

age 18

1843

Natchez, Mississippi

Jamie had been called to the Mississippi Jackson Mission, which encompassed parts of Louisiana, Shreveport, Jackson—and Natchez, Mississippi.

James looked down at the book in his hands and read on the fly-leaf, written in almost a childlike scrawl:

Fletcher Gordon

Natchez—

Beyond that, silence.

Still holding the book he walked to the window, his memories suddenly vivid and very real. His friend had arranged a meeting with the missionaries and they, of course, had begun to teach him the lessons. He wasn't a golden contact by any means. He was busy with his own life and, he thought, quite contented. He was in love with a beautiful girl and next year, after law school, he would join the exclusive firm of McClellan & Stewart. He had his future all mapped out—or so he had thought . . .

But bit by bit the truth penetrated his spirit and with it the realization that here was *commitment* in a way he had never imagined before. He knew what it was to discipline his nature, work hard for something, follow a tough set of rules: He was fifth in his class, always a high achiever. So perhaps it wasn't only the degree of commitment: Mormonism represented an entire new way of life.

He had pondered that thought and then ignored it for as long as he could, not mentioning his interest to anyone in his family. But Sydney was different. Sydney would share his life. And if his life ended up including Mormonism . . .

He remembered that last spring day they had spent together. They sailed in the morning, then picnicked along the Sound on a sandy stretch in the lee of a promontory, free from the wind but still soothed by the ocean's dim roar.

She had opened a hamper of food and he bent to help her, trying to sound conversational, merely casual as he told of his sessions with the Mormon elders. She had laughed at him, even cracking a joke or two—the old, tired jokes about Brigham Young and polygamy.

"Those are history book leftovers, Sydney," he had chided. "Mormonism contains some very plausible explanations, some exciting possibilities."

She had cocked her head, her blonde hair falling like seaweed, silken against her bare shoulders. "James, don't tell me you're *serious* about this in any way."

"I am. Did you know that the Mormons have a prophet and a priesthood where every man, every worthy male, is given authority, Sydney—"

She interrupted, uncorking a bottle of wine and pouring a glass, then purposefully handing it to him with a smile. "Did you know, James, that the Mormons are terribly stodgy? They don't smoke, or drink—" she ran a slim finger along her own wine glass— "and they certainly don't spend their Sunday mornings out sailing, then show up at the country club for afternoon cocktails."

He had tried once more, explaining to her the concept of eternal progression, of life before life on earth.

"It stretches your mind to try and comprehend it." He could

remember how deeply excited he had felt, how intense had been his desire to reach her. "There's so much depth and dignity in it, Sydney."

She had stared up at him with innocent, wide blue eyes. "I can't see it, James. It's a bunch of religious nonsense." She shook her head and the blonde hair shimmered. "Forget it, James dear, it's certainly not for *us!*"

Not for us. She had meant not for *me*, and he knew it. He had known all along how terribly spoiled Sydney was. But she was warm and fun and clever and very lovely—a classy kind of girl that a man could be proud of . . .

He had taken her home early, intending to work on a paper, but instead he had opened the scriptures and started to read. But he knew where his reading, where his thinking would lead him. He went for a drive, a long drive, then walked by the seashore. Walked and walked. Then, taking off shoes and stockings, he ran along the sand till he fell in exhaustion.

There on the edge of the sea and the sky there was no more hiding. He knelt in prayer. He knew what he had to do. And when he rose to his feet he knew he would do it. He had made up his mind and nothing would stand in his way. No thing—no person—no matter what pain it cost him.

And yet there was something missing. Some awful, aching emptiness inside. It took him a while, but he put his finger on it. He was missing the satisfaction, the sureness—the joy.

Perhaps if he stood back from it all, got away for a few days . . . He packed a bag and went home to his mother's house for the weekend—the old house in Philadelphia where he'd been born.

His sister, Lynda, was there with his mother and they welcomed him warmly. They knew nothing of the trial he was going through. That ought to have been some relief, but it ate at his conscience. *One day I'll have to tell them, and what will they do?* Would they be ashamed, afraid to tell the neighbors? Or would they laugh at him condescendingly as Sydney had done?

But oh, it was so sane here, so wonderfully normal. He could bask in that for a while, just to coat the pain.

It was the weekend his mother began her spring cleaning. "I warned you," she said, as she handed him a broom. "Cobwebs."

"Cobwebs?" he echoed.

"Upstairs in the attic."

He followed them up. He enjoyed working with his mother. Even drudgery couldn't be dull when attacked with her spirit. The three reminisced as they worked, surrounded as they were by such an accumulation of old reminders.

"There are so many things stored up here that I'd like to have. May I start filling a box?" Lynda asked.

His mother nodded. "As long as you cart them off to your own apartment. If you leave them downstairs they'll end up right back here again."

They worked for a while and their happy chatter suddenly made James feel lonely and somewhat removed. *I might ruin all this*, he thought, *by what I'm planning to do.*

"Here's something you might like, James. You're the history enthusiast." His mother pushed back a lock of brown hair with a dusty finger and handed him a small book. He turned it over. *Book of Mormon* he read in faded gold lettering. Emotion rose in his throat. He traced the faint letters. "Where did this come from?" he asked.

"Heavens, I don't know. It's been in the family as long as I can remember. Well, look inside—" She wiped her hands on her apron and opened the leather cover. The daguerreotype was there. She blew on it. "Yes, of course. That's—let's see—your great-great-grandmother. You know, James, the one mixed up in the Civil War, lived on some Natchez plantation . . ."

Lynda came over, bent close to take a look. "She's a beauty, isn't she? Why didn't I turn out that pretty?"

"Was she a Mormon?" James asked.

His mother had gone back to her sorting. "Heavens, I don't believe so."

"Then why the book? Not very many families back then owned a Book of Mormon."

"I'm sure you're right. Well, it's yours if you want it."

"I do." He picked up an old rag and dusted the cover. "I think I'll take it down to my room right now. I need a break."

They looked at him rather strangely, but he smiled and added, "I'll bring back some cold lemonade."

It had come. When he handled the book it had rushed in upon him. The joy he had been waiting for. *Strange*, he pondered, *the power unlocked by a picture and an old book* . . .

That was so many years ago. Before he met Katie. Even now he could tremble to think of a life without Katie, of what he would have missed if she had not been his wife. Tears came to his eyes and he didn't try to stop them. If he'd only known what blessings the gospel would bring. He would never have feared then, or wondered, or hesitated.

On and off through the years he had searched, but he came up with nothing. The Civil War had played havoc with what few records there were. There was no mention anywhere in the Church archives of an Angeline Gordon. Or of Fletcher. He had very few dates, and even less information.

It was strange how it bothered him still, how the feeling ate at him that something was missing, some pieces were out of place. Perhaps now with Jamie going right there to Natchez, back where it happened, back where the beautiful girl had been more than a photograph, brittle and faded . . .

There was a knock on the door. He set the book on the table beside him and rose a little heavily. "I'm coming," he called.

"It's just me, dad." The voice was Jamie's. James opened the door and smiled at the tall young man who stood waiting.

"I was just going to go out and find you. Come in here, Jamie. I have something I'd like to give you, son . . ."

6

Book One

Natchez, Mississippi
1842-1844

One

The evening was mild, the air warm with that velvet softness characteristic of the country known as "the Natchez." The two brothers rode together, "for companionship," as Hamilton put it. But he said it with a glint in his eye; each knew that he made poor, incompatible company for the other. Yet here on the edge of spring, on the edge of the bluff overlooking the sweep of river far below, watching the night sift down with a gray, soft settling, there was a peace that even the brothers could not ignore. And beauty. Nothing was fair as the Natchez country, and pride for her ran in the veins of her native sons. The flags of four nations had flown from the bluffs of Natchez and the frenzies of conquest, the passions and fears of struggle had worked into the very soil of the place. Dreams do not die as easily as men do. And Natchez was a conglomeration of dreams, a beacon set on a hill, a proud voice crying, "Men can live like kings. Men can make their dreams come true."

Young Aubrey Stewart and his brother, Hamilton, riding along Cemetery Road toward the approach of the city, were part of a dream that had flowered for men to see. The oldest settlement built on the Mississippi, dating back to the dateless days of old Indian tribes, now boasted more millionaires than any other American city. Millions made from the boll of the puffed white cotton and the labor of men and women whose skin was black.

They turned right where Clifton Street ran into Cemetery, drawing a little closer here to the river. Hamilton breathed in deeply; the river air could be an intoxication to certain men.

"It's too splendid a night to be stifled with fans and flounces. Why don't you come on down the line with me?"

There was a hint of gentle mockery in the question, a mockery that danced in the blue-gray eyes. But Aubrey didn't look up to answer his brother.

"Come, come, little brother, you're brooding on something tonight."

This banter between them was something that Aubrey hated. He had learned very early not to try to best his brother; if he did the barbs would grow sharp, deep enough to hurt. So he'd taken instead to this sullen-seeming withdrawal, while actually he was seething inside. And tonight his brother had struck too close to the truth. He was restive with spring, in his mind and his body—aching for action, for freedom, fresh air. Yet he was committed, with no way out. And the prospect of hours spent with adoring females— smiling and paying compliments not truly meant, playing the games that society decreed—sat hard with him, and knowing his brother knew it—

"All right. What if I came?" he said suddenly.

"If you came? I'd be delighted. I'd make sure you were introduced to some real women, Aubrey, not bloodsuckers like your 'ladies' up on the hill." Hamilton leaned forward in the saddle and the gleam in his eye betrayed him. "Coming, then?"

Aubrey hesitated, glancing down.

"That's right, we wouldn't want to rob the young belles of one of their richest prospects, now, would we?"

They had reached the point where Broadway crossed Market and Market Street wound its way on down the hill, becoming Silver Street, going under Natchez to the narrow mud flats where the river licked the land. Natchez-Under-the-Hill where clustered the gambling dens, dance halls, barrooms, houses of harlots, and where it was boasted anyone could get away with anything if he had a quick trigger finger or hard enough fists to back him.

"It wouldn't work for you, Aubrey." Hamilton's voice was a little kinder. "You're too worried about becoming corrupted. You wouldn't see that I'd given you anything. Just taken something away, that's how you'd see it."

10

Aubrey pulled his mount to a stop, watching as his brother slowed and took the curve that led to the river. Hamilton turned in his saddle with a grin. "Now, yon hill folk, they live with their heads in the clouds." He murmured the words, and his tone was lazy, honeyed. "That's the place for you, brother. Farewell. Have a pleasant evening."

Aubrey watched his brother, his feelings cold within him. With Hamilton he always felt less of a man—awkward, stumbling, dull beside him. Yet he was the heir to Lairdswood, not his brother. He knew crops and machinery, horses and slaves. He was respected by wealthy planters—and he was their equal!

He talked himself up as he turned his horse toward the city. But he knew inside that even if all were true, there was something lacking, some confidence within him. Or perhaps a hardness; perhaps that was what he lacked. He wished he knew. He gazed at the clean, white city. "Head in the clouds," Hamilton had said. Natchez had her head in the clouds this evening and they painted a golden rosiness over her streets, running along the columns of tall brick mansions, pricking with shimmers the glossed picket fence lines—warm and alive, like a light from another world. The beauty caught in his throat; he urged his horse forward, the beauty drawing him like a spell.

Angeline moved away. It was hard to breathe here. She felt suffocated by the giggling, gay-skirted girls, chattering with bright flushed cheeks together. She had never been quite at ease in this kind of company.

"Angeline!" Dyanne's voice laughed out to reach her. "Don't you dare run off and disappear into some corner. There are half a dozen young gentlemen yet to meet."

There were dimples by Dyanne's full mouth and her eyes were shining. She was in her element flirting and entertaining. She drew her friend close and whispered, her young voice silken. "The best are yet to arrive, dear. Hugh McAlister and his brother Henry, and that adorable Gilbert Grant. You know, Gilbert's daddy is buildin' a simply outrageous mansion out Windy Hill way. They say it's meant for his son and his bride when they marry."

It was all very serious business to Dyanne. Angeline tried to look duly impressed and attentive.

"Oh, and Aubrey Stewart. I don't believe Aubrey's arrived. My gracious, honey, perk up a little." Dyanne bent and hugged Angeline and her blue eyes widened. "Why, here's Gilbert Grant this minute."

Dyanne turned, her entire body eager and graceful as she swept across the room to greet her guest.

Angeline knew she was expected to follow, but she moved in the other direction toward the veranda where the arched French doors stood open and inviting. It wasn't that she was antisocial. It was more that she wasn't acquainted with all the fine points, the subtleties and perfections of being a belle. Perhaps if she had a mother to tutor and push her. She smiled to herself; it didn't appeal to her senses, this careful, practiced, learned coquetry. And besides, she didn't have much to offer—not as a prospective bride for "the county's best," as Dyanne called them in her light, irresistible way. She didn't expect to land that kind of a marriage. Her house was too small and her father too unimportant. And she had no connections; connections, above all, mattered.

She reached the doors. The soft evening air was fragrant, a caress against her skin and in her hair.

Unconsciously she held her head up higher, tasting the air, as some men taste their wine. Aubrey watched her. She had a look about her, a way that seemed different, spontaneous, spirited. That word came to his mind in the passing instant it took her to cross the veranda and reach the stairs.

"May I?" He reached her side, his hand extended.

She looked up flushed, surprised by his presence. "I was just . . . well yes, thank you."

He helped her descend the stairs. She drew her small hand carefully away. Something about his closeness discomfited her. He could sense that and it gave him a surge of elation. He realized then that she wasn't simpering and flirting, but gazing back at him with clear, uncertain eyes.

"Thank you, Mr. Stewart." Her voice was gentle.

"You have the advantage of me. I'm afraid I don't have the pleasure of your acquaintance." He paused and looked very

12

expediently around, but his eyes returning to hers held a merriment in them. "I fear there is no one to properly introduce us."

Angeline smiled at the thoughts that tumbled inside her. Not quite meaning to she expressed them aloud. "Yes, and what's more, you have somehow escaped Dyanne's notice. She doesn't believe you've arrived yet, Aubrey Stewart. She will be most upset to discover your clever evasion."

"It wasn't as wicked a thing as you make it sound." He furrowed his brow in mock consternation. He felt a sense of conspiracy with this girl. It was a wonder, this freedom, this honesty between them. "I just couldn't face the ordeal of introductions, and promising dances and carrying cakes and punch—"

Her laughter was warm and deep, as sincere as her eyes. "It's spring, I believe. She sows mischief in the air. I feel it myself."

She turned and they both began walking, away from the house to where brick-set, flower-edged pathways meandered in well-planned abandon through the gardens that were Dyanne's mother's pride and joy. They were lovely gardens, but tonight they were only a backdrop, their beauty and fragrance a spice to the excitement that would have surged into existence without them there.

They found a seat, half-concealed behind yellow forsythia. She didn't bother to spread her skirts carefully, but sat with a natural ease beside him.

"Your name, I don't yet know your name." Aubrey longed to touch her, to draw up the little hand that rested so near.

"I am Angeline Gordon. My father practices law here. In one of the less ostentatious firms on the Row. I'm Dyanne's best friend; she includes me in all her occasions."

Aubrey regarded her intently with warm brown eyes. He felt light-headed, intoxicated. He had never been a rebel before—never said what he was thinking, done what he'd wanted. Though the younger son, he had early taken a role of being responsible, someone to depend on. *Docile,* Hamilton called it. Well, that was all right. It had given him lands and property, given him power. Why had he never seen it that way before?

"Should we go back?" She was sorry as soon as she said it. But the brown eyes were causing a tingling under her skin and a burning inside that left her breathless.

"Most definitely we should. But does that matter? Is that what you want to do, Miss Angeline?"

He waited for her reply. She could hear his breathing. Slowly she began to shake her head. "I'd like to stay in the garden and talk with you."

It was that simple. They sat behind the forsythia and nothing existed save the spring night and each other.

Two

It was early afternoon and the hours were dragging. Angeline fidgeted under Dyanne's sharp gaze. She'd felt empty all day, as though she were missing something. The excitement of last night still clung to her, like a fairy garb that no other eyes could see. And the contrast of the day's ordinary hours left her feeling restless and discontent.

"The tongues are wagging, they surely are wagging, honey." Dyanne's voice held reproach, but her eyes were bright with interest. "Alone all that time together, and nobody knowing. That wasn't very prudent, Angeline."

Dyanne's accents were richly stressed, like all else about her; there was something so intense about Dyanne. She seemed to wither the magic, reduce it to tatters. Angeline made an effort, struggling to snatch back the fragile dream.

"It was wonderful, Dy. It wasn't meant to be prudent."

"Angeline Gordon! How frightfully naive."

"Why? There was nothing wrong about it. We just—"

"Proper!" The word burst forth from shocked indignation. "My goodness, nobody said you were wicked." The lines around Dyanne's round eyes crinkled up with mischief. "Proper's much more important than wicked, honey."

Angeline stared back, feeling vaguely rebellious. Dyanne, watching her, sighed and shook her head.

"It's how you get *along*, you know that, Angie." She talked as though she were instructing a willful child, a child who stubbornly refused to learn. "There are women men marry and women they . . . dally with. You must do nothing in public to compromise your position."

Dyanne took a sip of peppermint tea and leaned slightly closer. "Especially with Aubrey Stewart. You know his older brother's reputation. You don't want smudges on your good name, Angie."

Dyanne settled back; she was pleased with her own instructions. Angeline sat facing her, feeling even more empty inside.

The two honey mares, the color of straw in the sunlight, drew the light buggy as though it weighed nothing at all. Aubrey, holding the reins, felt exhilarated. There was the smell of fresh earth in his nostrils and wind in his hair, fingers of wind like the fingers he'd touched last evening, cool fingers that had lain like silk against his hand. Aubrey knew what he was doing and he was happy. For the first time in years he really wanted something, and he was determined to have his way. He had made a pleasant discovery and it thrilled him: What he wanted was good and right and within his grasp.

Aubrey slowed the horses and drew up before Harmony House. Angeline had been modest; the house was lovely—fine elegant lines, more substantial than he had expected. But the house could have been a shanty, a clapboard cabin. It made no difference to Aubrey at all.

He alighted and began to approach the house. But the sound of voices slowed his step—light, feminine voices floating over the air. He found the girls at the edge of the small back garden where the yard sloped broad and unbroken to curve down the bluff and end where the river snaked silently on its way, weaving like a ribbon along the land. Angeline was gazing down at the river, watching the sparkles of water that caught the sunlight. The river seemed full of joy at its own existence, the way she had felt last night when she looked at Aubrey and saw the sparkles of pleasure in his eyes.

Dyanne was chattering on; she pretended to listen. But she closed her eyes for a moment, just to remember.

She opened them, aware of the sudden silence. Then aware the next instant of something, something else. Drawn, and yet dreading, she turned.

He stood close beside her. She noticed that the sun streaked his hair with brushes of bright auburn, she noticed that his skin was brown and tanned. But his dark eyes stood out in his face, deep and compelling, overshadowing every other feature. They smiled now, and she realized he was speaking.

". . . give me great pleasure, Miss Angeline, if you would accept my invitation. Lairdswood would be honored by your presence."

"You should ask her properly—she isn't dressed. You should have sent word ahead!" Dyanne fairly bristled.

"But I can assure you my intentions are most honorable. I give you the word of a gentleman on that."

Dyanne was disarmed, Angeline enchanted. The excitement she felt was bubbling over now. He gave her his arm. Dyanne said nothing, and Angeline walked with her eyes straight ahead. And a few moments later her friend was forgotten. There was so much more to be wondering over now.

She had heard of Lairdswood. It was one of the large plantations known for its grandeur but also for its taste. Aubrey explained to her as they approached it how his great-grandfather had initially settled a three-hundred-acre tract with a mortgaged team and half a dozen Negroes. He had first arrived in South Carolina, a dispossessed small farmer from the Scottish highlands, robbed of his livelihood there by the expansion of sheep grazing, and other measures enacted by the infamous English Duke of Cumberland. He carried a burden of bitterness in his heart, unwilling to accept Culloden and the defeat of the Bonnie Prince, then the ensuing breakup of the clan system. It took the pulse and the breath out of Scotland, he said.

But here he had found enough challenge to sink his teeth into. Knowing how to work and how to manage he had nurtured small holdings into larger ones; with each successful crop he acquired more. His son, Duncan, was drawn by the lure of the Natchez country, claiming it to be closer to paradise than anything he'd ever seen. First he settled close to the thriving town, then moved his home further out as his holdings increased. It was he who built the original wing of Lairdswood, who gave it name and identity. In Scotland it was only the large landowners, the "lairds" or lords, who dominated the land. But he, the son of a humble highland farmer, was now "laird" in a manner the Scottish clans never dreamed of.

It was a romantic beginning, but most of the planter barons had romantic stories somewhere along the line. Angeline knew, from information that circulated, that Aubrey's father, Samuel, had wooed and married Miss Eliza Bragg, Charleston's "Belle of the Year," and brought her back to an enlarged and elegant Lairdswood to be mistress of the manor and bear his sons. So tragic that Samuel had met an untimely death, too bad that Eliza—but that Angeline didn't know, only vague rumors, nothing for certain. Perhaps today she might discover . . .

The carriage rounded an easy curve in the road. Opening before their eyes spread an avenue, broad and straight, and lining it on both sides stretched rows of oak trees arching to meet each other, touching with graceful fingers across the path. From their branches draped the familiar Spanish moss, soft green and shimmering gently in the sunlight. Angeline was accustomed to beauty, but she drew in her breath at the startling perfection of the sight.

"The live oak have been here as long as the estate has," Aubrey told her. "My grandfather planted them just as the century turned."

"I've never seen anything like it." Her voice was a murmur.

Aubrey leaned close and slowed the horses. "Here is Lairdswood, Miss Angeline. She's been waiting for you to come."

He shouldn't have said it, he shouldn't have said those words. Idly chosen, perhaps, but they seared into her, like a prophecy, like a fate that was meant to arrive. For already some deep response had awakened within her. And the house that sat like a lady with skirts finely spread, watching them from the end of the alley, spoke to her, as one spirit would to another.

There was a boy to take the horses as soon as they stopped. Aubrey was holding her hand and helping her down, then up to the long white porch and into a chair. There was shade here and the view still stretched before them. A large black woman came with a laden tray. There were cool mint juleps to drink. Angie took a long sip. The liquid was both smooth and sharp, sweet and biting.

"Thank you, Hester," she heard Aubrey saying. "That will be all now." He turned and faced Angeline. "Are you really that taken, Miss Angeline?"

He was smiling at her. His voice held a boyish pleasure.

"Yes, I am. I wish I had known your father."

"My father?"

"He built and planned this, didn't he? But then, those gardens I'm just beginning to notice, the air of peace and order, that must be your mother. May I meet her?"

He paused. She could feel his pausing.

"My mother . . . she's indisposed—she—she's not receiving." He took a deep breath and plunged on. "What you've heard of my mother is true. She's only a shadow of the woman she used to be. I wish you could have known her . . . before."

Angeline reached for his hand without even knowing, instinctively, as she would to a wounded child. "Show me the parts of Lairdswood you like the best, please."

He began to protest, but she insisted, with a sparkling determination in her eyes. He gave in and took her hand. "You may be sorry."

"I don't believe so," she answered, and meant it.

He took her first to the stables and the horses, introduced her to his favorite mare, telling her with pride that she'd even won some purses. "Minor purses," he hastened to make clear. "I've never been allowed to really indulge."

"Do you always do only the things you are allowed?"

The question sounded saucy, but Aubrey ignored it. He showed her the tack room, the saddles that were his favorites, the liniments used to rub down the horses' legs, all the interesting accoutrements so foreign to her.

"You're indulgent with your horses," she teased him.

"Heavens no," he replied. "Henry Chotard could be called indulgent. I'm only a careful husbandman."

They laughed together, both familiar with the stories of Chotard's magnificent stables: mahogany, hand-paneled, hand-carved stalls, marble troughs and silver name plates with the horses' titles spelled out in lettered Gothic. Before each stall were silver posts and chains, and a great gold-bordered mirror was mounted inside so each filly could toss her mane and admire herself. Men like Chotard were part of the legend of the Natchez.

The pair walked carefully on to the low kennels that housed the dogs, blooded hounds more high-strung than the horses, pacing, pushing their noses out to be petted.

"You don't relish the sport of hunting—do you?"

Aubrey had sensed a withdrawal from her as soon as they entered the kennels. Angeline hesitated. Until now her spontaneity had served her, being sympathetic with his own.

"I don't know animals, I've never been much around them. They make me nervous. I suppose that's all."

"I suppose it isn't." What was the tone of his voice? Warm—indulgent?

"No, I suppose it isn't. I suppose the whole thing makes me squeamish. And I suppose, Mr. Stewart—" she threw back her little head— "you're enjoying all this immensely. Is that not true?"

He nodded and they laughed again together.

A working plantation the size of Lairdswood, with nearly two thousand acres and more than two hundred slaves, was not a place that could be gone over in one afternoon. Beside the main house, which Angeline had not even entered, there were auxiliary buildings, galleried lesser versions forming kitchen, dairy, office, and schoolrooms; though the schoolrooms of Lairdswood were now billiard rooms, Aubrey informed her.

In addition to the stables there were barns and shops where Negroes trained as millers, draftsmen, smiths, and carpenters turned out the work of the plantation community. There was an ice shed, a brick kiln, and even a gin on the place where the cotton was processed and pressed into bales. Far to the back stood the slaves' hutlike village, long rows of low buildings with networks of brick walls between. These quarters boasted their own underground well with water as cold as ice, Aubrey told her.

"When we were boys Ham and I would sneak out there," he confided, "and drink from that well and play with the pickaninnies. There was nothing else in the world tasted so good."

It was the first time he had made reference to his brother.

Back from the village began the fields of cotton. It was late March now and the fields were planted, the small plants pushing up in endless rows. Soon it would be time for the first cultivation. To Angeline it seemed as if the fields never ended, stretching on and on, even and brown, bordering the little world in which they stood. As the blue sea borders a lush green island the brown earth bordered them—rich with its secrets, deep and still.

"Have you any idea how many plants are out there?" she wondered aloud.

Aubrey was amused by the incredulous tone in her voice. "We plant Dr. Nutt's Petit Gulf seed he developed at Longwood, right here in Natchez, and every planting is carefully counted. Trouble is, a nigger can plant more acres than he can ever hope to harvest. If there was some way to make the picking faster—"

"Then you'd have larger plantations, right, and more slaves, and bigger houses to care for and money to burn. Isn't all this enough?"

She waved her arm, encompassing all that spread around them. For a moment he felt uncomfortable, ashamed. Of greed, or excessive pride? He wasn't sure. But the moment passed, she took his arm, and they walked through the terraced yard to a low-lying garden, wild and sweet, more overgrown than the rest.

"The gardens have suffered some since my father's death. Mother's erratic—at times she tends to forget them."

"I like them this way, unconfined and full."

There were bushes here of camellias and azaleas, with roses and wisterias twining round their tallest branches, pushing and stretching for more room and height, their lavender blossoms pale against the vivid blue of the sky. There was a white latticed pavilion half-smothered with vines and flowers. They sat in the stillness with only the drone of bees and an occasional muffled sound from off in the distance.

"You are responsible then for running all this?" she asked him. For the first time she saw conscious pride leap into his eyes.

"My father's trained me for nothing else since I was a boy."

"Is it fascinating? There must be so much to learn, so much to keep track of."

"I always found it so. There's a lot of routine, but even routine has a certain quiet appeal of its own."

She nodded. "What of your brother?" She watched him closely, saw the wariness cloud his gaze. "If you are . . . in charge here . . . well, what—what . . ."

"What's left for big brother?" It was the first thing he had said that startled her.

"It is a little unusual, you must admit, the younger son inheriting all."

"You're curious as a cat, and you'd better be careful. You may get your whiskers singed poking round the fire."

Angeline arched an eyebrow and gazed, but she didn't back down.

She was disquieting. She kept his mind churning as well as his emotions. He didn't entirely like it. He wanted to say, "I'll trade you a kiss for your answer," like an awkward schoolboy. Instead he said, showing very little emotion, "There's another plantation out Pine Ridge Road past Landsdowne. It's called Echodell; it belonged to my mother. She willed it to Hamilton."

In lieu of the prize, she thought. *Because the boy was naughty.* This was fascinating. Angeline pushed on, aware of the undercurrents of danger, but spurred by them, determined to know. "But I thought your mother was a Charleston belle."

"She was. But her favorite uncle lived in Natchez. He had only one son, and she spent time here with them often. In fact, that's how she and my father first met. He saw her and was determined to have her."

"So your father won, over all the other suitors. He must have been quite a man." She said the words softly, gazing at him so he knew that the words reached out and embraced him in their meaning as well.

I'm not the man he was, but let her think so. She must think it! I can be that kind of man for her.

"How did the plantation come to your mother?" The question drew him back to reality with some difficulty.

"The son was killed in an accident on the river. She was like a daughter to them. It was only natural."

Angeline pulled a rose and smoothed out its petals, placing it next to her lips and breathing its fragrance.

"It is close here; I am unthoughtful to keep you sitting. Come, I'll show you the house now."

He took her hand. Her fingers were cool against his. He felt foolish that he could tremble at her touch.

"Aubrey." The small hand closed around his with a brief pressure, then she bent and left the pavilion before him.

At the house she checked the small rose-enameled watch that was pinned to her collar. "It's much later than I had thought. I must return now. My father will come home and grow concerned."

Aubrey was dismayed. He had been awkward. How *did* one entertain a lady? Certainly in the parlor, in some proper manner, with cakes and candied fruits and music—it was all very vague, very lost to him. She had not even set foot inside his house.

"Miss Angeline—" How could he apologize?

"It's been delightful, Mr. Stewart, every minute. Next time you can show me the house."

Next time. Of course. Tomorrow and tomorrow.

"Yes, there'll be other days, Miss Angeline. Many more."

It was what she wanted most to hear. She sat beside him in the buggy and rode back along the avenue of oaks. She was taking her first little piece of Lairdswood with her. She glanced at the profile of the dark young man. She had never spoken a word to him before yesterday. Yet already he held the power to make her unhappy, for he held in his hands something she knew she wanted. And because of that, no matter what way things happened, she would never again be quite the same.

Three

Fletcher watched till the street was free of buggies, until the men on horseback and the women carrying bundles, scurrying across the road with their crinoline skirts flouncing, had all disappeared down side lanes or into shops. Then he started out into the street with his shoulders hunched and his head held down. He wanted the licorice; the pennies were warm in his pocket. But small beads of perspiration stood on his forehead. He pulled open the door; there were very few people inside. He loped over to the counter, his face still hidden.

"Licorice today, Fletch?" the storekeeper asked him.

Fletcher nodded and mumbled something incoherent.

"Let's see how many pennies you've got. There you go." He counted out the long strands of shiny black candy, placing them into a small paper bag. "I've thrown in a few lemon drops for your pretty sister."

Fletcher hazarded a smile as he snatched the bag and handed over the moist, warm pennies. No one else in the store had said a word. He slipped back into the street and they shook their heads and whispered to one another behind his back. But Fletcher didn't see, so it didn't matter.

"Too bad," Mrs. Halverson said, as she'd said so many times over the past fourteen years, "that a girl so pretty as Sarah Anne Gordon should die giving birth to a child like that."

"Edmund's never been the same," Miss Peabody added. "Well, can you imagine the shock to a man like Edmund? And this being his only son, his only male heir."

"Fletch ain't so bad." The storekeeper scratched at his whiskers. "He keeps out of trouble, he don't get in anyone's way."

"They may say there's nothing really the matter with him," Mrs. Halverson blustered. "But his voice when he talks, all garbled and stammering-like." She shuddered.

"Fletcher don't talk much. I say he don't bother most people."

The ladies didn't agree with the staid storekeeper. They kept up their prattle, but lowered their voices a little, turning their broad backs on the unsympathetic third party. By this time Fletcher had made it across to the other side. He felt particularly lucky today. There had been no bands of boys on the street to throw rocks and make faces. He relaxed a little and slowed his gait.

He turned off Commerce Street onto Market where the Presbyterian church, tall and imposing, dominated the landscape of the block. As he neared it his footsteps froze and his heart started beating. The voices his ears had learned to pick up so quickly: loud and angry, with a biting edge of derision. He slumped down with his head between his shoulders, prepared to shuffle off in the other direction. But he paused. There was something different here, other voices, talking back to the angry ones. Fletcher listened, but he couldn't tell what they were saying. He edged closer, more curious now than afraid.

". . . and we don't want none of your angels and gold bibles. You too stubborn to see that, Yankees?"

The angry voice made Fletcher tremble. But he stood his ground, though he moved no closer.

"They'll string you up, you make trouble around here, boys." This voice was mean and little, more mean than angry.

"The good folk under the hill—you gone down there yet, boys?" The first voice laughed, sounding pleased with itself. "There be ladies there would take care of the likes of you. Wet behind the ears, hey, Lester? Natchez Under's the place for a couple of Yankees like you."

There was much sniggering and scoffing that followed. Fletcher made himself small against the stone church wall and watched till the angry voices at last went away. The two young men the voices had been addressing picked up their hats—knocked from their heads in the scuffle—dusted them off, and headed in Fletcher's direction. For some reason he didn't fully understand Fletcher shuffled out from his hiding place to meet them. He stood at the side of the walk as they approached him, clutching the bag of licorice with both hands.

"Another one?" The young man's voice sounded wary.

"I don't think so. Look at his face."

The two men stopped. "Hello there," the second one ventured. His voice was warm and his eyes were kind. Fletcher grinned; he knew these men wouldn't harm him. After all, he had something in common with them. Didn't he know what the angry voices could do? Hadn't he cowered the way he had watched them cower, with no way to fight the angry voices?

"I'm Elder Carlyle and this is Elder Logan. I don't believe we've met you before."

Fletcher licked his lips. He swallowed. "Fletcher," he said.

The young men nodded. "Glad to meet you, Fletcher," they said.

Fletcher grinned again; he stood grinning at them.

"Fletcher is your friend." The words came unexpectedly forth from the grin, formed carefully and spoken with effort.

"That's good to know," Elder Carlyle responded. "We need a friend or two around this place."

"Licorice. You have some of Fletcher's licorice." He opened the bag and extended it with great ceremony.

The men looked into the bag, then at one another.

"Thank you, that's most kind of you, Fletcher." Elder Carlyle's voice had grown very soft. He reached into the bag and drew out the licorice. He handed a piece to Elder Logan. Their eyes met and held for a moment. This was the first kindness they had received in Natchez, the first ray of hope after five weary weeks of rejection. They went home and wrote about Fletcher in their journals; they looked upon him as some kind of an omen.

This was Angeline's fourth excursion to Lairdswood and she had met neither Aubrey's mother nor his brother. She had seen at least parts of the inside of the mansion, Aubrey having contrived ways to entertain her more conventionally. But his mother was "indisposed," Hamilton "occupied." Dyanne thought it all extremely singular, even peculiar.

"In his own way he's ashamed of them both," she scolded. "Seems to me, honey, there's too much he wants to hide."

Angeline laughed at Dyanne's morbid fears, but she was stubborn.

"I don't know," Dyanne had cautioned the last time they were together. "May be a strain of insanity runs in that family. If I were in your shoes I'd be careful, Angie."

If you were in my shoes, she had wanted to answer, *you'd grab for all you could get and you know it.* Instead she smiled back and replied, "Aubrey's frightfully normal. Kind and quick-minded and ever so sweet and attentive."

Today she and Aubrey sat in the music room, furnished in blues and burgundy, rich with gold-gilded crystal-drop chandeliers, French needlepoint rugs, and heavy silk damask curtains. She sat at the Chickering rosewood piano playing some of her favorite pieces for his pleasure: Beethoven's "Für Elise" and Mozart's Turkish Rondo. Aubrey sat close, so close that she could have touched him, and the gaze of his brown eyes fell full across her face.

She was just finishing Chopin's wistful Fantaisie Impromptu and he sat with his eyes closed, lost in the melody, wrapped as she was in the somnolence of the mood. Then suddenly Angeline sensed it, a subtle difference, a presence that made itself felt without really intruding. The hairs on the back of her neck began to prickle; she felt an irresistible compulsion to turn around. She played a few more notes, then turned very slowly.

Eliza Bragg Stewart sat in the small winged Regency chair, her hands busy with the needlepoint in her lap, her brown eyes, glinting with gold specks that made them sparkle, regarding her son and the stranger at the piano.

"Charming, my dear. Go on, please finish."

The voice was a girl's voice, young as the eyes were young, set in a face unusually arresting, amazingly lovely in spite of what age had done.

How long has she been here? How long without my knowing? Angeline's fingers stumbled over the keyboard as she completed the last few strains of the piece. The small woman in her chair seemed to take no notice. Aubrey was sitting upright, his eyes wide open, like two dark pools of wonder reflecting the scene. He flexed his

26

fingers nervously under his chin. Angeline turned from the piano to face Mrs. Stewart.

"You play well, my dear. Though—here, let me show you."

She rose quickly and crossed the room, and each movement was graceful. She bent over the piano, standing close beside Angeline. The faint scent of lavender came like a whisper behind her.

"There's a trick to getting through those passages sprinkled with grace notes. And emotion, you need more emotion to make it alive."

Still standing, she placed long white fingers against the white keys. Sudden melody came alive at her touch, a fluid harmony Angeline had not been able to achieve. She listened with admiration and a sense of excitement at the spirit of this frail, slight woman which electrified itself through the spirit of the music, bringing something magnificent forth. Eliza Stewart finished with a little satisfied sigh.

"There, does that help some?" She smiled at Angeline and her expression was both sweet and singularly alluring. It was easy for Angeline to return the smile.

"Thank you. It was a delight to hear you. Did you ever—do you ever play for . . . company?"

"I used to. Oh my, years ago I used to." She laughed, a light, intimate sound. "I've three grown men to take care of now, you know. They demand all my time."

Her warm eyes began to sparkle. She leaned close to Angeline, the clean lavender scent growing stronger. "But then I always did enjoy the gentlemen's company more than the ladies'."

Angeline smiled and nodded. Eliza Stewart turned and examined a tall, expensive-looking oriental vase that rested on one of the Hepplewhite tables. She brushed a long white finger across the surface.

"Does Valencia dust here daily? I hardly think so. You see, there are so many details to look after."

Of a sudden Eliza turned to her son. "Aubrey, what are you doing here this time of day? You should be out helping Hamilton and your father." She shook her head and her annoyance seemed to grow. "You know your father drives himself too hard."

Aubrey didn't respond, but she didn't give him time to. She

drew a step or two closer, her hands on her hips. "How long have you been entertaining this young lady? Why haven't you brought her up to meet me? Why haven't we had tea together? Aubrey, it isn't like you to be so unthoughtful."

She whirled upon Angeline, the small features of her face drawn and thoughtful. "Even Hamilton, my oldest son, has not married. My boys . . . my boys are timid with the girls. Unlike their father—" She laughed and the sound was like her, warm and melodious. Her eyes grew brighter, almost feverishly bright. "Samuel was so bold in courtship. He had less to offer than all my other suitors. But that did not deter him. Oh no, he knew his advantage."

"What was Samuel's advantage?" Angeline murmured, fearful that the older lady would not reply, would turn abruptly to something else.

"He knew what kind of a man he was."

She spoke the words as though she were telling a secret. It was a strange reply; Angeline was puzzled. "I'm not certain what you mean," she ventured.

"He knew his own worth," Eliza expounded, with the same solemnity of expression and voice. "He had strengths—qualities to offer that far outweighed the other men."

"You must have been an extremely wise young lady." The response was out before Angeline could check it.

The woman paused and her smile became very tender—beautiful, so that Angeline caught a vision of the exquisite loveliness that was slipping away.

"Not really. From the first I found Samuel fascinating. Totally irresistible, my dear."

She stood near the door. Suddenly she raised her hand to her forehead; the movement was almost a flutter, a stir of dismay. "My goodness, I'm going on. I shall check on the tea now. I don't mean to tire you, dears."

She left them. The room was subdued, instantly still—but pulsing, Angeline thought as she turned to Aubrey, with the trailings of the woman's enchantment.

Four

It was very important this evening what dress she wore. If she chose a light, floating, diaphanous fabric she would appear more like the other belles—vague and delightful, innocently alluring. What about the pale pink satin with wide lace trimmings? The satin was more subdued but it carried its own implications: here's a woman who knows what she is and what she is after. The evening was somewhat cool with a breeze off the river. Angeline chose the satin gown.

The play was a melodrama out of New Orleans, wildly popular, and this was its opening night. All Natchez would be there, and all Natchez would see her on the arm of the young Stewart heir of Lairdswood.

She was choosing which jewelry to wear, the pearls or the locket, when Fletcher entered her room.

"Come in, Fletcher." She made her voice sound pleasant, though she wanted so much right now to be left alone.

"From Mr. Davison," Fletcher said, holding out half a dozen lemon drops. "'For your pretty sister,'" he quoted, with a shy smile.

"Thank you, Fletcher. Wasn't that thoughtful of him?" She placed the candy carefully on her dresser. "Did you have a good day? Did you have a nice walk into town?"

She watched to see the little furrows of perplexity gather on the boy's brow, waited for the torrent of explanation, the trembling recital of some unkind prank or abuse. Instead a wide smile lit his eyes and swept over his features.

"Friends today. Two new friends for Fletcher."

Angeline stopped what she was doing and turned to face him. "Tell me about it, Fletcher," she requested, pulling him down to a low seat beside her.

He could hardly contain his excitement, but the telling, even to her, was quite a chore. She gathered that the men wore suits and top hats, that the mean men had hurt them, that Fletcher had hidden by the church, that he had shared his licorice with them and they had thanked him. But the mystery of who they could be yet remained.

Angeline, watching the joy in the face before her, felt a stirring of gratitude toward the unknown men. She wished she could somehow find and thank them. So little joy crept into her brother's life. Impulsively she drew the boy toward her and hugged him briefly.

"I'm happy for you, Fletcher. Friends are such nice things to have. Now run off and let me get ready. I'll tell you all about my evening when I get back."

"Promise?"

"I promise, Fletcher."

She kissed him on the forehead and hurried him off. He went slowly to his own room. The night would be lonely, but Angeline would come. He had no doubt of that. If Angeline promised, then she would be there. He hugged the promise to him like a secret, remembering all the other times she had come, how good they had been, especially the first time. He remembered the first time, although he had been very little.

It had been deep night then, with darkness all around him. He was crying; he had been crying for so long that a pain throbbed in his head and his stomach was curling. Suddenly Angeline was there beside him, her young, soft fingers smoothing back his hair.

"Why are you crying?" she asked, but he couldn't tell her.

"I know why you're crying," she answered with ten-year-old wisdom. "You're crying because you want mother. I cry for her, too. I miss her all the time, Fletcher."

She paused; her own voice had started to quiver. "'Cept you don't remember her, Fletcher, and I do."

She laid down beside him, curling her young warmth against him. A feeling seeped through him he never had felt before. He clung to her, afraid and longing.

"It's all right," she whispered. "I guess I can be your mother. Poor thing, it isn't your fault you don't know how to talk."

She cradled his head; her arms were around him. "Don't cry, Fletcher. I'll be your mother. Don't cry, Fletcher, please don't cry."

So he'd learned it was a mother he was lacking. What a mother was supposed to be, he didn't know, or what other mothers were like, but that didn't matter. He felt certain no mother alive could be better than Angie. He felt safe and content in her love, in her being there. It was his one sheltered spot in a world that was cold and uncertain.

The roads approaching Choctaw Auditorium were choked with blithe, convivial crowds. While the ladies perched in light carriages driven by Negro coachmen, many of the men rode *a cheval*, their spirited animals proud with the burden of ornamental saddles. The gentlemen in wide felt hats and broadcloth suits looked casually elegant beside wives and sweethearts whose tight-waisted, expansive skirts spread out around them in shades of pale gossamer, shimmering masses of color.

Thus the "quality" rode out for their entertainment, though not every lady sitting high in her carriage was the mistress of a Natchez river plantation. Some had nice, discreet houses provided by unnamed gentlemen; some held residence only under the hill. As some visitors were wont to express it, Natchezians lived "rather more freely" than others were accustomed to doing. There were even free Negro citizens of Natchez who ran successful businesses and owned slaves of their own. The press of human diversity: anything with pluck and class and spirit was bound to be accepted Natchez-way.

The seats Aubrey had secured for them were good ones. Angie sank into hers with a sense of relief. She would like nothing more than to see the house lights dim and to be lifted away from the curious faces about her to the make-believe reality of the stage. Aubrey, turning in his seat, still smiled and waved to some of the faces.

"Aubrey, what is it?" His face had turned dark. She tugged at his arm. "Aubrey!"

"He did it. He said he would, but I didn't believe him."

"Your brother?" she guessed. "What did he do, Aubrey?"

"He couldn't give me even this one evening. He brought his— woman—to belittle me, Angeline. He's a wretched, egotistical—"

"Shhh. You mustn't." She hadn't known he could be so bitter. "He has nothing to do with us, Aubrey. Don't let him spoil things."

She wondered if he had even heard her. Again she followed his gaze; there were too many faces. As she scanned them the lights receded and dimmed. She sank back in her seat. Aubrey's face was veiled now; she couldn't see if the scowl still sat on his features.

She watched the villain step out into the stark yellow pool of stage light. The voice of the crowd rose to hiss and boo him. It would be good to boo for evil along with the crowd—the evil with black hat and mustache—so clearly defined, so simplified.

This Hamilton Stewart, what would he be like? Shaded, she was certain, unlike the villian who stood revealed and smirking before them. The play swept on, but the natural ease of the evening was jarred, and Angeline found her unquiet attention straying from the scenes before her.

Afterward she waited for Aubrey to find Woodrow and the carriage. The night was a velvety darkness, softened by lanterns that bobbed in the hands of servants or, mounted on carriages, spread trembling rays of light like bright streamers around them. The cool air, smelling of soil and the river, was stronger than the ladies' perfumes. To Angeline the air was refreshing after the closeness of hours inside. She took deep breaths, enjoying the earthy fragrance.

Hamilton watched the girl as she waited. He had not planned to approach her tonight. But he was curious now to observe her more closely.

Occupied with her thoughts Angeline heard nothing. All at once the man and woman were there beside her and two laughing blue-gray eyes were scanning her face. Instantly she knew and a flush spread through her, confusing her thoughts, threatening her composure.

"So you're the little girl who's enchanted my brother."

She was lovely, much more lovely than he had expected. Unpretentious, clear, fine features—an air about her—

"You are quite ill-mannered, sir. Would you do me the courtesy of an introduction?"

Hamilton's eyebrows shot up and the girl on his arm smiled slowly, almost appreciatively. "I stand rebuked. And justly so," he answered.

What on earth is Aubrey doing with a girl like this! Spirited, no-nonsense. She didn't look it. Slight and feminine, large tranquil eyes.

"I am, as you have most likely determined, Hamilton Stewart. And the lady, my companion, Miss Melody Norman."

"I am Angeline Gordon," she responded, returning his gaze as levelly as she could.

He bowed slightly, but his eyes never left her.

He's quite handsome, Angeline thought. *He must look like his father.* Long, acquiline features, hair that was thick and golden, with every red shade of firelight in it. He wore his vanity like a fine suit of clothing: unconcealed, accepted as requisite to his attraction, but never flaunted distastefully. There was a definite air of excitement about him, a vague enticement.

"Are you staying to see Aubrey?" she asked.

He inclined his head, continuing to regard her. She wished she could read the expression in his eyes. It was difficult to hold her own steady before them.

"How did little brother ever find you?" He wanted to add, *and what will he do with you now?* Instead he continued, enjoying a surge of mischief, "I am pleasantly surprised at his—what shall I call it—discernment? At his taste in women, as I would put it."

He was hoping to discomfort her but she parried, much to his delight, successfully. "Then by your own admission you do not know him. Perhaps there is more yet in Aubrey to surprise you."

"The prospect is pleasing, not threatening, Miss Gordon, as I perceive you would wish it to be." When had he ever felt this intoxicating mixture? And she was young, so unaware of her powers. *I must be extremely careful,* he thought; *I must be wary.*

"It is not my desire to spoil my brother's evening. Nor yours. That would prove most ungrateful when you have so enhanced the occasion for me." He drew up her hand and pressed his lips to it briefly. His touch held the same throbbing warmth as his eyes. "Give Aubrey my regards, Miss Gordon. I trust I shall see you again—and again."

Purposefully he drew the words out, made them linger. He turned with the girl and was gone, soon lost in the crowds. But he left her trembling with something that could have been anger, though she knew instinctively it was much more. She refused to allow him to draw her thoughts out to follow him. Resolutely she put him out of her mind, so that when Aubrey came up with the carriage a few minutes later she could look at him with a clear gaze and remark quite casually, "I met your brother."

"He was here?" Aubrey's voice stiffened, his eyes grew dark. "With his—"

"Please don't, Aubrey. He had a girl with him. I met her—"

"He had the impertinence to introduce her to you?"

He helped her into the carriage. "What did he say, Angeline? Was he rude and insulting?"

"He tried to be, but I don't think his heart was in it."

This drew a little smile.

"That's much better, Aubrey. There was nothing, really, no reason to worry."

The crowds thinned, and the carriage moved with a little more freedom. Jefferson Street was widening into St. Catherine's. Aubrey had failed to take the turn onto Pine. Was he planning a country ride in the moonlight, or was he only preoccupied? Angeline sighed. She must put an end to this nonsense.

"He'd be pleased to know that you're letting him ruin your evening."

It took him a moment or two, but he turned to her slowly. "I know, Angeline, I know that you're right. It—well, it just goes so much deeper than you can see."

"Then stop it now. Don't let it go any deeper."

It sounded so simple. Yet he was afraid that he didn't know how to do it. He remembered the first day at Lairdswood, alone in the garden, when she had seen him to be like his father, strong, in command. He mustn't do anything to destroy that image.

Forget Father and Hamilton both! he told himself fiercely. *This moment is yours. Nothing else can matter!*

And it all became very clear to him suddenly. In Angeline lay his fulfillment and his freedom. Without her he could go on, but all would be pretense; he would never really amount to anything.

34

Later that evening, along the high bluff by the river, Angeline struggled alone with her thoughts. She had come to be very certain of Aubrey's affection, certain that he wanted her for his wife. She knew she was meant to be part of Lairdswood. But was she meant to be part of Aubrey; did she love him? She laughed out loud in the clandestine stillness. What, after all, was love anyway? She had never really seen it between two people. She knew that her father had not only loved her mother, but worshipped her after a fashion. But was that good? Look at him now, in many ways wrecked and useless, with no love left over for his unfortunate son, and what she suspected was only a remnant of caring, a tenderness of remembrance he felt for her, seeing her mother in her more than he saw herself. She loved Fletcher — she knew she really loved him. But that was a very different kind of emotion, based on pity and loyalty and need. The love of a wife for a husband, a man for a woman? That was all uncharted territory to her.

Far below her a steamboat sat in the water, nothing from here but a star-prick of glittering light, one speck in an immensity of blackness, alone against the dark water. She was much like the boat, alone upon unknown waters. But, like the boat, she had lights to guide her: her love for Lairdswood and Aubrey's love for her. They were strong together.

If Life saw fit to steer her toward this future, she would do all she could to reach out with both hands open, not looking back and not asking any questions.

Five

Aubrey was drawn to him like a moth to the blaze that is bright and fascinating but can destroy. Hamilton was at work repairing the cotton gin, instructing Rufus so that one of these times he could handle it on his own. His shirt sleeves were rolled up, his arms and face streaked with grease and dirt and sweat, engrossed in the task so he didn't see Aubrey approaching. Or so Aubrey thought as he stood and watched for a moment.

"That will do, Rufus. We'll continue with this tomorrow. Aubrey has something to say and he's bustin' to say it." Hamilton grinned at the black man and winked. All the Negroes liked Hamilton. He could somehow speak on a level that made them comrades, that put an ease between them in spite of the fact that he could be more the cold, hard master than Aubrey was with them.

"You're all spruced up for courtin' again, I see," he said to his brother.

Aubrey tried to ignore the remark and the jibe that went with it. "You'll do well to find yourself a wife half Angeline's equal," he replied.

"A wife, is it? Well, I wish you'd hurry and ask her. How do you expect things here to keep running while you gad about?" Hamilton wiped his hands on an old rag and raised himself leisurely, standing an inch above Aubrey.

"I'll thank you to keep your nose out of my affairs."

Hamilton raised his eyebrows a little. "I just don't want to upset the balance, brother. After all, you wouldn't want to discover that old Ham could carry on without you. No, that wouldn't be good for anyone to know, would it, Aubrey?"

"You have to be a little twisted, Hamilton, to gain pleasure from causing other people discomfort."

"You cause your own discomfort, and when you know that you'll be halfway to overcoming it."

Hamilton turned and walked off with long strides, forcing Aubrey to either follow or stand there gaping foolishly at his back.

"She's a fine girl. I don't want you to frighten her, Ham."

"Scare that one off—I hardly think so!" The words were almost a protest. "I happened to notice that she can take very good care of herself. She has a tongue like an adder and a mind twice as quick."

"Is that all you happened to notice?" Aubrey couldn't help asking the question, though he wished he hadn't.

They were nearing the barns and Hamilton had not broken his stride. He stopped dead now and threw a long look over his shoulder, veiled and calculated, and then replied, "She's a beauty, Aubrey, an enchanting combination of the innocent girl and the sensuous woman. Much too much woman for you, I'd wager."

Of course the insult, always the insult. Then came the inevitable smile, playful and taunting. "You know that's the first thing I'd notice, little brother."

Angeline hadn't been expecting Aubrey. She had Minerva usher him in to what she called the morning room, the small west parlor that overlooked the river, all creams and yellows and flooded now with warm light. She stood so the soft light sifted about her, enhancing the glow of her skin, the silken shades of her hair. She sensed that he had come today for a reason. She was ready; she had been ready since Saturday night.

He paused when he saw her, not attempting to conceal the effect her beauty had upon him. The admiration she read in his face and eyes was like a strong intoxicant, sweet and burning. She stood poised and perfect, savoring the moment. When she moved it was to glide very close beside him and place her fingers lightly against his arm.

"Aubrey, what is it?"

He trembled beneath her fingers. "Angeline, forgive me. I hadn't planned it this way. But I cannot go on one more hour without knowing."

His eyes were distraught, impassioned; they gave him away.

"Angeline, will you do me the honor of marrying me, of becoming my wife?"

He was quaintly romantic. That was one thing she liked about him.

"Yes, Aubrey."

Five seconds . . . ten seconds to change the whole course of her life.

"Yes, Aubrey," she repeated and watched with wonder as the joy leapt into his eyes. He drew her against him.

"Angeline, I love you, I'll love you forever. You shall never regret this moment, I promise you, never."

"And I shall love you, Aubrey," she whispered, "and serve you and Lairdswood well for the rest of my life."

Then she held up her face to be kissed. When he embraced her she could taste love that was stronger than passion. But love is intoxicating to a woman and his kisses were sweet and easy for her to return.

After a few moments they separated and talked of their decision in detail. But to Angeline the details didn't matter. Her tomorrows at last had merged into her today.

There was still an ordeal for Aubrey to go through. He had to formally ask Angeline's father for her hand. They had only met twice before, and then only briefly. Aubrey knew little of the man's history, his withdrawal after the death of his wife. It was the one thing Aubrey held in common with him: they both had loved a woman to the point of worship.

Now, sitting across the desk from Edmund Gordon, waiting for the man's reaction to his request, Aubrey noticed a depth of sadness in the dark eyes, a sorrow it was almost intrusion to look upon. He dropped his gaze. Edmund Gordon cleared his throat.

"It's time she married, isn't it? Yes, I know that. I haven't given her much of a home—let me finish—" He held up a hand as Aubrey began to protest. "A girl growing up needs tenderness, needs a mother. She's gone too long, she's got love of her own to give. You know what I mean, son?"

Aubrey nodded without really knowing.

"This is what Angeline wants. I believe she loves you. What I want to know is, can you make her happy?" He rubbed his chin in an almost absent manner, but his eyes bored into Aubrey's like hot prongs of fire. "Can you love her half as much as I loved her mother? Oh, I know you've got wealth, but I don't give a tinker's curse for money. It's love holds a marriage together."

"Then you can rest assured that Angeline will be happy. I love her, sir, with all my being."

"I can see that, boy." A smile played about his thin mouth, but his eyes had grown expressionless, dull with old sorrow. "The young have to get on with the business of living, don't they? Young Stewart, let's get down to terms then, shall we?"

Aubrey nodded; the worst was over. He felt himself moving inexorably toward a happiness hard to imagine, a happiness nothing could hamper or destroy.

Aubrey rode home alone through the shadows, his spirits still soaring. The need to share his joy, to tell somebody drove him to near madness. If he were Hamilton he could solve the problem quite simply by dropping over the bluff for an evening Down Under, drinking himself into oblivion with a roomful of sympathetic comrades. It wasn't that easy for him. He needed *someone*.

He guided his horse through a gully where the low spots were water, and the branches of old trees trailed over the path. Remnants of the Natchez Trace—it made his skin prickle each time he passed here alone in the gathering dark. Generations of Spanish, French, and English had trod here, wearing deeper the trail that the buffalo first had broken, which even the Indians could not improve upon. By the time American pioneers looked for a road to the Southwest the narrow twisting trails had turned almost into tunnels crawling ten, fifteen, sometimes as many as twenty-five feet between walls of earth that towered along each side. But no other passage by land was open to them, so in the cool gloom, with the roots of old trees reaching for them, like gnarled fingers thrusting and grasping, with the wet smells of soil, damp leaves, and thick vegetation, all America passed: peddlers, preachers and schemers, grand ladies and farmers' wives, and all in between.

Aubrey bent over the saddle and pressed his horse until the low road began to climb, the gloom sank below him, and he could spy the crown of a slope up ahead—then he was within safe distance of Lairdswood and home.

Aubrey didn't see Hamilton that night, but the following morning in the breakfast room over hotcakes and coffee Ham looked up from his paper and fixed his gaze on his brother.

"You asked her to marry you, didn't you?"

For a moment Aubrey felt hot and embarrassed, as he had when they were boys and Hamilton had caught him doing something he shouldn't be doing and showed him the fool. He met the steady blue eyes.

"That's right, I asked her. And her father as well."

"Well, well—you don't waste any time."

"She said yes, Hamilton!" The excitement crept into his voice unbidden.

A slow smile spread over the face that was watching his. "Oh, I knew she would, little brother. I knew she would."

How in the world could you know that? Aubrey wanted to ask. But Hamilton was rising from his chair, folding the newspaper, walking over to Aubrey.

"Congratulations, Aubrey." His hand was extended; there were no glints of derision or ridicule in the blue-gray eyes.

Aubrey took the hand and returned the warmth of the handshake.

"I have to hand it to you, little brother. You've one mighty fine girl there—and you're right, I don't know if I could do half so well myself."

There was an awkward moment, then Hamilton clapped his shoulder. "Well, the hands are barring off and scraping that long southwest field this morning. I think I'll ride out and see how the work goes along."

He turned and cleared the room with his long, easy strides. Aubrey sat there after his footsteps had died, not really trying to figure out the moment, but savoring what it had given him inside.

"I'm thrilled; yes, Aubrey, I know how much you love her. Yes, I think she's a lovely girl. But you know there are other things that must be considered."

The brown eyes gazed up at him, bright and unblinking. He thought, as he often did when he looked at his mother, *She has the most beautiful face I've ever seen.* Even now with the blank unawareness that crept across it, the glaze that might sometimes cloud the expressive eyes, there was nothing could really mar the depth of beauty, the delicate symmetry of color and line.

"I must discuss all the fine details with your father. This has been most singular from start to finish; you know that, Aubrey. We must meet with her father and mother, there are *conventions—*"

He turned away. He had told her a dozen times that Angeline's mother had died many years ago. She didn't retain things. She lived so much in the past now—or rather in that strange world of her own creating where Samuel hovered forever in the wings, more real, more acknowledged than anything else about her, yet phantom only, and lost hope and memory. He shuddered. What good did it do to attempt to reach her? When he came home with Angeline would she even remember? Or would she demand to know why this strange girl was in her house?

He bowed himself out of the room. What would he do about her? He stalked to the card room and slumped on the old settee. Hamilton found him there half an hour later, brooding. He rose awkwardly when his brother came in.

"I don't mean to chase you out. What's the matter, brother?" Hamilton lowered his frame with ease and relaxed on the spot Aubrey had vacated, seeming to take up twice the space another man would.

"Nothing." Aubrey turned and walked to the window.

"Nothing! You never could hide your feelings, Aubrey. You're as dark as a spring thunderhead and twice as wound up."

"Well, it's nothing I can do anything about."

"Mother."

"Blast you! You always were good at guessing." Aubrey ran his fingers roughly through his thick hair. Perhaps he ought to see how his brother reacted. "I don't think she ought to be at the wedding, Ham. You know what she's capable of doing. I can see her halting everything and demanding we wait for Samuel. I can't put Angeline through that."

"What does Angeline say?"

Aubrey paused. *Confound you for asking!*

"She says we should have her. She says it doesn't matter one whit to her what happens or what people say."

A smile that was unreadable touched Hamilton's features, just briefly, with a fleck of emotion, and then was gone.

"I thought as much. So stop worrying, little brother. I won't let her shame you."

Aubrey shrank at the undertone. "Hamilton —"

"Never mind. I'll talk to her, Aubrey. I'll take care of it, you understand?"

Aubrey nodded darkly. Hamilton rose. "Get back to work now. Stop brooding about it."

He stood and waited, as though he expected instant compliance. Aubrey felt a stubborn rebellion building inside. He threw himself onto a chair, reached for a decanter, and poured a glass of whiskey while Hamilton watched.

"Even I don't drink during working hours, brother." He crossed the room and picked up the glass, walked to the open window, and emptied the liquid.

"Don't put on airs with me," Aubrey shouted. "You do more than drink when you've a mind to. But 'not during working hours'"—he mimicked his brother. "You think that makes you some kind of saint?"

"It makes me a realist, Aubrey, nothing more. You'd do well to —" He broke off with an impatient gesture. "Never mind. Have your own way, Aubrey, and see how long you can keep it."

He walked out, his footsteps muffled by the thick carpet. But Aubrey heard him taking the stairs two at a time.

He's gone up to mother. More power to him.

He reached for the decanter and poured himself another glass. But Angeline's face came into his mind and he couldn't shake it — the image and all the thoughts it awakened. He didn't touch the drink, and an hour later when Valencia came to straighten the gentlemen's room she found it there. She was young and enjoyed being daring and putting on airs. She poured half of the whiskey back in the decanter and drank the remainder with careful, appreciative sips.

Six

The long hourglass had finally emptied its plunder; the last minutes were sifting soundlessly away.

Tomorrow, Angeline thought, *I will be a new person. Never singly myself again.* It was a solemn thought: not little girl, not maiden, not daughter—but woman and wife.

She had been trying for days to prepare Fletcher. But tucking him in bed tonight, realizing it would be for the last time, she had caught him up in her arms and held him fiercely, fighting back the tears that would frighten him.

"Remember, always remember, Fletcher, I love you. Promise me you won't forget!"

He promised. She blew him a kiss from the doorway. He caught it and tucked it under his pillow—a kiss for tomorrow night when she wouldn't be there. But that was only the first tomorrow ahead.

A slice of light showed under the closed door of her father's study. Angeline stood for a moment gathering courage, then lifted her hand and knocked. It seemed long minutes before she heard him rise and come to answer.

When he opened the door and saw her his features softened.

"Angeline! It's late, can't you sleep? Come in."

It was awkward, the two of them alone together, the big house folding around them, empty and still. He stirred the dying embers of the fire. With his back still turned he spoke to her over his shoulder.

"The house will seem strange without you."

"I hope not. I hope you won't miss me too badly, you or Fletcher. He'll need you now, father."

He poked at the embers; it was as though she had not spoken. When he turned and saw her curled up in the chair, looking so like her mother, his face turned ashen. She saw the look in his eyes and went to him and took his hands in her hands.

"When you leave me it's the last of her gone," he said.

She could barely make out the words but they pierced her—like shafts of pain, like shadows across her heart. She had come here prepared to spell out his duty, to brave the bold-faced encounter, to make him see that he could no longer neglect the son he had fathered. In her idealism she had thought in one moment to wipe out the past, to set everything right.

She knew now that such an endeavor would be hopeless. She could not fight the intricate complexities of heart and mind. All she could hope to do was love them, knowing as she did so that her love would not be enough. She drew the gray head against her shoulder.

"Papa, papa." The childhood endearment came and she held him, as he had held her that night long ago when everything had been pain and darkness and the only comfort was in his arms. She held him until at last his long arms lifted and circled around her, and the comfort came to both their hearts.

The minister had arrived and the guests were gathering. Aubrey stood and greeted each one who came through the wide front door. He smiled, remembering Dyanne's shrewd appraisal: "The county's best, all come to outdo each other." Something within him responded with pleasure to the awareness that all this was happening just for him. The house in polished elegance behind him, the sheds and barns, the animals and acres, the labyrinth of gardens, the woods, the lane—all this was his, and he was master. And Angeline was the finishing touch.

Dyanne had dressed Angeline to perfection and she stood waiting in all her wedding attire, secreted in an upstairs room until the moment when she would make her grand appearance and sweep magnificently down the broad curved stair. Her dress was crepe over white satin with flounces of satin looped up with white tuberoses. The graceful pompadour sleeves with ruffles of Honiton lace fell very low at the back of her arm and the points of her bodice were cut fine and deep. She wore short white gloves trimmed with swansdown and laced up the back of her hand with pale silken cord.

"I wish I had your thick hair," Dyanne lamented. "When I

marry I shall have to add a false braid or two. But then what will my husband say when I take down the masterpiece and all my beautiful hair falls out before his eyes?"

Angeline smiled gently. "Perhaps the fashion will change. Or begin a new one; you're just the person to do it."

Angeline stood in front of the mirror and regarded her image. Her rich brown hair, parted in the middle, was brought down in smooth bands to cover her ears, then braided in nine separate strands and interwoven into a graceful coronet at the back of her head. Her deepset eyes, dark as her hair, were fringed with thick lashes. Her cheeks looked rosy today, her skin very pale. She had a small, well-shaped nose, not too thin nor given to sharpness. The line of her chin, the curve of her throat—all seemed faultless before her exacting gaze.

It was good to look in the mirror and find yourself pleasing; the waiting eyes, the eyes that would be staring could do her no harm if she remembered this moment. She drew herself up and turned. The door opened. "Miss Angeline?" Minerva's broad face was shining. She took a deep breath. At last it was time.

It was time. The *Wedding March* was playing. All stood in anticipation of the bride. There was a brief stir in the room of muffled silence; a murmur, a greeting or two. Aubrey turned his head. Hamilton had quietly entered and on his arm, looking elegant and frail and holding herself like a queen, walked his mother. He drew in his breath. So this was Hamilton's way of "taking care of things." Aubrey's high rolled collar felt suddenly hot and tight. He shifted again. He would not seek their eyes nor acknowledge their presence, not until the ceremony was safely over.

Like the gentle sigh of a wave he heard the sound, a trembling response that passed through everyone present. He lifted his eyes— and when he saw her, poised at the top of the staircase like an angel, glowing and soft and pure, he forgot everything else but the love within him, and the knowledge that this wondrous perfection belonged to him.

The words were brief, but the words were solemn, and the kiss Aubrey gave her was like a seal, spreading through her with a thrill of promise. She turned and for a moment there was silence. In that quick moment she slipped through an opening in the crowd. The regal lady stood watching her, waiting. Angeline reached Eliza's side, put her arms around her, and kissed her very gently.

"I shall try to be a good daughter to you," she whispered.

For a moment Eliza's eyes misted over. "You are a lovely bride, my darling, a credit to Lairdswood."

"I'll drink to that," someone nearby suggested. Black servants were already circulating with trays of liquid refreshment, directing the guests to the porticos and porches.

"Samuel, I believe I should like a little sherry. Would you be so kind?" Eliza turned to Hamilton. He took her extended hand, bowed briefly, then turned and steered her expertly through the crowd. Those standing the nearest saw and heard her. Angeline, staring after her, felt dumbfounded.

"Good luck with that one," an ample lady chirped, patting her arm in a motherly way. "Not much you can hope to do with her kind. She's lost to the world, as some folks would say."

"Humor her," another woman suggested.

"She's got that handsome son of hers to do that."

The two ladies laughed as they wandered off together. Angeline, standing on tiptoe, searched for Aubrey. Suddenly from behind two arms were around her, hugging her waist, a warm breath against her neck. She turned in the embrace.

"It's my turn, little sister."

The blue eyes that gazed into hers were bright and piercing. She had never been this close to the eyes before, nor the lips that laughed at her with desire. She twisted in his arms but he didn't release her. *Let him kiss me then!* She relaxed and his face drew nearer. She readied herself, half closing her eyes. Then the lips brushed past her lips and touched her cheek briefly, feeling cool and tender against her skin. In a moment it all was over, but Angeline trembled, confused at the impulsive, unpredictable actions of the man.

"So you have what you want now." His voice was masked and careful.

"What do you mean?" she asked.

"Well, I don't mean Aubrey."

"You mean Lairdswood." She made the words a statement. She forced herself to meet the hard gray eyes. She blinked; the eyes looking back at her were friendly.

"I love Lairdswood," she said. Another statement. He nodded slowly.

"I don't begrudge you that. You belong here," he said. "Welcome home, Mrs. Stewart."

In his mouth the words became a caress. She stared at Hamilton. What was his meaning? Others were pressing to congratulate the bride. He nodded briefly, turned, and left her. What was his meaning? She wanted to know.

There had been food enough to feed all of Natchez. Long tables covered with snowy linen cloths and spread with what Angeline thought was a staggering assortment: turkey, duck, Virginia ham, roast mutton, chicken salad and chicken fricassee, sweetbreads, and an assortment of delicacies—jellies, blancmange, meringue baskets, secrets, mixed cakes, macaronas lady fingers, grapes, bananas, pineapples, fresh ice cream, and Roman punch. Not to speak of coffee and liqueurs for the ladies, brandy, wine, and, of course, champagne. And when the guests had floated away at last there was food left over to feed the entire plantation household for a week. The slaves, of course, were to have their own celebration. But Angeline and Aubrey would not be there to make an appearance and accept their congratulations. When the steamboat *Natchez* set off for the port of New Orleans in the last pale hours of daylight, they were aboard.

It was an exciting, romantic way to begin a marriage. Aubrey had made arrangements for one of the few grand cabins, ignoring Hamilton's dampening prophecies.

"You'll have to take turns in the bed," Ham had warned. "They're so confounded narrow. It's no way to begin a love affair, little brother."

But Aubrey didn't agree. He wanted the freedom, with no one

stalking his steps, watching every move. When he and Angeline got back they'd be used to each other. Time enough to deal with Hamilton and his mother then.

Around the second—boiler—deck, which held passengers' staterooms as well as the barroom and dining salon, ran a promenade like a narrow white veranda. Here Angeline stood with her husband and watched the sunset. The end of the day was as beautiful as its beginning. The clouds were trailing ribbons of light like streamers. Gold seemed to be spilling out across the horizon and the sun itself was a boiling curve of gold, etched just above the gray line of water.

"Shall we go in now?"

"Oh, Aubrey, no. Just a few moments longer."

He smiled. He had not been watching the sunset, but the beauty that stirred beside him, young and alive. "I'll go check and make certain our cabin is ready."

"I'll be along in a moment," Angeline promised. She leaned over the railing. The sky seemed to be scattering sprays of fire across the dark water below. There was no other sound but her breath and the sigh of the water. Then a door banged open and sharp voices drew near.

"I don't give a _____, he's a _____ and a liar. Let him drown in five fathoms of hell before crossing Tom Leathers."

The voice was a boom and a snarl together. Angeline turned. She had seen Tom Leathers before, but only from a distance on social occasions. Leathers owned the *Natchez* and had named her after the city. People said Tom had a love affair with Natchez; it was the one place on earth the Kentuckian wanted to live. Angeline's brief movement caught the captain's attention. When he saw the young woman he strode the short distance between them, stood with his legs stretched apart, and stuck out his hand.

"My pardons, ma'am. Thomas Leathers at your service."

He towered above her, six foot four, wide girthed, broad shouldered, weighing close to three hundred pounds. His keen eyes looked out from under a ledge of bushy eyebrow. His nose was large and the line of his mouth a hard slash. But the deep eyes sparkled and the smile was boyish and friendly.

She took the extended hand. It was a thick, large paw and her own lay small against it. He patted her hand in an almost fatherly manner.

"I always say what's the use of being a steamboat captain if you can't tell the world to go to the devil, eh, Mrs. Stewart?"

"'Tis a luxury I've wished for myself a time or two."

He threw back his head and laughed in loud pleasure. "A beauty, I said when I first laid eyes on you. It's gratifying to find you have spirit as well, my lass."

"Thank you for both the compliments, Captain Leathers."

Ben, the mate, had been waiting through all this, watching. Leathers turned to him now with a smile and a broad wink.

"I'm escorting the little lady to her cabin. Excuse us, Ben."

Angeline took his arm. She liked the burly captain and was quite certain that he felt the same easy friendship for her.

"You remind me of my little wife, very small and dainty. She weighs ninety-eight pounds, never's topped a hundred yet." He spoke the words with a lover's apparent pride.

"And how does she manage to handle the likes of you?"

His eyes twinkled and he shook his great mane of hair. "Don't ask me, ma'am. She must use some kind of magic. But she knows how to keep me in line, I'll assure you of that."

Aubrey heard the two voices approaching and recognized them. He smiled to himself. *So she's already charmed the captain.* When she came in her color was high and her eyes were shining.

"I've been with Tom Leathers. He's fascinating, Aubrey."

"So you've charmed 'Old Push.' That's no small feat," he replied.

"I remind him of his wife. That's the only reason."

"No it isn't, and you know it."

She sat down beside him, her fingers working at the gold pins and braids that bound up her hair. At last it fell loose and she shook it about her shoulders. He traced the line of her chin, the curve of her throat. Her skin was soft as rose petals under his hand.

Something deep and wonderful stirred when Aubrey touched her. She kissed him, hungry, suddenly eager. What swept them both must be something eternal, as deep as the river, as endless as the skies, as brilliant and burning as all the bright stars above her. She sighed, content. The promise had not been a lie. Love was joy and life was loving, and she was one with this man who held her in his arms. The mystery didn't dissolve in the knowing but grew, a brighter treasure within her hands.

_____Seven

Of all the towns along the lower Mississippi, New Orleans was the undisputed queen. In January of 1815, two weeks after the War of 1812 had ended, American troops successfully defended the city against a British assault and the glorious Battle of New Orleans became history. Free now to grow, the busy Mississippi, crawling with barges, keelboats, and ambitious little steamers, made people feel that everything was possible. By the 1840s the river and her enterprise had transformed New Orleans from a charming Creole town into one of the largest shipping ports in the world.

Angeline discovered that something exciting took place in New Orleans on every street corner, at any time of the day or night. From the rougher sports such as cock fighting, bull and bear baiting, horse racing, and gentlemen's duels—more popularly known as "games of murder"—there were excellent plays and concerts and outstanding dining with menus boasting crawfish bisque and gumbo filé, Spanish mackerel and pompano, fried plantains and baked bananas, claret and bourbon, absinthe, Sazerac, and silver fizz. She found street shows with everything from jugglers to portrait painters, street vendors selling fresh fruits and sweet, sugary pralines, and open-air markets with street after street of wares. It was like a circus, sensation after sensation, each experience more exciting than the last.

The pleasures and sensations merged together except for two things that stood out in Angeline's mind. One was a chance encounter with a stranger who passed the candlelit table where they dined. He was a distinguished man, a little older than Aubrey, but not older than Hamilton, she remembered thinking. He paused beside them and spoke and his voice was Northern in accent, but respectful and very kind.

"Excuse me, sir, but aren't you Aubrey Stewart from Lairdswood? Hamilton Stewart's brother?"

Aubrey nodded—coldly, Angeline noticed. She watched more closely.

"What a stroke of luck running across you this way. You may not remember me, sir. My name is Warren Ellis. Your brother and I have a business association."

Aubrey stared, and his voice when he spoke was as cold as his eyes. "I know very well who you are."

The man raised an eyebrow, disconcerted, but he stumbled on. "Very well, then. Uh...Mr. Stewart, it would be most helpful if you might—"

"Mr. Ellis, I'm on a pleasure trip with my new wife. I am not interested in what would be helpful to you."

Aubrey! Angeline nearly spoke right out loud. She was shocked at his rude behavior. So was the stranger, but he made one more attempt.

"It is not my own interests, but a matter your brother is very anxious about."

"I am not interested in your concerns or my brother's. Is that clear enough, sir?"

"Most emphatically, Mr. Stewart. Forgive the intrusion. Sir—Madam."

He bowed and left them. Angeline felt herself trembling.

"Aubrey!" She had never scolded him in public. "You behaved like a mannerless brute. I can't believe it."

He scowled at her from across the table. "I had reason enough."

"I don't care what your reasons were. There's no excuse for belittling others with such behavior, not to mention what harm you cause yourself."

"Angie, I don't wish to talk about it. It's been a bone of contention between us for years." He made a gesture half of anger, half of frustration.

"What has?"

She was pushing him; he knew she would keep on pushing.

"Hamilton believes in dealing with Northern entrepreneurs, investing in Northern business with Southern capital." There was emotion in his voice that he strove to control.

"Several Natchez 'big bugs' have Northern holdings. What about it do you object to, Aubrey?"

"Everything! Lining their pockets, giving them power. Nearly a dozen plantations outside of Natchez are owned by Northerners. Land, Angeline! That's Southern land."

She leaned forward a little; she was listening now intently.

"Steel mills, bank stock, railroads—it's so much malarkey. It could all blow up in smoke. But not the land. When everything else goes to pieces, there's still the land."

Angeline was surprised by the depth of his emotions. Nor could she really take issue with him. She thought to herself: *Don't I love the land? Don't I love Lairdswood as though it had a spirit, a life of its own?*

The encounter stuck with her and colored her thinking, though at the time she had no feelings or premonitions concerning the part Warren Ellis would play in her life.

All the arteries of trade ran to New Orleans, as lifeblood flows through the arteries of a man. The main focus was on sugar and cotton sales, and on yet one more lucrative commodity: slaves. Planters from all parts of the expanding Southwest, coming to New Orleans to market their crops or touch base with their factors, called in at Gravier Street or Bienville, where the slave dealers set up their wares. There were sales going on the morning that Aubrey took her there. Angeline had never witnessed the business on this kind of scale before.

"I'd like to check out the market," Aubrey told her, "see what they have to offer in young field hands."

Angeline hung back. Her father owned only three Negroes; she wasn't accustomed to slave trade as such.

On the auction block she noticed an older Negress, light in color, who stood a little apart, her hand on the shoulder of a very black little boy with thick kinked hair and large brown eyes. The auctioneer was speaking and the boy moved forward, but his mother's hand detained him and he paused. The dealer was up beside them in a moment, his forked whip cutting skittles along the floor.

"You listen here, Nancy, you promised you'd give no trouble. You want me to get harsh with you now?"

He grabbed hold of the boy and pulled him to the front of the platform. The bidding began and it seemed to drag on forever. Angeline felt a stirring beside her and turned to find Aubrey there.

"Bid on the boy," she said, surprised at her boldness.

"We don't need him, Angie. He's not old enough for a field hand."

"Use him in the stables. The man said he had worked with horses."

"Angie, I don't think—" Aubrey stopped and frowned and drummed his fingers against the green painted column where Angeline leaned. He *was* in need of someone new in the stables. He didn't like Jonas's way with the horses—he had no natural instinct, he wasn't gentle with them. This boy would be gentle. And what was more, Aubrey could train him exactly the way he wanted. He could always turn Jonas back into the fields.

He moved a step forward. Tim Ostler from St. Francisville seemed to be highest bidder. Aubrey knew him; he was overseer for old "rascal Randolph," pig-eyed and little and meaner than Randolph himself, who had no small reputation in that quarter.

"I'll give five twenty-five for the boy." Aubrey spoke up loudly. People shifted and turned to eye him. Ostler hunched his thin shoulders and spit in the straw at his feet.

"Mr. Aubrey Stewart of Natchez has entered the bidding. He has topped Mr. Ostler with the sum of—"

Angeline didn't listen. She was watching the boy's mother, wondering at her excessive reaction. As soon as the auctioneer spoke Aubrey's name the woman had clasped her hands at her breast and begun to sway back and forward, at the same time muttering brokenly under her breath. Her face was transfixed, like the Negroes at gospel meetings when some influence overtook them and left them dumb. She kept swaying back and forth, her low voice mumbling, and her keen eyes never strayed from Aubrey's face.

Tim Ostler raised the bid, but Aubrey went higher. Ostler spit out a wad of tobacco with a crude oath; then Aubrey knew he had him. In a few minutes it was all over. He approached the broker to conduct terms and arrangements. As he walked past the woman she reached out a long, slender arm and touched him very timidly.

"Massa Aubrey, I'm old Nancy, your mother's servant. I come wid her to Lairdswood when I was a bit of a gal—"

The dealer approached. "Git back from the gentleman, Nancy. Ain't no business of yours no longer."

Aubrey held up his hand. "No, leave her, let her continue."

He turned to the woman. She didn't cower but stood at ease before him. She was light in color, slender, fine high cheekbones. Something stirred in his memory. "You belonged to my uncle and came with mother to Mississippi when she was married."

"Yes! Yes, suh, dat's me. But I shore had no sense as a youngun. I run off wid dat man I marry, and your daddy, he sole me. I had nothin' but trouble and sorrow eber since."

Aubrey remembered the story suddenly, very clearly. "I'm too young to have known you," he said.

"Dat's ah-right, young massa. You ges gib your mammy my best. You saved my youngun. Dat's the lass child I have left, and you saved him, massa." The dealer grabbed her roughly and drew her away. Angeline, who had watched the exchange, was fascinated.

"Angeline, wait for me by the door there. I'll be but a minute."

There was something in Aubrey's voice that made her comply. She walked toward the open door; from behind her she heard him.

"I want the woman as well as the boy."

The dealer blinked and rubbed the stubble along his chin. "She ain't—"

"I don't want her qualifications, I want to buy her. Pay a decent price, but don't you try to skin me. I'll be back to settle up and make transfer arrangements."

When they were out in the warm, clean air walking together Angeline hugged his arm and smiled shyly. "I'm glad you bought the boy, Aubrey. But who was the mother? Did she really know your family?"

"Much more than that." His voice held a note that she couldn't decipher. "She was one of my uncle's illegitimate daughters by a house slave he was particularly fond of."

Angeline said nothing, but her eyes grew wider. They crossed a street, dodging horses and potholes. On the other side he continued again.

"He was old, you see, he doted on the young slave girl. When this child came along, his wife had had her fill and more. But he wouldn't sell the girl to just anybody. So when mother married and moved so far away, he saw the perfect out and he took it. Presented her as a gift to his baby sister."

"What do you think your mother will say when she sees her?"

"I don't know." Aubrey rubbed his hands together. "That's the only thing I'm concerned about."

But that wasn't true. If for any reason the transaction upset his mother he'd have more to pay where Hamilton was concerned.

"I'm glad you purchased her, Aubrey. There's something about her. I believe she'll serve you faithfully and well."

"Do you believe so? I just had this feeling...but now I'm not certain..." He wondered at the weakness in himself, feeling manipulated by some softness he carried inside.

Eight

Coming home was a quiet affair but very pleasant. Lairdswood was a hive of activity, but homey activity, peaceful and somehow ordered, so welcome after the hustle and noise of New Orleans. The bedroom suite of furniture they had chosen their first day in the city had arrived by boat and was set up and waiting for them.

Angeline walked slowly over the threshold of the north bedroom. She thought: *This will be the center of home to me. It will be Aubrey and comfort and love. It will be quiet talks on a winter's afternoon, or watching a bright spring sunrise together. It will be crying alone where nobody else can see me. It will be hope and laughter* . . . She touched the smooth, carved rosewood of the half-tester bed where she would sleep with Aubrey. The footboard was delicately worked with two sweeping scallops. She traced these now with her hand as she gazed around her. There was a double armoire, a bureau, and two bedside commodes, ivory-covered. She must set out her belongings—her books and her pictures, her needlework and doilies, her special perfumes. *It will seem more me,* she thought. *So this is Lairdswood. I am Lairdswood—and I am home.*

Aubrey's mother came down that evening to join them for supper. She welcomed Angeline with gentle enthusiasm. As they ate she asked chatty questions that seemed very normal. Then suddenly, out of nowhere, "Good heavens, Aubrey. Your father's not back for supper again tonight. It was rude of him; I shall speak to him of the matter. He certainly should have been here to welcome you home."

For a moment or two the table was in silence. Angeline became suddenly aware of the swish of the punkah. Her eyes were drawn to watch the cotton-dyed flowers and cotton blossoms swish, arch and disappear, then swing back again. It was a warm evening so a small slave boy worked the "Shoo Fly" back and forth, back and forth . . .

Angeline laughed brightly. "Eliza," she said. "May I call you Eliza?"

"Of course, my dear, we are friends already, you know."

"I must try to describe for you the fashions I saw in New Orleans. Outlandish, and some so bold—"

"I'd love to hear, though I'll wager before you begin, dear, there'll be nothing so bold as the fashions of my own day. When I was a girl short wigs were the going rage. You couldn't be seen in public with your own long hair showing. Five dollars for a wig to tuck it all under and show yourself in the height of style."

Angeline smiled. "Please go on. I want to know what I have to compete with."

Everyone laughed. After that it was easy, the conversation was natural and spontaneous. *I like Eliza Stewart,* Angeline thought. *I'm sure she could teach me a lot, and I mean to learn it. She knows how to be the great lady of a great house. It seems safe to me to follow in her footsteps.*

May evenings in Mississippi were long and languid. Angeline sought a few moments alone on the wide front porch that extended along the second story of the house. Six identical rockers sat in a row. They looked cool and inviting. Angeline chose one and sat back, relaxing against the smooth wood. Here more than anywhere else she felt mistress of Lairdswood. Before her were the wide lawns, finely boxed in with hedges or bordered round with an edging of flowers. Just beyond stretched the oak lane she had ridden with Aubrey. From here she could see the intricate lacing of branches and the long gray moss that trembled in the slack air. With that peculiar clarity of light that sometimes comes before sunset the trees seemed three-dimensional, far yet near, as though she could reach out and touch one with her hand.

The rocker creaked, so she didn't hear the footsteps. She felt a hand on the back of her chair and turned to find Hamilton.

"May I?" He indicated the seat beside him. She nodded. "I thought to find mother here," he continued. "This is her favorite spot."

"I can well see why. There's a feeling of space here, of symmetry, of freedom—" She paused. "I'm sorry. I must sound a little dramatic."

"Not at all. We've already established your love for Lairdswood."

She took a deep breath. "What about you?" she asked him. "How do you feel about Lairdswood?"

"Now, that's a strange question to ask." He contemplated her sharply, his blue-gray eyes questioning, probing. "There's something behind a question like that."

"You're right. There is a reason behind the question. Something that happened, something I think you should know."

He listened quietly while she told him of their encounter with his Northern business associate, Mr. Ellis. His only visible reaction to his brother's rude behavior was a tightening of the muscles around his mouth.

"It was kind of you to tell me, Angeline. Thank you."

"I just hope it wasn't too awfully important."

"It was important. But that's neither here nor there now."

She could see it was costing him something to bridle his anger and control the reactions her story had stirred.

"That brings us back to the motive behind your question. How could I love Lairdswood and the land when I'm content to sell out to cold-hearted Northern capitalists who are unworthy to set foot upon sacred Southern soil?"

She stared at him. "You knew all along—"

"As Aubrey must have told you, it's an old trouble between us." He rose as if to go.

"No, please. I want to know what you think."

"And why is that?" He whirled to face her, the lines of his lean face drawn and set. She could never feel sure of herself around this man. She tried to return his gaze unblinking, squarely.

"I want to know more—I want to understand."

He sat down slowly. "All right." He nodded. "I'll tell you. There are too many Southern leaders," he began, "who fight unity with the North upon any premise. Men such as Randolph, John Taylor, and now Calhoun, who argues that a state should continue fully sovereign with the right to decide whenever a Federal law violates the Constitution. Then that state could refuse to obey and could nullify the measure. That's as powerful a states' right stand as you can come by."

He leaned forward, eager, engrossed by the things he was saying.

"Many of the protective tariffs the country has are advocated and maintained by Southern votes in Congress. We cotton planters pay duties only on what we consume of foreign goods. A large part of the duties paid in the country as a whole come from goods for which there is no demand in the South. We have fought for a state of being that favors our system. And the opposition, the controversy rages."

Angeline nodded. "I think I understand. The rest of the country is angry at us, and jealous."

He laughed, but the laugh was kindly, not cutting. "You could put it that way. But we Southerners do tend to act, my dear, without temperance and bring much of our trouble down upon our own heads."

"Do you fear for the future?"

"Yes, I fear for the future. There may be war with Mexico, did you know that? And worse—much worse. You see, Angeline, Northern money goes into what you might call industrial improvements: schoolhouses, mills, railroads, waterworks, gasworks, new labor-saving devices—it is constantly distributed, reinvested. Do you know where Southern cotton profits go?"

She shook her head.

"You may think into libraries, furniture, precious art pieces. The blunt truth is, Southern profits go almost exclusively into Negroes."

Something about the intensity of his gaze when he said the words sent a cold chill through her.

"They're the basis of our system; we're tied up with them. Of course, not *all* Southerners—but planters like me and Aubrey. You can bet your bottom dollar on one thing for certain: When the North decides to go for blood it will be men like us and places like Lairdswood they'll be after."

She rose and walked to the balustrade, fighting emotions that were new and mature, emotions she wished to reject. *I don't want to think of such things!* she told herself fiercely. He came up behind her and stood very close, with his hands on the railing.

"The last thing I want to do, Angeline, is upset you. What I'm trying to do should, I hope, make you secure. The *only* way to protect what we have is with Northern investments."

His voice was intense. She turned and studied his profile. He wasn't looking at her, but out over the land. The contours of his face were finely chiseled, his chin line firm, his red-gold hair disheveled.

"It's childish to hoard all your eggs in one basket, turn your back on the future as though it will never exist. All this—" he threw out his arm, almost in anger—"all this could tumble into chaos about us, and how many people would be able to pick up the pieces?"

She trembled again. He felt it and turned to face her. "I'm sorry." He shook his head at his own folly. "I'm not doing much better, am I?"

He took hold of her shoulders. His grip was firm and compelling, like all else about him. But when he spoke his voice was gentle and persuasive.

"Listen, we'll be able to hold things here together. I promise you that. And no matter what else about me, I have never been known to go back on my word."

His eyes held hers, there was something solemn in them. Even when she returned to her room, with all the impressions churning, all the fresh ideas juggling in her head, it was that one last thing she turned to to restore her. Why she should believe him she didn't know. But the strength and peace she sought came from those last words: *I promise you that. And no matter what else about me, I have never been known to go back on my word.*

"So when are they due to arrive?"

"Day after tomorrow."

Aubrey played nervously with the pen he was holding, drawing circles and lines across the marked-up sheet where he and Hamilton had been doing some accounting. He had just told his brother of the purchase of the slave woman Nancy and her son. Hamilton had listened with little expression or outward reaction. Now he stretched and leaned back in his chair with his hands cupped behind his head.

"You were really feeling your oats off alone in New Orleans, weren't you, brother? Well, what's done is done."

"Maybe not. We could always resell them."

Hamilton shook his head. "No, let's play the thing out now."

"It's a chance we're taking." Aubrey's brow was creased in a faint line of worry.

Hamilton chuckled. "Which side are you advocating, brother? Everything in life's a chance. That's how I see it."

"Well, I do feel rather responsible—"

"Yes, and you ought to! There's only one point about it that really concerns me. The sale of Nancy is one of the few things they disagreed over. As I remember the story, mother was young and headstrong and opposed father pretty strongly on the matter."

"And he didn't give in?"

"Not that time—you know what a principle it was with him. Having the girl around," Hamilton mused, "was a constant reminder to him of something he could neither sanction nor understand. I think he sold her to come to some peace with himself on the matter."

He rose. "Well, let's see what happens. We'll play it by ear. Trust you to keep things lively, little brother."

It was a barb, but not as unkind as it might be. It seemed to Aubrey that Hamilton had been somewhat subdued since Angeline came here. Whatever the cause, he was pleased with the difference. Though maybe the difference was in himself, he decided. He felt more sure of himself, less uncertain in making decisions, in taking actions he would have agonized over before. And with himself he *knew* that Angeline was the difference; he knew, and he thanked his lucky stars for the change.

_____Nine

Eliza Stewart was always the first white person astir in the household. Angeline learned this after a day or two and asked her mother-in-law if she might accompany her on her daily rounds.

"I see no reason why not, Angeline. You must sometime learn the management of the place and, as far as I'm concerned, the sooner the better."

She cocked her head and the girlish sparkle came into her eyes.

"I've no daughters of my own, so I've had to be patient until one of those slow boys of mine decided to bring home a wife. Don't you think it's about time I sat with my feet on a pillow, ate comfits and sipped mint juleps all the day?"

Her tingling laugh spilled forth and Angie laughed with her. So the following morning when shadows clung to the corners and sifted like cobwebs along the high windows and walls, she took the big ring of keys that Eliza gave her and began her first duties as mistress of Lairdswood Hall.

Eliza was in the habit of kneading the light morning bread with her own hands, at the same time instructing the kitchen servants concerning the meals of the day. Angeline had learned to make her own bread, being substitute mother, so this posed no problem for her, and she liked the black woman, Hester, who ran the kitchen. Wide and ample she was and she wore a bright blue bandana wrapped round her head, and about her waist an apron whose deep pockets contained bits and pieces of hidden treasure ranging from sugar lumps, moist and linty, to pins and needles, herbs for the headache and herbs for the belly cramps, a spool of thread, a small ball of yarn for the kitten that sneaked in to sit by the huge brick fireplace. She grinned a wide, toothy grin at Angeline.

"This chile needs fattenin' up some, Miss Eliza, if I do sez so myself."

She handed Angie a hot sweet roll fresh out of the oven, winked broadly, and said in a conspiratorial way, "Now, listen, chile, you done marry dat nice Massa Aubrey. You's a wife now and needs to know som'pin about a man. Ain't nobody knows more about men dan does ole Aunt Hester—"

"That's right," Eliza agreed in a sweet, easy manner. "Hester's raised both boys from babies, she knows them well. Besides that, she's had five husbands of her own—"

"Six, mistress, dis Rufus done make six—"

"You've had six different husbands?"

"Lan', missus, she's turnin' pale at the thought, jes' see her."

Much fussing and laughing and teasing ensued until Eliza scolded the Negroes back into working and took Angeline through the passages, porches, and work rooms checking for cleanliness, her sharp eyes missing nothing, not a corner unswept nor a basket or tool misplaced. She checked the order of pantry and larder and chastised a young girl who had placed apricot jars where the plums ought to be. Before breakfast they still had time to go into the gardens and set four small boys to hoeing weeds and raking debris. Angeline found that she ate with great appetite that morning, and was glad she did, for the rest of the day was as busy: mixing medicines, cutting clothes for the slaves in a back room, scalding glassware and china and drying the pieces themselves, overseeing the dusting, the baking, the flower arranging, until finally in midafternoon they stole a few moments and sat in the music room, where Eliza played for her, and there were cool drinks to sip on and a few lazy hours to fill writing notes to friends, or resting awhile in her own room. Angeline loved it. There was a balance, she came to know, and she found that she loved the busy, pushing hours almost more than she did the ones she could call her own.

Supper wasn't served until seven-thirty, and usually that was the first she would see of Aubrey. It was nearing June and, the cotton stand being a good one, there was much cultivating to do to preserve the crop; not only the Lairdswood fields, but the Echodell acres as well needed hours of care and preparation.

One humid July morning several weeks after Aubrey and Angeline's return, Fletcher arrived at Lairdswood. His own world, very confined and carefully limited, was known and secure, but this world that was now his sister's seemed too far-flung and large for his liking. He clung like a shadow to the one thing he knew and trusted: the mistress herself.

Angeline humored him a little; his eyes were so frightened. But she knew he was talked of in whispers behind his back. She didn't want that. So one morning she went to the stables and found the boy, Moses, and drew him away from his work. His black eyes were like saucers. What could the mistress want of him? he wondered. She sat down on the low bench beside him.

"My brother," she told the young boy who watched her intently, "has come to visit me. He is taller and older than you—" she marked the space with her hand. "But he seems much younger.

Because he can't talk well, he can't make the words to express himself. Do you understand me?" Moses nodded solemnly, swallowing once or twice. "I want you to let him help you work with the horses. Be kind to him. Let him do a small job or two—"

The boy's face brightened. "Yes, ma'am, I knows what you mean. He kin carry the bucket, an' han' me the brushes, an' pour the oats in the bin."

"Yes." Angeline returned his smile. "I know I can trust you. Be careful with him—and be kind—and there'll be a reward."

Moses jiggled on the seat with his own excitement. "Yes, ma'am, yes, ma'am, you knows you can count on Moses."

"I'll bring him by a little later this morning."

She rose to go. He leaped up and cleared a pathway, pushing the heavy door open, then stood aside to let her pass through. The boy would serve her well, she knew it: make Fletcher happy and ease the pressure on her. She stepped lightly, happy to know she was solving the problem.

For Fletcher the days, full of fears and shadows, took on a new color when Moses entered his life. They not only worked in the stables, but fished together, chased frogs and coons and anything that moved, stole green apples from the trees, and begged goodies from Hester. Fletcher had the first real friend of his life.

At night he would stammer and struggle to share with Angie the wonders of the days. He failed in the effort, for nothing could reproduce the feelings inside him—most definitely not the dull speech he was capable of. But she tucked him in bed and kissed him and that was better than even the day's adventures with Moses had been. He took one day at a time and he was happy.

There were not many slaves who could be trusted with cutting fine patterns. But Valencia had a way with a needle and thread. For years Eliza had worked with her and trained her, until now she was quite a seamstress in her own right. So she was called to do a gown for the new young mistress.

The three of them bent together over the work, Angeline faint with the heat and the closeness and somewhat uncertain of what to do or how to do it. Eliza was confident, happy in giving instructions, offering little encouragements here and there. Valencia's dark hands held the shears that cut through the lawn fabric—fine, cool fabric, smooth beneath her hands. Her body had never worn a dress of lawn fabric—cool and swishing across her legs, light, loose weight on her arms. She thought of the coarse cotton cloth of the shift she was wearing. She smoothed the fabric and cut a few inches more. She didn't like the way the older master looked at this woman—Hamilton, who had always been kind to her, whose lean, sinewy looks stirred a sense of excitement in her. Now he never seemed to notice if she was there.

Everything had changed with this woman's coming—this pretty white woman whose body would wear the fine dress and who poked in her nose where Valencia didn't want her. The scissors moved and slithered, serpent-quick—noiseless and sure and immutable in their cutting.

"Oh!" Angeline saw the move, but was too late to stop it. She grabbed for the scissors; they slipped and fell to the floor. Valencia hung her head. The tears were coming—by the time Eliza spoke the big tears were there, ready to show the mistress.

"My goodness, what's here? You've ruined this piece, Valencia. That's not like you." She turned to Angeline, disturbed but unsuspecting. "She's never made such a mistake before."

Angeline gathered and folded the pieces of ruined material. She didn't trust herself to make a reply.

"It's a shame. There won't be enough to finish the dress now. Stop that sniffling, Valencia. Accidents happen. Though I don't expect one of this kind to happen again."

The girl bent down to pick up the fallen scissors. Angeline caught the glance of pure hatred from the dark eyes. It stunned her like a blow. She stood frozen, unmoving. When the girl stood up again with the scissors her eyes were lowered, long lashes hiding whatever emotion they held.

Full mellow August was here and with it the first days of cotton harvest. Angeline obtained permission from her father to keep Fletcher a little longer. He was working out well now, no trouble at all. And what did he have to go home to? As far as she could tell from questioning him the two Mormon missionaries were still his companions, still talked with him, took him fishing now and again. His only friends . . . she wondered what things they talked of, what strange notions they fed into his head. She supposed they could do little harm with a boy like Fletcher, but nevertheless he was much better off out here.

Now the fields were dotted with gangs of slaves, men and women, like sets of patchwork, bright beneath the sun: red and blue bandanas, faded browns and yellows. Each slave dragged behind him his own long bag where he stuffed the cotton. When it was fat and full it would go onto mule-drawn wagons waiting to take the cotton to the gin. There were overseers to work the gangs and Negro drivers to aid in superintending the slaves, setting the pace for the work and acting as policemen. Yet Aubrey would come home every night exhausted—ravenous, but nearly too tired to eat. And tense, wound up like a top with some strange excitement.

Hamilton was noticeably absent during those evenings.

"He has his own ways of relaxing," Aubrey tersely said.

"You think he'd be too exhausted," Angeline countered. Aubrey raised an eyebrow.

"No, it's the tension," he said. "You have to unwind before you can face tomorrow."

So Hamilton spent his evenings Down Under, and she spent her evenings learning to be a woman, discovering little ways that a woman had to settle a husband, to calm him, to bring him comfort. And as they talked of slaves and cotton, discipline, weather, and profits, some of the cotton madness seeped into her veins. She chalked up the profits with Aubrey and felt the tense waiting, the awareness that every day—long, golden, and shining—came laden with armloads of treasure to fill their laps; and she found herself hungering, hankering after the treasure.

It was a hotter day than most, with a thunderstorm building— a day when the clouds would dapple and darken the sun, and the roll of distant thunder would sound and then echo, and any strange noise made a person start and jump. The slaves worked harder than usual, feeling driven, as though to escape the black heavens that crowded and spread. When darkness came the storm had still not broken, but a wind was rising, a noisy, whining wind.

Fletcher heard the wind at the casement around his window, laughing at him, trying to get inside. It was late; he had drifted into and out of slumber. The big house beyond his shut door was empty and still. But the wind still laughed and an angry rain was beating in brittle, incessant tappings against the glass. A cloud rode over the moon and the shadows trembled. Something moved. Fletcher saw the long, dark wedge of shadow cut into the dark of his room. From behind the shadow came something gray and whispery, moving his way. He tried to scream. He clutched at the moist bed covers. The gray shape stopped by the chair where his pants and shirt lay carefully folded; it paused a moment there. *It will go away,* he thought. *It will turn and leave now.* But the shape moved on till it stood beside his bed.

He could tell by now that the shape was some kind of person, and the person was mumbling strange sounds under its breath, and the person was reaching out with long fingers to touch him. Then the thunder tolled like a bell and a splinter of lightning seared across the darkness and showed the black face and the wide dark eyes, hate-filled in two pools of whiteness. And the fingers touched his face, and Fletcher screamed: long and high and keening, like a child.

By the time Angeline was there to hold him the gray shadow had disappeared and he was sobbing, and there was no way to make his sister understand.

Aubrey stood in the doorway watching the scene before him. There was nothing to frighten a boy his age into hysterics. Aubrey felt a wave of repulsion; he turned aside. "He's all right. Come back to bed now, Angeline."

He spoke over his shoulder and she didn't turn to answer.

"I'm staying with him for a while."

"Well, I'm going to bed." He stomped off in slippered feet, feeling strangely rejected, but not being quite able to define the feeling as such.

Angeline knew by his tone of voice what Aubrey was thinking. She resented it just a little. How many times had she ever imposed on his kindness and understanding? She felt he was deserting her when she needed him. She held the trembling boy and tried to still him, and felt much the way she had felt as a little girl: alone in the world, unloved and helpless.

Hamilton, sitting in the gentlemen's room that was called the card room, was nursing one last drink before going to bed. He had come from Under the Hill with his hungers still in him; there was nothing there that could settle his hungers now. He heard the patter of running feet on the staircase and reached the doorway in time to see the girl. The figure moved with the litheness of a young tiger. But before she disappeared he recognized her, and knew instantly what the trouble had been upstairs.

It took a long time to settle Fletcher. Angeline made very certain he was sleeping and pushed his door open wide before she left him. She felt cramped and exhausted, but far from sleepy. Aubrey would be long asleep by now. She felt her way down the stairs and into the library. She could read here awhile undisturbed, and perhaps clear her thoughts enough to go back to bed.

Drawn by the light in the room, Hamilton found her. He stood watching a moment before he made himself known, taking in the slender girl in the long white robe whose hair lay like silk down her back and along her shoulders. She was reading a book; her eyes were veiled. But he could see the line of her cheek and the curve of her lashes, and the throat more smooth and white than the lace resting on it.

"'O long and tedious night, abate thy hours. And sleep, that sometime shuts up sorrow's eye, steal me awhile from mine own company.'"

She looked up with a start and saw him standing in the doorway, framed golden, like a young god, in the light. "That's Shakespeare."

He inclined his vermilion head a fraction. "I'm pleased to find you know him, Angeline."

She turned back to her book. He entered, uninvited.

"Poetry as well? What have we—Shelley?" He took the book. She folded her hands in her lap, then rose. He had such a disruptive influence over her.

"I'm sorry. Don't go." He stood looking down upon her. "I'm sorry about your brother."

She turned with a movement shy and embarrassed. "He's all right now. He's asleep. Aubrey thinks nothing happened. But I've never seen him that way before. There must have been something—"

"Most assuredly something happened."

She turned to face him. "Do you think so?"

"Yes. Stop distressing yourself with doubts. Let's talk Shelley and perhaps you'll calm down some. Isn't that what you came for?"

She nodded slowly, her lips beginning to smile. "How is it you read poetry?" she asked him.

"I was educated, much to my father's shame. University of Virginia."

"I didn't know that."

"You wouldn't. It's not talked about much around here."

"Why ever not?"

"My dear, how can I explain it?" He walked a few paces, then sat on the edge of a chair, facing her, trying to second-guess her reactions. "I disgraced myself—wine, women, licentious living. And my father had never approved the idea at all. He was of the old school and felt that a boy's education could be handed down like his property, father to son."

He paused, still watching her face. "Do I bore you?"

"No, I'd like to know what happened—please go on."

"All right. Much better you hear it from me than from Aubrey. It was more than just the wild living. Take Jefferson. He founded the University of Virginia. He's a hero of mine, but my father could not understand that."

"Why not? What could he find to object to there?"

Hamilton smiled, and the expression, she thought, was more sad than bitter.

"Take the motto of the school as a good beginning. 'Here we are not afraid to follow the truth wherever it may lead, nor to tolerate error, so long as reason is left free to combat it.'"

"That doesn't sound too threatening."

"You don't know Jefferson. Join that with this: 'Can one generation bind another, and all others, in succession forever? I think not.' Jefferson—and that's really quite mild."

"Do you countenance all he said?"

"He set me to thinking. I was young, with youth's fiery sense of justice. I asked questions and made demands. I broke out of the pattern."

"And you challenged your father." She spoke the words quietly.

"It's no matter any longer. I got what was coming. I asked for it. I pushed him, and kept on pushing . . ."

He rose. She could feel his pain almost reach out and touch her.

"I was his eldest son. He had so much riding on me." He ran hard fingers through his unruly hair. "I became an embarrassment, a disappointment." He took a deep breath and stared at her—hard, unrelenting, as though he was somehow determined to punish himself. "In the end he died believing that I had failed him. I don't think I can ever forgive myself for that."

"*Hamilton!*" The word, as a whisper, escaped her. If he heard her, he did not acknowledge that he had heard. He walked over, took hold of her hand and raised her. In the silence she heard for the first time the thunder, and the lonely sobbing of rain against the dark glass. He handed her the candle and stood aside.

"Go ahead. I'll not be coming up until later."

She went. There was nothing else she could do. She crept into bed and lay very still beside Aubrey. And when she slept she slept from exhaustion, not from a sense of comfort or peace.

_____Ten

September was still consumed with the cotton harvest. There was work enough to last well into December, and the days had now settled into their grueling routine. Fletcher went home and Angeline missed him, though she was too busy to think about anything right now.

Cotton. It seemed they ate, drank, slept and breathed it. Cotton, born in those far-off countries of India and Africa, was admirably suited to gang slave labor in the South. True, the cotton crop required a long growing season, over one hundred fifty days free from killing frosts. Here in the Natchez country men could depend on two hundred to two hundred sixty frostless days. So cotton grew into the shape of dreams and legends, pulling the strings of prosperity round the land—white cotton bringing beauty and wealth and laughter, grown from glossy black seeds of hunger and pain.

But with September returned the social season, and who would host the first party, of course, but Dyanne? Angeline hated to admit it, but she was excited. These last few weeks had been trying and somewhat strained. It would do her good to laugh and chatter and gossip, to show off her handsome young husband again.

The day of the party dawned warm and cloudless. _This is a good day to make someone happy,_ Angeline thought. So this morning she walked alone to the stables and again drew Moses away from his ordered tasks. She walked with him awhile, discussing the horses, impressed as she always was by the boy's quick knowledge, by his memory, his sharp and accurate eye. They came to a stall where one small brown colt sheltered. He was a dusky brown, not glossy and richly coated. His legs were short and a little too stocky of build. His ears were too long and his nose would never be slender.

"What about him? Do you hold much hope for him, Moses?"

Moses stopped and scratched for a moment behind his ear. The pony, spying him, came and nuzzled his shoulder. She could see the warmth, like lights in the boy's black eyes.

"He won't never be no hunter or jumper. I know dat's true 'fore Massa Aubrey sez it."

"What would you suggest we do with him?"

"Don' axe me. I spose—" He struggled, hating to be honest, yet not canny enough to be anything else.

"I spose he ain't much good for nuthin'." He pushed away the wet, persistent nose and dropped his eyes so the lady couldn't read them. He felt her soft hand very lightly on his head.

"I don't agree with you, Moses. I think this colt could do very well if one kept him to roads and lanes, if one used him just for pleasure, or running small errands—"

He stood almost breathless, not daring to raise his eyes.

"Moses, the master and I have decided to put him into your care and keeping. He is yours to teach and ride when your work is finished. And Master Aubrey has agreed to free you from the stables during afternoons when I need your help with my errands."

She felt the young boy tremble beneath her hand.

"You've earned him, Moses. Master Aubrey is pleased with your work here. And I am not only pleased, but grateful, for the way you helped my brother and made him your friend."

He looked at her now, though his eyes were misted over. "Missus, I thank you, I don' rightly know how to thank you—"

"Take good care of him, Moses, that's all I ask."

His grin was broad and white and lit all his features. "I gwine ter do dat, yes ma'am, I gwine ter do dat!"

She carried his happiness with her throughout the day. And when she stood ready and gazed at herself in the mirror she knew there was something about her that had been missing the last time she attended one of Dyanne's parties. What was it? Confidence? Some sort of graceful assurance? She felt it, without being able to give it a name. She had been but a girl before; now she was a woman, with all of a woman's secrets and skills. She would wear the strand of pearls that had been her mother's. Somehow they would be right for her tonight.

But where had the pearls gone? How could the pearls be missing? A sickness rose from her stomach up into her throat. She had missed things before and never found them. She paced back and forth while the hands of the French clock moved. She knew there was only one answer: the black hate she had seen in Valencia's eyes.

"Are you coming, Angeline?" Aubrey stood beside her. She looked up, not able to hide the distress in her face.

"My pearls—my mother's pearls are gone."

"Missing? They must be somewhere. Have you looked well?"

She nodded, tears threatening to fill her eyes. "Aubrey, this isn't the first. I've found other things missing."

"Well, then, why haven't you told me before?"

She shrugged, a helpless little-girl gesture that made him draw her against him and gentled his mood.

"I'm sorry, darling. Don't let it spoil your evening. We'll settle the matter, I promise, first thing in the morning."

She went, but there was no happiness left in her spirit.

In the downstairs hall they met Hamilton. He was just leaving, but he paused, for he saw the dull sorrow on Angeline's face.

"I thought you were looking forward to going this evening. You look as though you just lost your only friend."

"Her mother's pearls, they seem to have come up missing." Aubrey's voice was brusque and impatient. He took Angie's arm and started to walk on by, but Hamilton placed himself in their path and there was no way to avoid him.

"Is this the first thing you've found missing, Angeline?"

She shook her head, not sure how her voice would serve her.

"Have you any idea who took them?" She didn't reply. "Angeline?" He could see that her eyes were frightened as well as unhappy.

"Really, Hamilton, we can settle this in the morning. You'll upset Angie, and the whole mess will make us quite late."

He pushed past now and Hamilton made no protest, though his hands were clenched into fists at his side. *I know her so much better than you do, brother. She'll enjoy nothing until she gets back those*

73

pearls. She's scared of something—and she needs to be loved and protected.

He had never disdained his brother so much before. And the bile of his need and envy unsettled his system. He went out to his horse and rode down the oak-flagged passage, then doubled back and tethered his horse by the path—the wooded, meandering path that led to the Quarters. *I'll settle this thing right now, brother—and in my own way.* He bent low and moved quickly and noiselessly down the rude pathway.

The party was every bit as lovely as Angeline had expected. It was good to see Dyanne's winsome smile, tucked in by dimples, and to hear the sound of her sugared voice.

"Why, Angeline, honey, what's happened to you? You're by far the loveliest belle of the ball tonight." She turned and winked at the smiling listeners. "Marriage must agree with our Angeline."

Angie blushed, and the crimson blushing became her. The women may have eyed Aubrey and cast him glances, but many handsome young men sought her gaze tonight, kissed her hand, and whispered compliments for her hearing. It was new, and it sent a pulse of excitement through her, to see the unmasked desire in other men's eyes. *This is good for Aubrey,* she thought. He was fierce and attentive, and aware of her in a way she liked. So long minutes would pass at a time when the pearls were forgotten. But as soon as something would bring them again to mind the hard knot would twist at the pit of her stomach and an unreasoning feeling of fear flicker through her mind.

Aubrey didn't mention the loss of the pearls all evening. Back home, getting ready for bed, she expected he might. But he had drunk several glasses of brandy, as well as champagne, though he swore it wasn't the drink but her bewildering beauty that sent fire surging through his veins. Whatever the cause, he was interested in far more important things than lost jewelry. For the first time she felt her response to him less than total. Some barrier cast up between their spirits threw a shadow across her pleasure in his love. *How complicated,* she thought, *are a woman's emotions.* And she longed for the freedom the shadow had darkened and marred.

When she came downstairs next morning a small group had gathered, under Aubrey's direction, she was sure. Hamilton stood a little apart, his long arms folded, assessing each move and each word with his watchful eyes.

Aubrey looked ill at ease and restless, Eliza wide-eyed and slightly confused. Only Valencia's face showed no expression as Aubrey questioned her concerning the pearls.

"Goodness, but this is a dreadful business." Eliza fussed like a little wet hen. "If you didn't take the pearls, girl, you must know something. I won't accept that they vanished into thin air."

The black girl stood straight and unbending, her deep eyes sullen. When she turned them on Angeline they seemed to smoulder. Angie felt hot all over; her skin went pale. Aubrey rolled his eyes and tapped his foot on the hardwood.

"We've no time for this kind of nonsense."

Valencia sniffled and turned enormous, innocent eyes on the young master. "I don' know nuthin' about de pearls, I swears it, massa."

Her voice was soft and low, and contrived to sound wounded. Hamilton saw that Angeline trembled. He sauntered forward. All eyes turned to watch as he pulled from his waistcoat pocket a long white strand of pearls.

Angeline gasped; Valencia's dark eyes widened. He dangled the pearls in front of her face. For the first time fear washed over her like cold water.

"Where in the devil—" Aubrey began.

"Shut up, little brother; I'll handle things from here on."

He stepped closer to the girl and she seemed to cower.

"Mistress—" She turned appealing eyes to Eliza.

Hamilton's hand reached out and the slap hit sharply—once across each cheek, as hard as he would have hit a man. Eliza made some little noise and, without even moving, Hamilton spoke to her with quiet authority. "Mother, go up to your room. Aubrey, take Angeline out of here—now! Do as I say!"

They were stunned into compliance. Hamilton grasped the girl's wrist and twisted her arm behind her. She moaned slightly but did not struggle against his hold.

"This isn't all, is it, Valencia? You've taken other things as well as the pearls. And it was you in Fletcher's room that night—I saw you." His voice was as full of venom as her eyes. "You do not harm the young mistress, whatever your feelings! I will not hazard her safety. You ought to have known that. You've gone much too far to turn back now, Valencia."

She broke into a long, low moan, her dark eyes rolling. "Don' sell me, massa, don' sell me, please."

He turned and pushed open the office door with the toe of his boot. A man was standing outside—a man in his forties, lean like Hamilton, but hard in a different way. From his hand dangled the overseer's knotted black cattail.

"Give her twenty-five lashes," Hamilton instructed him. "And I want her off the place within the hour."

The overseer licked his lips and spat into the bushes. "Yes sir, Mr. Hamilton."

Hamilton turned and left them. But the slight black girl watched after him with hate-filled eyes.

"Just what in blazes do you think you're doing? Punishing my slaves and then selling them out from under me, without so much as a by-your-leave." Aubrey was as angry as Hamilton had ever seen him.

"I don't need to ask your permission, little brother."

"Oh, don't you? They're my slaves—all Lairdswood is mine."

Hamilton stared with disdain at the man who stood trembling before him, this brother whom accident had shoved into his rightful place. "First of all, let me remind you, the slaves are held jointly, to be used both here and at Echodell. And second of all, who will challenge what I do here? Who besides you." He smiled, sarcastically benign. "You've no weight to throw around, Aubrey."

Aubrey's mouth curled into a petulant, angry snarl. "Big brother, whether or not you like it, I'm master here. I could have you thrown off the place."

Hamilton's laugh was frank and sincere. "But I don't think you'll try it. Do you, little brother?"

"You don't belong here!" Aubrey paced back and forth indignantly. "You ought to be back at Echodell—"

"Oh, really? And who is it that begged me to come here when father died? Who is it who didn't know how to run the plantation—who found the Natchez lawyer to rent the Echodell house to, so that Hamilton would be forced to stay by his side—"

"Shut up; I know all that. I've changed my mind now. I don't want you here. I don't want you near Angeline."

Spoken at last! Hamilton moved, his back to his brother, pacing himself now. "Someone has to look after the girl," he countered reproachfully. "You do a sorry job yourself—you know nothing of women."

"I know all I need to know about Angeline!" The words were a cry of defense. Hamilton gave no quarter.

"That's where you're most wrong."

The words were too smugly spoken. Aubrey whirled on his brother, but Hamilton caught his arm, wrenched it painfully, throwing his brother off balance.

"You don't want to come to blows with me, brother. I'd hate to send you to Angeline bruised and bloodied." His voice like an instrument spoke for him, harsh and disparaging.

"Just what do you have to be smug about?" Aubrey challenged. "You're cold and empty-handed—you've got nothing to boast of."

Hamilton raised an eyebrow but didn't answer. That thrust had gone home; he winced inside. "I know myself, and I can live with the knowledge. That's more than you'll ever be able to do."

Hamilton left, though Aubrey shouted behind him, seething and unsatisfied. All Aubrey's doubts and fears came crashing back upon him—feelings he thought he had conquered and left behind. And a new one: Was he inadequate as a husband? Like a poison the question penetrated his mind. And he knew the victory had been his brother's, the last revenge of a planted seed that would canker and grow.

But he didn't know that the infallible, self-contained Hamilton walked the fields of Lairdswood under the cold moonlight, with the night like a velvet paw that tore him to splinters. He couldn't lie to himself nor conceal his own knowledge that Aubrey had all that he, Hamilton, most wanted in the world. Had it and didn't know how to appreciate it—how to enhance it, how to make it shine. And Hamilton was bound to watch, self-tortured and helpless, with no way to heal the wound he suffered inside.

Eleven

In the days ahead Aubrey tried a little harder. Angeline, feeling the difference, responded—the trying bore fruit. But the brothers carefully avoided one another, Hamilton disappearing sometimes for days, seldom coming to dinner with the rest. Only when Eliza grew restive without him would he appear and quietly take up his routine. There was none of the caustic banter, the old sarcasm. Angeline thought the blue-gray eyes looked clouded, but he seldom spoke to her or sought out her company.

A fox hunt was planned for the first part of October. Hounds and horses were Aubrey's passion and, like a boy, he looked forward to the day with restless pleasure. When the morning came it was right; the air was chilly, the ground moist and warmer than the air.

The day before they had carefully chosen their horses. Ill luck perhaps that Hamilton entered the stables while Aubrey, drawing out the enjoyable task, compared horse against horse and savored the moment of choosing.

"You'd best take Ginger. She'll show you off to advantage." The usual quip, but Aubrey picked it up.

"It's I who excel in the riding field, remember? I think I'll mount Tormud."

"You're foolhardy if you do. He's skittish and his back leg is weak still. Besides, he's not ridden the course in nearly two years."

"What you mean is you think he's too hard to handle."

"You're being obstinate, Aubrey, for no good reason."

"I don't see it that way."

Here we go again, Hamilton thought. *Have your way, little brother. It's your neck, and you're big enough to take care of yourself.*

So now with the sun still wet and the river in shadow and blackbirds scolding across the empty sky, the noise of men and dogs broke the early stillness.

Angeline watched the men ride out, and the sight of Aubrey in his velvet cap, white stock, and brass-buttoned jacket, sitting high on the tall black horse, made her heart sing with gladness. The colors of coat and horseflesh flashed under the sun and Angeline thought the riders a romantic, disorganized sight with the spotted hounds running rivers around their feet. She watched until they became small and then she lost them, resigning herself to the hours that held nothing but a woman's waiting for her.

At first the field was slow getting started. The horses spread out, their excitement slightly quelled. The tall grasses were still wet with shadows and heavy dew. The hounds did much checking and once or twice started to feather. Then heads down, sterns high they found the scent and gave tongue. The huntsman blew his horn and, from a distance, someone called "view halloo!"—the fox was sighted.

Movement began up the hill, in the thick of the covert. There was a low wall and a muddy stream and some horses had trouble. But Aubrey on Tormud cleared it with little effort. *He does look fine on a horse,* Hamilton admitted. *As though for a change he knows what to do with himself.* There were a couple of hundred yards of riding full out, dodging bushes and brambles and jumping ditches. Then the hounds checked, and there ran through the riders a poised sense of pausing. Hamilton used the brief moment to slip ahead of Aubrey. And when the hounds took off in a wide arc toward open fields, he followed full pelt and drew several yards beyond him. He kept his lead, though the heavily plowed fields here slowed him to a trot. He was warming up now and the air in his lungs was delicious. Let Aubrey stew for a while—it would do him good.

Back at Lairdswood Angeline waited through the hours with her own excitement stringing her feelings high. When Aubrey rode back he would be boyishly flushed and happy, and then the time to tell him would be just right. She savored the picture and painted it for her own pleasure, practicing for the moment to arrive.

The riders in pink and black had ridden their fox to the ground and the hounds, hackles up, tails stiffened, gone in for the kill. The mask, pads, and brush had been duly awarded, then waved high for the riders to cheer; it had been a good run. But a fresh fox had been winded, the hounds were baying, the riders making ready to ride off again. There was the blowing and neighing of horses, the jostling of bodies, the creak of warm leather, the squashing of mud underfoot. And always the cry of the hounds that the hunters called music, the rhythm the horses rode to, the pulse of the hunt.

Aubrey and Travis Breckinridge were riding together. They were old boyhood friends, but Aubrey was twice the rider, so he was forced to check his horse often, and Tormud balked. For a few minutes they blundered about in blind country, jumping ditches thick with leaves and broken twigs and a high fence that Tormud took beautifully.

Then the close wooded area leveled and opened out and the field veered to the left and up a slight ridge. The horses pulled for more speed, strung up with excitement. Aubrey waited until Travis had a fair lead, until he was well away, then gave Tormud his head, and immediately the gap between them shortened.

Up where the low ridge crested stood a stone bridge; the riders followed the stream to the left down a smooth embankment. To the right the ground dropped sharply, turning to sand and gravel that slid down a broken ravine. There was a tangle at the bridge as they approached it. If Aubrey had been in the lead he could have worked round them and easily cleared the obstruction. But Travis panicked, checking his horse on a sudden late impulse.

It all happened quickly; afterward no one was sure of the details. One of the youngsters, attempting to be helpful, moved his mount just as Travis veered. Travis dragged on the reins, but too late; the horses collided. His horse reared, then stumbled, trying to regain firm footing. Aubrey coming up made an instant decision.

He could bear off to the far right and avoid them all. The drop was close and the surface loose and sandy. It was a calculated risk, but he thought he could make it. He would have if the frightened youngster, his horse no longer under control, had not suddenly bolted straight into his path.

Hamilton was approaching the bridge and he saw it. He opened his mouth to call, but it was no good. The thought flashed through his mind as he saw the horse shie and rear: *If he were riding Colonel or Ginger he could make it!* Tormud came down at an awkward angle. He slithered then stumbled, still fighting his rider's control and his own fear. He pulled back as he fell and Aubrey somersaulted forward, hitting the ragged embankment again and again.

Hamilton was the first to reach him. He was lying motionless, face down. Hamilton turned him over and with his silk stock began carefully clearing the mud and wet leaves from his face and nostrils and mouth. There was one good sign: he was breathing still. People gathered behind but Hamilton didn't heed them, except to shout once, "For mercy's sake, take care of that horse," and somebody put an end to Tormud's suffering and his shrill, inhuman scream that had wrenched them all.

There was no possible way to move or transport Aubrey. Someone rode for a doctor, and all they could do after that was wait. Hamilton loosened Aubrey's scarf and collar and folded his own coat under his brother's head, covering him with the one that Travis thrust forward. Hamilton thought he looked cotton-white and his breathing was ragged. It seemed a long wait. When the doctor finally came Hamilton rode along in the wagon holding Aubrey, refusing the dark thoughts that pressed against him, knowing that pain and guilt were nobody's friend now, forcing his mind to function and stay clear.

There was no one in sight when the wagon drew up before Lairdswood. Hamilton felt a wave of relief for that. If he could just get the boy inside and settled, then go and find Angie and ease her into the thing. He lifted the limp, still body, surprisingly heavy, and carried his brother gently into the house.

Angeline had heard the wagon and the voices. She came down a little perplexed, but eager. She heard the door open and was there when Hamilton entered, cradling her husband's body in his arms, limp and white and seemingly lifeless. Her hand flew up to her mouth, but she gave no cry. A terrible tightness constricted her throat.

"He's alive, Angeline. I'm sorry you're here to see this." He moved past her and in to the long sofa in the card room, laying his brother's body out carefully.

Then the doctor took over and ordered Angeline's departure. She hovered outside. There was nothing but muffled sounds, no voices she could discern from behind the closed door. She didn't want to think, but the thoughts came unbidden: *He'll die and he'll never know, he'll never know! Dear heaven. How will I bear it if he dies?*

She bit her lip. The waiting was torture; there was no way to make the pain go away.

The doctor, really, could do very little. He cleaned the cuts and set Aubrey's broken leg. But the concussion was another matter, and if there were internal injuries, well . . .

He departed, leaving instructions for Aubrey's care. The fever must be watched especially. When he was gone a terrible quietness seemed to settle, so that even their voices seemed loud and out of place.

"I want to stay with him," were the first words Angeline uttered. Hamilton nodded agreement and left them alone. She sat and stared at the still, white face. She had never seen Aubrey so still before—his eyes so closed, his features so frozen. Even in sleep he usually seemed warm and stirring with life. She moved her hand and brushed back the hair on his forehead and stroked his cheek; there was nothing, no kind of response.

By the time Hamilton came back Aubrey's fever had risen—his skin where she touched it felt burning and dry.

"I talked mother into taking supper upstairs," he informed her. "Nancy's with her."

"She'll have to be told sometime."

"No. He'll improve," he argued. "Then she can see him."

Protective. Always protective with Eliza. For a moment Angeline felt pity for herself. How fiercely she wanted someone to protect her, to make it all go away—to be able to see Aubrey stride laughing toward her, to throw herself into his arms, to whisper her wonderful secret into his ear . . .

As is was they didn't have time to tell Eliza. In the darkest time, the soul's midnight, when they say men's spirits are restless to leave their bodies, Aubrey moved with one great shudder. He opened his eyes, but they stared empty and unseeing. Her hand was there—he groped for her hand. His fingers found and pressed it ever so briefly. Then the shudder passed, and he sank back into the stillness.

Angeline knew—she threw herself upon him, screaming, "Aubrey, Aubrey!"

Hamilton drew her away. "Come, Angeline, please."

"No!" she shouted, pushing him from her, struggling against his hold. She sat down in the chair. Her eyes were dry still. She folded her hands in her lap and stared up at him. He turned away from the pain in her eyes.

At last he left her there and closed the door upon them. He sat on the hardwood floor outside, his knees drawn under his chin, and kept vigil until the darkness dissolved and a brittle white sky brought the unyielding day he was dreading.

That day was never a reality to Angeline. She stayed beside Aubrey; even after they took him she remained sitting, her hands in her lap, staring straight ahead. Hester came with hot soup and tea and coaxed some down her.

"Chile, poor little chile," she murmured. She was frightened by Angeline's blank white face. "She needs to cry," she told the kitchen servants. "Needs to grieve 'fore she kin start to mend."

It was Hamilton who found some way to tell Eliza. She stared at him with a look of wide-eyed surprise.

"Hamilton, don't frighten me with such stories! You must be mistaken. Whoever would spread such tales?" She fussed with the lace at her throat and pulled back the silk curtain, looking down on the long oak drive from her open window. "He'll be along directly, I suspect, with some kind of explanation. Don't worry me, Hamilton."

He had anticipated that kind of reaction, but hoped against it. He felt helpless, and inside him an anger was building. Why did men die and leave pain behind them? He had seen it before with the death of his father: hearts shattered and broken, lives left in disarray, pain streaming like the flood waters of the river, choking the spirit in wave after merciless wave.

Hamilton had been avoiding Angeline and he knew it. There had been other people to tell as well as Eliza, the funeral arrangements to make, and a dozen ordinary day-to-day details—enough to keep him busy, but in his mind her image sat, overshadowing every hour. And when the heavy hours at last were lifted, and the muffling darkness spread like a mantle over the pain, he shook himself and roused his tired senses and went to face the last and final chastisement. He went prepared to give, at the same time knowing how powerless he was before her pain.

He was alarmed to find her alone and unattended, and grew fierce when he learned she had kept her lone vigil all day. He approached her where she sat, feeling very uncertain, miserably out of place and inadequate. No one had been able to move her, not even Aunt Hester or her own old servant, Minerva.

"Angeline, you're going upstairs to bed now." He took her cold hands in his; there was no response. "It is time. There's nothing more you can do here. Shall I carry you, or would you prefer to walk?"

She didn't raise her face, but she stood up slowly. He took her arm and walked with her up the stairs. Had she uttered a sound. since that awful, anguished hour? He doubted it.

He had sent Minerva ahead. She was there now, with the bed turned back and waiting. He waited outside while she got Angeline ready and into bed, then he sent the woman out for a basin of cool water and he gently bathed her face and arms and neck. He made up a bed of cushions in the far corner and left a candle burning so there would be light.

She seemed to fall quite easily into slumber, but every muscle in his body was tightened and aching, and the thoughts he had been so long repelling knocked relentlessly on the door of his weary mind.

He was too weakened to parry them all and some gained admittance to perch like devils and taunt his sanity. He tossed and turned and fought his cruel tormenters, not aware when at last sleep mercifully ended the struggle with the black oblivion he craved.

The first sound he heard was a soft, muffled crying, so soft he wondered how it had wakened him. He sat up straight; the crying was gentle and even. He rose with care and walked noiselessly to her bed. She wasn't awake—she wasn't aware she was crying. She rested on her side; her eyes were closed and her body curled up for comfort. She looked like a little girl, innocent and defenseless.

She began talking, as though to herself. He bent over to listen.

"My baby . . . my baby . . . what will happen to my baby . . ."

She mumbled the words like a chant, but they pierced like a sword point to the core of his own hot pain. He grabbed hold of the bed while a wrenching feeling of sickness overtook him. She was crying again. He stared at her dumbfounded, while the terrible knowledge seeped into his tired brain: She was carrying Aubrey's child. She was facing that nightmare—alone—on the shattered edges of her world.

The words came again: "my baby . . . my baby . . . my baby . . ." Then the steady but unrelenting tears. She moved, as though in pain. Hamilton shuddered, then lowered himself very gently onto the bed. He lay carefully, on top of the covers, but she felt or sensed him beside her and turned, reaching for him in the darkness of sleep. She found his warmth and snuggled beside him, one hand curled softly against his cheek, the other flung protectively over his chest.

He lay very still and after a few moments he felt her body relax, the soft crying subside. She sighed a time or two as a little child would. He reached out then and smoothed down her crumpled hair, murmuring tender words of comfort, aching to draw her close against him, to make a nest of protection within his arms. But at last she was quiet and resting and he grew drowsy, and the thread of consciousness raveled thin and snapped. He slept, but in the sleeping there was awareness of the solace beside him that his lonely spirit craved, that the depths of his unconscious being could not deny.

The funeral was set for the following afternoon. Hamilton had risen long before Angeline awakened and had seen her for only brief moments during the morning. He shuddered at the thought of the ordeal she was soon to suffer, and at his own inability to remove or lessen its burden. At the same time an awful decision loomed up before him: Should Eliza attend the burial of her son? Would it help? Would it make any lasting difference? It might force her to face the reality, but what might that reality do to her fragile spirit? He decided to bring her alone to view Aubrey's body and feel his way, step by step. She bluntly refused him. Near despair, he left her to see to his other tasks.

Angeline was alone in the small front parlor with Aubrey's body. She gazed on the features, familiar, yet not the same—altered by the soul's leaving, so she didn't know whether to kiss the cold lips and cry, or run from the emptiness to the places that knew him: the stables, the accursed stables, where he had spent so many happy hours, where surely the sound of his voice would echo still; the room where they had slept and made love together, sharing the deepest longings and joys of their hearts. One thing she knew as she stood looking down upon him—she could never whisper into that unheeding ear the secret that now lay like a burden within her.

At first she didn't hear Eliza enter; it took moments for her to sense someone else was there. Eliza was already approaching the casket—the box cut out and carved through the long dark night. She watched. What could she say to the older woman who knew so much of suffering and shared with her this new grief?

Eliza stopped short. Her bright eyes widened. It seemed to Angeline she had ceased to breathe. Just as she decided to move Eliza lunged forward, throwing herself on the body with a scream that tore through Angeline with a thrill of horror, that trembled along the air in tormented waves.

"Samuel!" She clutched wildly at the body. "Samuel! Don't you dare to leave me and die!"

There was a strangling sob and her long white fingers tore at her throat, then she slumped and fell. Angeline caught her as she slipped, limp and senseless, and was holding her when Hamilton entered the room, his blue-gray eyes looking wild and frightened.

He knelt and put his arm around Angeline's shoulder.

"She saw your father." Angeline's eyes mirrored her horror. "I watched her face—she saw only your father."

Hamilton nodded, his throat too constricted for speaking. Angeline leaned her head for a moment against his shoulder and they remained thus with no sound save their own breathing and the stillness that pressed with the memory of Eliza's cry.

Then he raised himself heavily and lifted his mother and carried her with great weariness up to her room, laid his head on the bed beside her body, and cried as he had cried when he was a boy—never for anyone but her to see—but this time without her soft hand to soothe him, without the strength of her love to help him go on.

So in the end it was Angeline and Hamilton who faced the lonely ordeal alone: sat with stoic faces before the roomful of mourners, listened politely to the minister's vague assurance that the question mark we call death will be one day resolved, the only way we mortals can perceive as solution—with *life*, with *everlasting life*. So came the tribute to a youth so cruelly ended, the acknowledgment, then the letting go . . .

The hardest part for them both was at the graveyard when they lowered Aubrey's body into the gaping hole. A wind was blowing cold and the wet leaves went scudding, pasting muddy imprints against Angeline's gown, some swirling down the tunnel to rest on the coffin, withered reminders that dying will have its way, that all elements in the end will come to nothing.

The trees hung dark and brooding above them. Even the skies were ominous and gray as Hamilton led her back to the waiting carriage and they returned to Lairdswood in silence together. The dripping oaks along the drive seemed to weep upon them— Angeline felt them reach out to her with a force that was palpable. For the first time she felt a vague stirring inside her: This was Lairdswood, this was roots, this was home. This was strength to go on, and something to go on for.

At the cemetery she had dreaded the thought of returning to the lonely shadows of what had been before. Now she could scarcely wait to have Lairdswood fold around her, knowing in her heart that here was her joy, her security, her only hope for the future.

_____Twelve

Eliza rallied, Eliza's tenacious body clung to life in spite of her will to go. And Angeline knew that Eliza was her salvation. She threw herself into serving this woman she loved, and it gave her something to do and something to think of, some reason for getting up when the sun brought day, some reason for ignoring the other matter that she knew could not for much longer be ignored.

Evenings were hardest. Evenings brought the darkness, and loneliness, and thoughts she could laugh at by day. Her father urged her to come for a while to Natchez, but driving home from the funeral she'd made a vow to never set foot off of Lairdswood lands again. She began taking long walks alone, out past the gardens, to the wooded paths where the leaves were carpeted thick, and birds cried mournfully in the bare tree branches, and mockingbirds echoed the emptiness in her heart.

Two days...three days...four days...there grew a new pattern. But nights became harder, not easier like the days.

A week rolled around and they came to the day of the fox hunt —memories past bearing, hours that had to be filled! Angeline didn't know how she could make it. Eliza was bad, slipping into and out of awareness, calling for Samuel, not touching her food. Angeline wore herself out caring for her. She was sick as well; she shouldn't be sick in the night, she thought. When darkness came she was drained, too weak for the struggle—more vulnerable then she had been since Aubrey died.

Hamilton stayed close, and watchful. Angeline sat in the library restlessly scanning the pages of book after book. He suggested sleep, but she shook her brown head at him and her eyes seemed to panic behind their steady gaze. He brought tea and shortbread; she wouldn't touch it. It grew late—her eyes were dark and weary, but her mood of restlessness seemed to grow.

She has to let it out; she has to face it. He studied her face, searching desperately for a clue. _It's driving her crazy keeping it all_ *inside.* He took a deep breath. His insides were churning. He prayed, *Let me be right—let me help her!*

"Angeline," he began, "I'm worried about you. You're not taking care of yourself—you're not eating as you should."

"I'm fine," she answered, looking up at him with vague curiosity.

He kept his voice very even and normal. "But now you have the baby to think of."

Her eyes grew wide; she froze like a statue. He walked over and knelt down beside her chair.

"It's all right. You don't have to keep it inside any longer. When I think of the torment you must have gone through..." He didn't move or attempt to touch her, but his voice and the look in his eyes were like a caress. "You didn't have time to tell him, did you?"

She shook her head.

"Angeline, my dear." He touched her hand and her fingers closed around his, tight like a vise, all her agony trapped in her grip. He sat silent beside her. At last she spoke softly.

"How did you know—about the baby?"

"That night when I stayed with you in your room."

She nodded, said even more softly, "I thought it was Aubrey." A pause, then, "No, I knew it wasn't Aubrey. I wasn't quite certain—I couldn't remember..."

"It's all right," he said again. "It will be all right now."

The look in her eyes ate like acid into his soul. "It will never be all right, Hamilton. Aubrey will never see his child, nor this child his father. And I will be alone. And where is the joy? Where are all the things I thought my life promised?"

What answers do I have to give her? He sat trapped in her agony, and his own. When at last, too cramped, he moved, she drew back her fingers. He stood, but she made no move to rise.

"It's late, Angeline. Please go up to bed now."

She shook her head. "I can't," was all she would say.

So he sat at the end of the room to keep vigil, hoping perhaps she might talk again. But she couldn't stand his eyes upon her and at length she arose and walked slowly upstairs.

He waited for a while, then went to his own room. It was a long, long time before sleep would come.

When he awoke the waking was sudden and total. She was crying, but this time in wrenching sobs. He knew that no matter when it had happened he would have heard her; he would have known.

He made his way to her room. When he entered he could feel her pain like cold waves wash over his skin. She was crying so hard that it choked her breathing. She gulped in air, her whole body trembling.

Hamilton's fingers shook as he lit the candle. He had never heard anyone cry like that before. Perhaps if Eliza had cried that way . . .

He sat on the edge of the bed. "Angeline, I'm here now."

At the sound of his voice she sat bolt upright, drew the covers about her and stared at him wildly. "No! How dare you? Go away, go away."

She was crying still; her brown hair was tangled and her face wet with tears. She brushed at them angrily. He felt dissolved in helpless frustration.

"Please, for mercy's sake, don't send me away!"

The words rang out; he had not meant to say them. She gazed into the pools of pain in the blue-gray eyes. Then everything broke that was so near breaking, and she could no longer control the cruel anguish inside.

"Don't leave me, Hamilton, please don't leave me!" She threw herself against him. At last his arms could close with aching tenderness around her. He hushed her as he would hush a child, holding her in the fierce circle of his protection. She was crying again, but she wasn't sobbing. She spoke through the tears with her face against him. It seemed he could feel every word she said.

"Don't leave me alone. I can feel him dying—as if it has to happen all over again!"

He drew her closer to still the terrible shaking. He talked to her, never knowing what he said. There were times when he despaired, when he thought forever would swirl in circles of pain around them there, and he would hold her and she would never stop crying, and his heart would break . . . and break . . . and break again . . .

Even the unendurable has an ending. She fell asleep in his arms; he hardly dared breathe, or move a muscle to ease his position. He sang to her, the songs his mother had taught him.

He sang away his own shadows and thought to himself: *I have faced a terrible darkness and triumphed. I have learned more about loving tonight than some men learn their entire lifetimes.* And he slept, in peace, of his own accord.

Hamilton sat in the Natchez office of Bailey and Johnson, drumming impatient fingers against the arm of his chair. The large, stout man with the small eyeglasses gazed at him somewhat anxiously.

"That's most unconventional, Mr. Stewart. It's a pity that Aubrey never changed the will. But if what you say is true it should make no difference—"

"It makes a great deal of difference to me. See that it's done. I don't care how you do it—write her a letter, pay her a personal call. Just make certain that you convince her—that she believes you."

The big man smiled and his eyes grew narrow, his rosy cheeks bulging under the circles of glass. Phillip Johnson was a comical-looking character, but he held the reins of the city's largest law firm and the Stewart brothers were two of his most influential clients. *Too bad about Aubrey Stewart, really too bad. Now, here is an interesting, but ticklish development!*

"You keep people on their toes. You've a way for that, Hamilton."

They parted on friendly terms and when Hamilton left him he made copious notes on a long, legal pad.

Angeline received the lawyer's letter, couched in legal terms but assuring her that Aubrey's financial affairs were in order. After a decent interval, at her discretion, the firm would be glad to meet with the widow and go over the legal papers, etc., etc.

It was a great relief to her mind to feel safe about Lairdswood, though it caused her some inner uneasiness, too. Wasn't Lairdswood what she had wanted in the first place? Hadn't Aubrey taken second priority? Perhaps a just God had been angry at her deception and given her what she wanted, to see how she liked it. Now, too late, she knew how real was her love for Aubrey. How cruel were the wicked twistings of fate!

But the days moved into weeks and she started adjusting. She was young and alive—what else could she do? It was mid-November; the baby was due in April. Four months, nearly four and a half—nearly halfway along. The baby was real, she could not deny it. She would have to bring it into the world alone. And then—but she mustn't think any farther. She mustn't, else something would snap and go crazy inside.

She felt better now, and though the days grew nippy, she continued her solitary walks. Even late autumn was mild in the Natchez country, and something about the tangled and overgrown woods struck a harmony with the tangle of feelings inside her, the uncontrolled conglomeration of beauty feeding the unending need in her soul.

But she pulled within herself, became more and more private. One day shortly after the funeral, when Dyanne came to call, Angeline ran to Hamilton in a state of mild panic, begging him to go down and send her away.

"I can't face her sweetness, her well-meant kindness. She'll ask questions—Dy could never resist asking questions." She looked up into his eyes, plainly appealing. "I don't have any answers to give her, Hamilton."

He went down, of course. Dyanne had never met him face to face, only seen him from a distance. She was struck by how dissimilar the brothers were—there was no way to tell they *were* brothers. She was seized with Hamilton's compelling sexual attraction. *No wonder women are drawn to this one,* she mused. She was left not only with her questions unanswered, but with all sorts of new ones running around in her head.

Eliza did not improve. She seemed to grow weaker, sinking daily before their eyes. She was listless, no longer interested in living. She wouldn't eat, though Nancy so patiently coaxed her. She seldom left her rooms anymore, except to sit on the upstairs porch in her favorite rocker, going back and forth, back and forth, the old wood creaking. . . . Angeline learned to live with the sound, like a pulse beat that ticked off the day's tedious hours, oftentimes seeming to mock her own misery.

Bit by bit Angeline took over Eliza's duties, glad she had learned as much as she had before. She and Hamilton took their meals together; she was aware that he never went off of an evening now. She approached him once very boldly about the matter.

"I keep you from your own pleasures," she told him.

He returned her unblinking stare and replied quite simply, "My pleasures are here now."

She colored and dropped her gaze, and was careful to never bring up the subject again.

That night Angeline slept poorly, disturbed by vague, fitful dreaming. The following morning Nancy discovered Eliza dead. Her soul had fled from the body that caged it; there would never be any need to pretend again.

While Nancy stood screaming and wailing, Angeline was thinking: *I wonder if she's with Samuel? Is Aubrey there?* She could picture the happy reunion in her mind. The thought shot through her from nowhere: *They're together and happy, and I'm left behind!* Then she remembered Hamilton.

She found him in one of the sheds mending harness. He turned when she entered, a welcome in his eyes. But he saw her hesitate and knew there was something. He waited. He was at core a patient man. She picked up a piece of leather and pulled at the ravel where a strap had torn and given way. He knew he would have to help her.

"What is it, Angie?"

She looked at him with little-girl eyes and he knew, though she was able to say the words then, anyway. "Your mother's gone. Nancy found her this morning."

He nodded as though to say *yes, yes, of course it would happen. We knew it would happen, didn't we?* Then he bent to his work so his face was hidden.

"Go back to the house," he said. "I'll be there shortly."

She responded to the tone of dismissal in his voice more than the words themselves, and left him.

They buried Eliza the following afternoon. Hamilton was solemn and extremely silent. So many people came, so many old friends who remembered the gracious, feminine woman, who even now regarded her with some awe. And of course, in spite of sympathy, their eyes were curious: What would happen to the son and the young widow?

Angeline's father begged and then demanded that she come home with him, but she stood firm.

"No," she explained. "I've too much to do at Lairdswood. Eliza died very suddenly. Minerva's with me and I have Nancy. Perhaps later when things are in order."

He wasn't placated, but at the same time he had no authority over her. He felt vaguely uneasy about leaving her at Lairdswood. Too much tragedy all at once, and this baby she carried . . . His fears for her future were based on old memories. But he took her kiss and went back to his law books, because in the end there was nothing else he could do.

Angeline felt a real sense of relief in returning to Lairdswood, though she had to ignore how empty the big house felt. Hester brought in a hot dinner and Hamilton sat with her; she had been afraid he might disappear. He sat, but he didn't talk, and later that evening he retired to the card room and got royally drunk.

Angeline sat alone in the library, half a dozen lamps lit and the fire built high. She was aware that Hamilton sat in the card room drinking. She wanted to go to him, help him some way. But some stronger, unnamed emotion held her back.

He came of his own accord, searching for her. His eyes looked unnaturally bright, but his hand was steady when he poured from the glass decanter. His speech, unslurred, was edged with the biting sarcasm that had lately been missing.

"Have we nothing to drink to together?"

She didn't answer, but he drained his own glass and the one he held out for her.

"What an unlikely pair we have here. The innocent widow and the wicked wastrel."

She raised her eyebrows. "Hamilton, please."

"You're alone with the prodigal son, my dear, be wary." He perched on the edge of a chair and regarded her. "So you've come to this end already in your young life. Pity the pretty young widow and the worthless—"

"Stop it this instant!" She rose very suddenly; the book in her lap went flying to sprawl on the floor. "I don't like you when you're this way."

A caustic grin twitched at the corners of his mouth. "Ah, implying there *are* times when you like me." He cocked his head at a wicked angle. "Pray, lady, your pleasure is mine."

"My pleasure is to have you not drunk and disgusting."

He rose with a quick, lithe movement and grasped her wrist. "And my pleasure is this—"

He drew her roughly against him. His lips upon hers were like fire, but honey sweet, compellingly tender—she struggled and pulled away; she was trembling all over. He laughed, and the laugh was all bitterness and pain. She turned and fled and his cruel laugh followed.

"There's nowhere to run to, Angeline. This is Lairdswood, remember? This is what you wanted."

She reached her room and bolted the door into place, then threw herself onto the bed and cried, wringing out every emotion that tormented her.

Hamilton walked slowly back for another decanter. Nothing so far had touched the pain. He gulped down another glass; he had a long way to go yet.

Thirteen

Angeline rose late and, as she had suspected, Hamilton was nowhere to be found. She felt exhausted and ill, but she pulled herself together. Work, what a wonderful remedy! By noontime she was feeling much better and ate so well that Hester was delighted.

"Das de way, Miss Angeline. We got ta put meat on dis little baby."

Midafternoon she was out working in the tool shed, sorting and storing some of Eliza's herbs. It was one of those days when the thin sun shone strongly, and its warmth through the glass felt good. Hamilton entered quietly and, clearing a place on the cluttered bench, sat down as though to watch her at work. She moved nervously, nearly dropping the jar she was filling.

"Don't run away, Angeline. Hear me out, please."

She dared not face him. "Go on," she said.

"There's no possible excuse for my actions last evening. I cannot even ask your forgiveness; I ask only this—" He paused. She could tell how painful was the speaking. "Do not hate me, Angeline. Perhaps in the future I will have some chance to redeem myself."

His voice drew tenderness from her. "And of course I'll leave Lairdswood; that goes without saying. As soon as I make arrangements for someone else—"

"But I don't want you to leave Lairdswood." She turned very slowly. The masked hope in his eyes was painful to see. "I couldn't get along without you."

"On the contrary. It seems I only make things the worse for you."

"That was once. I have no fears it will be repeated." She busied her fingers in the dry plants, feeling suddenly shy. "Heaven knows you've a right to be human just one time, after all you had suffered—"

"Angeline, please. Don't make this any harder for me."

"What of the other times when you were my salvation? When you served me, with no thought for your own grief?" She drew herself up, not aware of her striking beauty, but vaguely aware of her growing dignity. "You and I are all that is left. We must stick together. You can't desert Lairdswood now—or me—"

He nodded. So much he felt was past expression! He nodded again. "You're right. We'll do it your way and somehow we'll make it—no matter what hell has to throw our way."

There was the hint of the old rakish smile at his eyes now. She felt more secure to see he could rally that way. She felt suddenly stronger, as though she could breathe now, as though surely tomorrow could somehow be faced.

In the end she broke her vow and went home for Christmas. It was good to be with her father and Fletcher again. How easy and routine her life had been then, before—before— *This ought to have been my first Christmas with Aubrey!* At times, out of nowhere, the thought would flash into her mind. She knew how much wiser it was to be here and around other people, rather than back at Lairdswood alone with the shadows and pain.

She stayed longer than she wanted to, longer than planned. Hugh McAlister had at last asked Dyanne to marry him, and she drew Angeline into her own excited plans. Shopping sprees again—how Angeline hated them! And Dyanne was enchanted with thoughts of Angeline's baby.

"You have a boy," she insisted, "and I'll have a girl. As soon as possible," she added, with a sparkle in her eye. "When they're older we'll marry them off to one another. What fun to watch our grandchilden grow up together."

Dyanne, of course, was crazy in her own right and took advantage of her assumed privilege to be outspoken. "You stay away from that Hamilton, honey. Does it make you jittery being alone with him?" Her eyes shone with her poorly concealed interest.

"Dyanne, really, I'm six months pregnant with Aubrey's child."

"Well, I know that, and it makes you safe for the moment. But, after all, you won't always be in this condition—"

"Dyanne, I assure you, you've no need to worry."

"It's most unusual you living alone out there together, and after the baby comes—"

97

"When the baby is born we'll go from that point. Right now there's nothing unusual about it. He runs Lairdswood; it would fall apart without him. We're surrounded by servants—I've Minerva with me always, and Hester to fuss over me and now Nancy as well."

"All right, all right, I concede. But you just watch him. He has a certain look in his eye—"

Angeline smiled, knowing full well her old friend's fascination with a handsome man with "that kind" of look in his eye.

Just as she made progress in extricating herself from Dyanne, Fletcher fell ill and Angeline stayed on to nurse him. One day, quite by surprise, Hamilton arrived. He didn't stay; he hardly stepped inside the door. She expressed her eagerness to get back to Lairdswood.

"There's not much going on there. You're better off here."

"I suppose you're right, but I won't stay much longer. Just until Fletcher is back on his feet."

She thought he looked drawn and fatigued, his eyes shadowed.

"Are you well, Hamilton?" She was afraid he had too much time now to brood, to—

"I'm holding my own—and I'm not getting drunk nights!" He cocked his head. How provocative his eyes were!

He took leave of her, then suddenly turned back to add, "By the way, I've stopped spending my evenings in Natchez-Down-Under. I haven't been back there once since Aubrey died."

She dropped her eyes. She could feel her pulse beat rising. "You don't need to tell me that."

"Oh, but I do. It's something I want you to know, Angeline."

Just one more day...one more...and a week slipped past them. Fletcher mended; he had never been really that sick. But he needed her, she could sense that from him, and so she had stayed: *why shouldn't someone be happy?* But at last she packed her bags and announced her departure.

"You'll come back here to have the baby?" her father asked. She knew how much it meant to him to have her. They didn't talk much, but just knowing she was there...

"I don't know, father. I'll think about it."

How could she explain that the only heir to Lairdswood had to be born on Lairdswood land? *Besides,* a little voice inside her whispered, *it didn't help my mother to have you there. You weren't able to save her, papa.*

Rufus drove her home on a sunny day in late January. She hadn't announced her coming, but Hamilton was there. Rufus took up her bags and Minerva insisted that she and Nancy could do the unpacking themselves. So she sat down to Hester's meal and her motherly fussing. It was so good to be home again!

After eating, Hamilton pushed back his chair. "Are you tired, Angeline?"

"No," she replied, "not really."

"Would you like to go over the place—say hello again?"

"I'd love to!"

She took a light cloak and they walked together, straight from the house toward the oak avenue, then veering right past the medicinal herb garden and through the parterre, Eliza's small ornamental garden where the flower beds and paths formed a circular pattern and the feeling, even now in the absence of blossoms, was one of gentle order and peace.

The arboretum and the old, tangled gardens were more her, Angeline felt, than they were Eliza. The two wandered there and he told her of small improvements, interesting things that had happened while she was away. They circled back by the barns, the tool and milk sheds, avoiding the kennels, skirting the stables. In late December the last of the cotton had been gathered; the land would lie fallow through February, perhaps into March when the plowing would begin. They gazed over the expanse of empty fields, stark in the pale sunlight.

"Do you know what a good slave picks in a season?" he asked her. She shook her head. "Well, let's start with the average hand who would bring in a hundred fifty to two hundred pounds a day. A good hand will bring in over three hundred. Now, Hester's Rufus, do you know what his record was?"

"Tell me!" Her eyes were bright with interest.

"Four hundred eighty-six pounds on December 18th! We threw him a little celebration. I presented him with a decanter of New Orleans whiskey and a new red tie to wear on Sundays." He chuckled, recalling the time with pleasure. "He says next season he'll break five hundred. It's the darndest! He's fifty years old, you know, if he's a day."

They walked back toward the big house together. "And Hester?" she asked.

"Hester I won't even guess at. She was old, I swear, when I was a little boy." They were approaching what was called Eliza's Garden. The summerhouse stood here; it was very quiet.

"What happened to Valencia?" she asked him. He didn't seem to react, though she was watching.

"She was sold. Didn't Aubrey tell you?" He looked at her now, his eyes sharp and discerning. "Angeline, Angeline, why must you try to spoil things? You're safe from her; put her out of your mind." He wanted to say: *I'll take care of you! I did before; I always will.*

They walked for several yards in silence. He placed his hand over hers, only briefly, but the warmth and strength of his flesh seemed to linger.

"You're home, Angeline," he whispered. "Be happy."

They walked on to the house. *What is happiness?* she considered. *Money and power, having someone to love? To some people health, to others children . . .*

She couldn't shake the thought all evening. *Why are some people happy and some people not?* She lay in the four-poster bed she had shared with Aubrey. *What has happiness been for me?* Her thoughts moved in tumbled confusion; she wasn't certain. Would happiness ever have a place in her life again? This baby . . .

She refused to think of the baby. She buried her head in the pillow and cried, and refused to think about anything at all.

That first night when she cried herself to sleep she heard nothing. But the second night the sound awakened her. At first she just pulled the blankets up higher. But the sound persisted; it grew neither louder nor dim, and at last her curiosity got the better of her fears.

The upstairs rooms of Lairdswood opened onto a large hallway, which widened at the south end. There was a Sheraton tea table there with an ivory chess set, some chairs, a French needlework rug or two—and beyond them the broad, white door with the half-arch above it leading to the upper porch. It was from beyond this door that the noise was coming. With a sudden chill Angeline recognized the sound.

She pulled open the door. A faint breeze was rising, perhaps enough to stir her hair. But the solid wooden chairs on their solid wood rockers stood still in the moonlight—all save one. It was rocking back and forth very gently, with a creak as the tips of the runners pressed the floor and another as the back ends swooped downward. She shuddered and stepped instinctively backward to the warmth of the hall, the screamed as she felt solid flesh behind her. She turned, then drew back. It was Hamilton standing there. So he, too, had heard!

"Hamilton, what do you make of it?"

He walked to the threshold of the open doorway. The chair was still gently moving back and forth—the chair where no one ever sat but Eliza, the one that was her favorite, hers alone...

He shrugged his shoulders and made a little sound. "Let's wait and see if it happens again."

That left her unsettled. She began to protest, but he silenced her with a look, then said, "Don't let your imagination frighten you, Angie. It will make all the difference, I think, if it happens again."

She went back to bed, but she left a candle burning and lay very still for a long, long time. There was no sound to reward her listening—only silence until sleep came.

Hamilton reached for the pen Phillip Johnson handed to him and carefully signed his name on the document. The stout lawyer rubbed his forehead along his hairline, his small eyes looking withdrawn and somewhat disturbed.

"I can't say I approve what you're doing, Hamilton. It's untoward and unnecessary, and—"

"No, no, Phillip. It's quite necessary." He blotted his signature and pushed the long paper back across the desk. "I've no complaints with how you've handled the matter thus far."

He pushed back his chair and stood smiling down at the lawyer. "You see, I've been telling her she's a wealthy widow. You wouldn't want to prove me a liar, would you, now?"

Phillip Johnson didn't return the smile. His small eyes screwed up like hard marbles behind his round glasses.

"It's a gamble, Ham, that you just might lose."

"I know. I'll take that chance. The child's due to be born soon. He has to be born as legal heir."

He picked up his brown leather gloves with his left hand and extended his right to the man behind the desk. "Buck up, my friend. Lairdswood never was meant to be mine. Isn't that what my father told you?"

Phillip found that the palms of his hands were sweating. "Hamilton, I don't like this—"

"Well, I do. It's justice, and there's precious little of that in the world."

He touched his hat. His grin grew a little lopsided, but he left the room with his usual cocky air—the air of a man who knew what he was doing, who was willing to play whatever cards he was dealt, and who wasn't accustomed to looking behind him nor harboring unnecessary regrets.

In Natchez country spring comes in February, or so the early flowers seem to think. The first things Angeline found were a few white hyacinths, then snowdrops and delicate violets. The days were warm, so in the arboretum some of the trees and shrubs began to bloom. She arranged her schedule so early mornings and late afternoons could be spent outside, wandering the paths in quest of discovery.

In Eliza's Garden the early trumpet daffodils, pale as new sunlight and graceful as a wild flower, had raised their heads to welcome her. And against the dark cedar trees in faint delicate pattern the silver bells had begun to bloom, their slender buds arched like a swan's neck, their petals bits of twisted sea-foam.

In Eliza's Garden the tarnished sundial mocked her with its innocent words: *I measure only the happy hours.* There was that old word *happy* again. But February was also a time of promise, and youth cannot for too long turn a deaf ear to such whisperings.

The day that Warren Ellis came to Lairdswood Angeline set aside her other tasks. Hamilton had asked her to entertain him and invited her to sit in on their meetings.

"You know enough now," he assured her.

He'd been instructing her in the evenings, so she was familiar with the Lairdswood accounts and had a smattering of knowledge of economics and the rules and theories behind the world of finance. Still she was very hesitant and uncertain to match her wits with the two men. What was more, she remembered too well their New Orleans meeting, when Aubrey's rude behavior had embarrassed her so.

But when they met he immediately set all her fears aside, bringing things frankly out into the open. "You're as beautiful as the last time I saw you," he told her.

Though not much older than Hamilton, his manner was benign, totally free from pretension or guile.

"You're a lucky girl to be carrying that child," he said, and his tone was emphatic. She gazed at him; she must have blinked her eyes. "Yes, you are." He went right on, as though she must hear this. "I know how awful it's been to lose your husband. But just think, you'll have him forever in this little mite. My wife and I have been trying for years to have children. Lost a couple. You see, it's not easy for some."

His resonant voice had become more tender. "She's expecting another herself near the end of this month."

"Oh, I do hope all goes well for her this time!" Angeline's sincerity rang in her voice.

"Well, thank you, my dear, I'll join you in that." And without more ado he walked over to Hamilton's sideboard and poured a generous whiskey for himself. She liked him; with great relief she liked him.

They certainly were solicitous of her comfort and even in the depth of a weighty discussion Warren Ellis would interrupt himself and explain, making certain she understood their wanderings and reasonings. She began to get a feeling, sense the intrigue of juggling back and forth with large sums of money, playing games of chance that were backed by power and skill, riding the tide to see where the swell would lead—she could read their excitement behind the careful, reasonable expressions they wore.

She was surprised by the extent of Hamilton's Northern holdings, but even more so to learn that Mr. Ellis held shares in Echodell, and that a small plantation out Linden Road past Melrose that had sold last summer—she herself remembered the sale—had been purchased for him through a Southern agent. She listened, she asked a few questions, she felt she learned ten times as much as she had in the sessions with Hamilton. This give-and-take, this actual dealing, this shuffling of properties and cash, for all its fascination was in deadly earnest and that knowledge, that weight, overrode all else.

When at last she went up to her room she felt exhausted, hardly able to go through the motions of getting to bed. As soon as she settled her head on the goosedown pillow she felt the soothing waves of sleep numb her body and mind.

Nothing should have awakened her. Then how was it that she sat upright in bed, her eyes open? *What had happened?* She felt a knot in her stomach. And then she heard it: the rocking sound again—the rhythmical, even, unnerving rocking. She moved onto her side, intending to ignore it, but she tossed and turned, and the noise seemed to pound in her head. Perhaps this time she'd discover an explanation...

She padded out into the hall. A lamp was burning; Hamilton leaned against the frame of the open door. He turned his head only slightly when he saw her.

"I'm sorry you have awakened, Angeline." He voice held that tight control which she had come to discover masked deep concern or emotion.

"Oh, I'm all right. I just thought that perhaps this time I'd find a reason, some explanation..." Her voice trailed softly away.

He shook his head. "I'm afraid not. There's no possible rationale I can find." *Except, of course, the one thing we both are thinking.*

She pulled her long shawl more closely around her shoulders. "Well, I hope it didn't awaken Mr. Ellis."

Hamilton's amused, lopsided grin grew slowly. "I doubt it. He can sleep through anything. A renegade's conscience, you know." He closed the door with a move that seemed brisk and final. "I'll remove the rocker tomorrow," he said.

"No, don't do that!" Angeline heard herself protest. "No, Hamilton, please don't touch the rocker."

He studied her with those eyes from which nothing could hide. "And why not?"

He could be so demanding, so unrelenting!

"There may be a reason," she stammered, "a need. I don't want to tamper..." Then she took a deep breath and repeated aloud the thought she had harbored inside. "If it's really Eliza, what harm does it do?"

A kind smile warmed his eyes and softened his features. "You're an extraordinary woman, did you know that? Quite as uncommon as Miss Eliza herself, and that's going some." He put his hands on her shoulders and kissed her forehead lightly. "Good night, Mrs. Stewart. Sleep well."

He turned and was gone. She walked to her room and climbed back into her bed, and this time she didn't bother to lie still and listen, but closed her eyes and slept with an easy mind.

Fourteen

It was down to a matter of weeks and, though she would slow them, they ran like fine sand through her fingers—and suddenly it was a matter of days. Only days before her child would arrive.

They received a letter from Warren Ellis telling that his wife had given birth to a healthy son. They were naming the boy, he announced, Niles Hamilton Ellis. She could tell how pleased Hamilton was. She thought to herself: *That's a good omen. One child safe—and one to go* . . .

She had given her father her last word on the subject: She would not return to Natchez to have the child. Hamilton and Hester had made arrangements with Dr. Humphreys, and Hester assured her that she knew just what to do.

"Was me put de firs' little clothes on Massa Aubrey. I reckons I kin do the same thing for his chile."

No one seemed unduly concerned, but she was frightened. And there was nobody to soothe her or talk her fears away: no husband, no mother. At times she found herself thinking: *I don't want Aubrey's baby. I don't want to have this child!*

She was alone in the arboretum when the first pains came. They were little more than a tightening sense of discomfort. But instinctively she knew them for what they were. She walked slowly to the house. She was undecided about whom to tell, or if she should tell anyone at all yet. But what if there was trouble locating the doctor?

She found Hester and Hester found Nancy, and in a few minutes Moses was riding one of the fastest horses down the oak path. Hester plied her with pennyroyal and urged her to lie prone. But moving helped her ignore the dull aching inside. Anything to keep from thinking, from staring up at the ceiling and imagining—and picturing—

By the time Dr. Humphreys came the contractions were steady, coming every two to three minutes. He lost no time preparing her and preparing the things he needed, scolding Hester harshly all the while.

"For goodness' sake, woman, you ought to have had things ready, and this poor girl off her feet. Hand me that linen."

His brusque manner, his taking over, relieved the strain: They could relax and follow instructions, for the matter was now in capable hands.

Hamilton rode into the yard nearly three hours later. When Nancy rushed up to him wringing her hands he felt his pulse quicken. So it had come to the moment at last! He poured a stiff brandy and found himself pacing the length of the entrance hall, back and forth, back and forth. He could hear his boot leather squeaking in rhythm with the dull tick of the library clock.

In the birthing room Angeline struggled against the weariness that seeped into her muscles whenever the tight pains ceased. At first she had experienced a sense of release, a flush of excitement: At last, no matter what happened, the time was here. She welcomed the doctor's instructions and ministrations, in spite of her qualms of embarrassment here and there. Every step brought her nearer the final moment, the culmination she both longed for and feared.

But that had been hours ago, in some vague beginning, when this body had still belonged to her, part of herself. She had long since slipped past that stage to a numbed detachment, when all the things that had so intensely mattered dissolved into one importance: holding on. She saw the subtle change in the doctor's expression. He had been cheery and hopeful at first, then concerned, now worried. And finally even the doctor no longer mattered. Nothing mattered but making it through the next onslaught of pain that gripped her and wouldn't let go, that built higher and higher, past the point when she said to herself, *I can bear no more!* — on still until at last it subsided and left her, trembling all over, and weak, and afraid.

Dr. Humphreys was frightened too, though he tried not to show it. The contractions weren't doing their work. They came long and hard and regular, as they ought to. But the head didn't want to lock into the birth canal. Conditions were within a hair's breadth of being ready, but meanwhile this terrible punishing of mother and child.

Evening came and passed on into night without Hamilton noticing. He could do nothing, think of nothing but Angeline's suffering.

Near eleven o'clock the child was at last delivered—unwillingly still, for instruments had to be used, then Dover's Powder administered to take the edge off Angeline's suffering. The baby was small, weighing just over six pounds, but he had a good color and a lusty cry and a head full of straight black hair. Hester held him, the tears running shamelessly down her cheeks, her round shoulders shaking. Angeline lay with her eyes closed, limp and exhausted. But a warm comfort spread through her body: her burden was gone. And a son had been born who was whole and well. And there was nothing to run away from now. She slept.

But the doctor watched with uneasy attention. She was hemorrhaging and that wasn't a good sign at all. After such a difficult labor, true, it could be an expected reaction. But she was too weak to continue to lose more blood. He had to do something to stop it, and the sooner the better.

At last he went out to where Hamilton was waiting. He hated to destroy the look of relief on the young man's face.

"Yes, the child is delivered and well. But we're not out of danger."

Hamilton lifted an eyebrow and watched him with narrowed eyes.

"The mother is hemorrhaging and so far I can't stop it."

"What have you tried?"

Dr. Humphreys chafed at the insolent tone. Young upstart—he well knew the type.

"I've given her ergotrate—the best treatment available. But there's little that has much effect in a case like this. We must wait and watch her closely..." He spread his hands. Best to be totally frank with a man like Hamilton.

"Is she suffering still?"

"No, she's peaceful now and resting."

"I see. Could you stay with her?"

"Yes, yes, by all means. I'd planned to."

"Thank you, doctor. I'll send Nancy to see that your needs are met."

He turned on his heel to leave, then thought better of it and paused, and held the doctor with his gaze. "I want to be informed of the least alteration, the least change for good or bad—and immediately."

William Humphreys swallowed and nodded. Ever so briefly the dark thought played at the edges of his mind: Heaven help the man who had to face his anger, who had to tell him if the girl died.

Hamilton sat in the wing-backed chair and thumbed the pages of the Natchez *Free Trader*. He had abandoned the liquor and now drank black coffee to stay awake. A dozen images tortured his brain, dark and teasing. This child, now alive and breathing beneath this roof, was a link between himself and the dead—he could not ignore it, however much he might wish it to go away. *A son, a dead man's heir!* He shuddered. The night was calm and still; it seemed unfitting. But wasn't that how death was? After all the wild storming: a sudden calmness, a sigh, a slipping away? He had sat in this same room scant months ago and watched it. But that time the woman upstairs had been by his side, not lying herself in the capricious clutches of death.

Near dawn Nancy came down; there had been no changes. Would he like to see the baby? He shook his head. *The baby! Aubrey's baby!* What if this child of Aubrey's should take her life? He lighted one of his father's old pipes, but he didn't smoke it. He dozed a little, fitfully; he dreamed.

In his dream he stood once again by his fallen brother. There was the sharp gully, the high keening cry of the dying horse, Aubrey face down in the leaves and the heel-marked mud. With a fear that trembled inside him he touched the still body and turned it to face him.

The dead man opened his eyes. They were two orbs of glowing red light with no iris or pupil. But they bored into Hamilton's eyes like two prongs of fire. And his mouth, now a chalk-white line, grew grotesquely twisted and laughed, like the demons would laugh in their boyhood stories.

"She is mine, she will always be mine," the thin lips taunted. "Even in death I can take her from you, Hamilton. Watch me!"

He laughed again and the white lips turned blood red and spread like a stain cheek to cheek, then earlobe to earlobe. And a cold hand grabbed hold of his jacket and pulled him down closer. Now the light from the glowing eyes was a pain in his head.

"She will never belong to you, Hamilton. Never—never—"

He struggled against the voice and the grip that held him. He fought and struggled, and woke to find sun in circles staining the flowered carpet at his feet. He rose, his skin cold, his joints stiffened. He stretched. He walked to the window. The day was upon them. A faint breeze stirred in the bushes beneath the window. It was just another ordinary day.

The patient's condition remained unstable; the bleeding continued. Each hour the strength to fight back diminished, the body's resources lessened and ebbed.

About noon Dr. Humphreys called Hamilton into the library. He stood with his hands clasped tightly behind his back. His face was shadowed with the stubble of beard that he hadn't shaved yet; his eyes were heavy and bloodshot. He told the young man, "I think we should send to Natchez for Angeline's father."

Hamilton's hand where it rested on top of the sofa closed into a fist. His eyes, though tired, were keen yet. They narrowed.

"Is it necessary?" he asked. The doctor nodded.

"I'll make the arrangements," he said, then turned abruptly and left without one more word. Dr. Humphreys stood rubbing his chin. His mouth tasted sour. He knew that somehow—somehow he had to pull this one through. There were some, no matter what happened, you couldn't let go of. With heavy steps he turned and walked back to the room where he had been imprisoned all night with the mysteries of nature and the terrible shortcomings of man's knowledge and tools.

Hester had located a wet nurse for the baby, so he ate and survived, unmindful of his mother, greedy in his own consuming need. And past the dark oak sentries through dapples of sunlight, alone in the awful silence, a white horse passed with a small black boy like a smudge clinging to him under a sea-blue sky that stretched empty of clouds.

They found and followed the sleek gray river, then the old Trace Road loomed up as the rough trail turned and the daylight was swallowed and walls of darkness rose up like the walls of a grave; the black boy trembled. At last he topped the rise and the woods fell behind him, and the river was there again and the city in sight.

He rode straight to the house and ran up to the front door. The name was printed right there, as the master had told him. He banged the heavy brass knocker. There was no answer. He banged again. His heart was banging. He could feel his quick pulse at the hollow of his throat.

At last the big door pulled inward. He blurted his errand before the black maid could shut the door. She pulled at her short tight curls in distraction.

"Massa ain' here, he gone to Vicksburg. Won' be back till late tomorrow." She rolled her round black eyes and wrung her hands. "Lord, don' let Miss Angie die, please hep us."

Moses stood rooted in place. The master had not prepared him, instructed him for such an extremity. Panic rose like bile in his throat. He swallowed against it. He couldn't ride back empty-handed! Then behind the black girl appeared a face that was most familiar and even more welcome.

"Fletcher!" He cried the name as he would a hosanna. "Come along wid me quick. Your sister, Miss Angeline's ailin'. Massa Hami'ton sen' me here to fetch your father. But you'll jes have t'do." He grabbed for the white boy's hand and led Fletcher to where Colonel waited.

"De baby done come, an' Miss Angie, she's very sick now. We got to git back to her quick."

At this Fletcher nodded. Moses climbed into the saddle and held out a hand to Fletcher, who scrambled behind. The black girl still stood at the door, mumbling and grieving.

"You sen' de ole master along, gal, soon as you kin."

Moses turned the horse and started back toward Lairdswood. But he felt an insistent tug at the sleeve of his jacket. He half turned back. "Whatcha want, Fletch?" he inquired.

"My friends. Fletcher wants his friends to come and help Angie."

Moses shook his head a little impatiently. "Ain't got time for no friends now, Fletcher. We in a big hurry." But the tight hand continued to tug.

"My friends come with us," Fletcher insisted.

Moses remembered the stubborn persistence that Fletcher could show. Calling on Lady Luck to save him a beating he followed Fletcher's instructions and pulled Colonel up before a large, run-down house with several entrances and several door knockers.

He ran his tongue over dry lips and looked back at Fletcher. But the boy had already slid down from the horse's back and was running toward one of the doors. The black boy watched him. A young white man answered and conversed with Fletcher. Another young man approached. They exchanged more words. Moses tapped his knee with staccato fingers. They were wasting time and courting trouble! Then Fletcher came back on the run, and the two men followed.

"Wait here, lad," one of them shouted. "We'll saddle up quickly."

"You bes' do dat!" Moses muttered beneath his breath, and he fidgeted till the horse caught his nervous fever. At last the two men rode up and Moses moved out, as fast as he could, with Fletcher clinging behind.

They reached Lairdswood just as the sun was setting, and it laid long purple shadows across their path. Elder Carlyle looked askance at his companion and added one more quick prayer to the ones he had already uttered.

A fine-looking, middle-aged Negress ushered them in. The mansion was one of the grandest they'd ever entered, but it seemed empty right now, with a quiet that was depressing. Fletcher followed at their heels, wide-eyed, not speaking. Outside Moses led the tired, lathered horses to the barn where his evening's work would begin.

"We're ministers of the gospel," Elder Carlyle explained to the Negro woman. "Fletcher would like us to give his sister a blessing."

She didn't reply. At the end of the hall she stopped them. "Wait here, please," she instructed and left them awkwardly standing.

Hamilton was at his desk in the card room when Nancy

approached and told him about the two gentlemen callers. He was disturbed. She had known he would be. He rose, with his brow knit, and strode out into the hall where the two men uncomfortably waited. He had already made up his mind and he started to tell them, thanking them curtly but politely for their concern. But Fletcher stepped out, his eyes large and troubled. He placed a small hand on Hamilton's sleeve.

"Fletcher's friends," he said. "Let them help Angie." Hamilton read the awful struggle behind the eyes. "Please let them help her. Please don't let Angie die."

Tears gathered around the dark eyes and along the thick lashes. Hamilton always had harbored kind feelings for the boy. What harm could it do? They certainly couldn't hurt her—

"All right, you may go up. You've got fifteen minutes. If you're not back by then, I'll come after you myself."

Well could they believe it! They thanked him and followed Fletcher up the long sweeping stairs to a second floor hallway that was as large as most rooms they had ever seen. They stopped before a closed door. Elder Logan knocked softly. No response. They knocked once again and then cautiously entered.

Angeline lay very still in the center of the large bed. She looked small and white with her dark hair seeming to float along the pillows. In a corner chair the doctor slumped, half sleeping. He started and clumsily rose at the sight of the strangers, but Elder Carlyle hastened to explain and urged him to sit still, while Elder Logan brought out the vial of consecrated oil. With his hands propped under his chin the doctor watched them. He thought the whole thing a bit strange, but if Hamilton had approved them then he certainly wasn't the one to interfere.

Fletcher stood by the bed with his hand over Angeline's cold one. Elder Logan performed the anointing, then Elder Carlyle, with one long look into the eyes of his companion, placed his hands on the sleeping girl's head, closed his eyes slowly, and with all his heart entreated the powers of heaven.

Angeline had heard the disturbance around her, struggled vainly to swim up and open her heavy, closed eyes. Was it Hamilton? She thought she heard someone say *Fletcher*. Could it be Fletcher and her father? She drifted away. Then clearly, ever so clearly—out of nowhere—the words fell like soothing drops on her fevered mind:

"In the name of Jesus Christ and by the power—" She took a deep breath and shuddered, relaxing— "we rebuke the sickness and bless you with strength to be well—" She came up from the deep dark pool she had struggled in, onto a calm, warm plain that was flooded with light— "we bless you with peace and strength and the ability to . . ."

Something was happening to her; something was different. She responded, she felt both a cleansing and a joy—strange, so strange . . . She moved her fingers. Fletcher felt and believed that somehow his sister was listening, she was there, she would be all right—she would be made well. Angeline took another breath and sank into a deep and restful slumber.

Elder Carlyle opened his eyes and stood still for a moment, watching the girl's calm face. It was so hard to tell. He had felt the Spirit moving through him, putting words into his mouth that he wouldn't have said . . .

They met Hamilton on the stairs and thanked him.

"Moses will have your horses ready," he said.

Fletcher followed them down, but Hamilton called after, "Would you like to stay with her, Fletcher?" The young boy paused. His face was more mature than Ham had remembered.

"No, thank you," he said. "Fletcher wants to go home. But she will be well now." He smiled, an expression innocent, almost angelic. "Isn't it wonderful, Hamilton? She will be well!"

He turned and followed his friends. Hamilton shivered with a current that seemed to drive into his very bones. He turned and continued his climb and went into the room where Angeline lay as silent and still as before, her hand resting over the coverlet, white and unmoving, and he sat with her through the long, unchanging night.

In the morning the doctor examined his patient. He had suspected something as soon as he looked at her face. Her chalk-white color had changed. There was now a floridness, almost a tinge of color in her cheeks.

"I'm better," she told him, and everything seemed to confirm it. He went out to where Hamilton waited in the hall.

"The hemorrhaging's stopped, her pulse is steady. It happens sometimes."

"That's no explanation." The young man seemed strangely displeased. Dr. Humphreys blinked his eyes. "To what do you attribute it?" Hamilton pressed him.

"The body's restorative powers suddenly rally. Things stabilize of their own accord."

"Without any stimulus or medication to alter conditions?"

Why this blasted scrutiny! Dr. Humphreys bristled. "It's not uncommon, yes, I've known it to happen. It's what we've been hoping for—we can only be grateful."

Hamilton nodded. "Yes, yes, of course," he said.

He had always believed she would live, but now that he knew it, the weakness he had resisted set in. He sat in the library chair, the one she was fond of, and looked out through the open window at the morning. A new day—another chance for him. Light, not darkness; hope in place of despair.

He rose. He bathed and dressed with a sudden new vigor. There was no reason left to look behind. Every moment now belonged to the future. And part of that future was lying alseep upstairs in the cradle that had held his father—the walnut cradle where he himself had slept.

He entered the nursery, disturbing Nancy. "Leave me alone with the child," he said. She looked up with frightened eyes, but she obeyed him. He approached and stood looking down at the sleeping boy, so tiny, so very perfect in every way. He had no idea whom the infant looked like, but his nose was finely shaped, his skin color clear, not blotched and mottled as were so many babies. He had masses of thick, dark hair, and fine long fingers. A superior child— what else! Hamilton smiled. He touched one tiny fist with his finger.

Ah, but babies grow, and this one would grow to a man. Would he be like his father? Would enmity rise between them? Perhaps the boy would favor his mother—or Samuel—or bear out some unknown ancestral strain. He rubbed the smooth-grained wood of the cradle. He knew it was a matter for deciding. Right here, right now. One way or the other. Not for Aubrey, not for Angeline's sake—for himself alone.

The faint movement disturbed the child, and his eyes opened. Deep eyes, blue-black. He didn't cry. The eyes seemed to look into Hamilton's; they blinked once. Then the tiniest smile curved along the lips. *Angeline's lips,* he thought. He lifted the baby, cradling him in his arms, and walked to the window. He placed the child gently against his shoulder and parted the long lace curtains.

"See there, that's your world." He spoke out loud to the infant. "Enough to keep you busy the rest of your life."

The new eyes continued to search; the hand on his shoulder was smaller than his thumb, so exquisitely small. They stood that way for a while, the man and the child: looking out, looking off to the future together.

_Fifteen

Angeline fell happily into her new role as mother. She was well and strong, her ordeal became memory, dulled more and more by each bright new day with her child. Nights only, sometimes, she would lie and ponder, with an uneasy sensation that something was missing. Something she ought to remember and know.

She remembered, really, so little of those few days. The doctor and Hamilton, Hester and Nancy—they were dream figures that drifted through clouds of unconscious haze. By the time her father arrived, exhausted and shaken, she had been sitting up in her bed to greet him.

But then, there had been that other uncommon occurrence when Fletcher came with his Mormon friends. No one brought it up; no

116

one spoke of the matter. Only once did she press Nancy for details, but Nancy knew very little. Her own strange memories served her better. Warm hands on her head, firm hands, and words that were spoken, and a difference she could instantly feel. She kept her own counsel concerning the matter, but she thought of it sometimes; she didn't think she would forget.

Summer came with a routine by now familiar: cultivating the cotton fields, repairing machinery, caring for slaves and animals, bottling produce, weeding the vegetable, fruit, and herb gardens, minding that the girls kept the dairy running. Once, sometimes twice a week a lamb would be slaughtered, the hides from the beeves supplying the plantation with shoes. Always something— always something. And this summer there was Edmund as well.

She had christened her son Edmund Samuel after both grand-fathers—Edmund Samuel Stewart, a dignified name. Much easier to bear than another Aubrey... The child was strong, with no problems of temper or health. She left Lairdswood only once, for Dyanne's marriage to Hugh McAlister in June. It was a gala affair, of course, with more guests in attendance than any wedding the county had seen for the past ten years.

She shopped, showed off the baby, attended luncheons and afternoon socials and theatricals and soirées—and ended up staying weeks longer than she had intended. When she finally went home to Lairdswood it was busy, true, but so quiet. So *lonely,* with no one to talk to besides the black slaves. She needed *someone—*

She was often awake in the nights with Edmund, and each time she was up she would hear the sound—the creaking, methodical sound of the rocker. Once, after putting the baby back into his bed, she went out on the porch alone. It was easy to think here, on top of the world, up above Lairdswood.

Was that it? Did Eliza look down on them all? And if so, what was there that still displeased her? Angeline had had a feeling that it might be the baby—concern to see that he got here alive and well. But he was here, and plump and plucky—and still the rocking. She shivered against the night air, though the air was warm. *What else can Eliza want?* she wondered.

It was September; they were in the midst of the cotton harvest. Late September—nearly a year since Aubrey died. As the date grew closer Angeline grew moody: sharp with the servants, impatient with the baby. She felt it herself, but seemed powerless to control it. She dreamed of Aubrey nights and woke up trembling. She wanted to lay him to rest and get on with her life. *But what life?* The long, bleak future stretched out before her. She would grow old alone, a dried-up, lonely woman.

The night of the twelfth of October came; she could not stay it. She had worked late in the gardens on purpose, then cared for the baby, then alone in her room gone over her whole toilette—washing her long hair, scrubbing down her body, seized with a passion for cleansing. She took great care with her creams and perfumes, with her hair and make-up. At last she went down, aware that the house was silent, that even the servants avoided her tonight. She was hungry, but in a dull way. Her eyes caught a movement. She half turned.

Hamilton stood in the tall, arched entrance that led to the candlelit dining room beyond. He wore dark green trousers and a warm gray coat. His hair, though long, was immaculately groomed. The eyes that regarded her were as gray as the jacket.

"Good evening, Angeline." He moved forward and a sea-blue color stained the gray eyes, and red lights danced along the tawny hair. "There's food and company for the night if you'll have it." He moved his arm to indicate what lay behind him. She could see that the table was laden with china and glass. The line of his jaw was tense. He waited. No cleverness, no cajoling.

She demurred. "It's very kind of you, Hamilton, but really—"

He moved closer. "It wasn't meant to be kind. I want you to spend the evening with me."

She felt bleak and trapped. "That will only make it harder. We were together a year ago this night, remember?" She sounded petty. She could see it reflected in his eyes.

"For your sake and mine, Angeline, don't do this. It will come to no good for either of us, you know."

"Why this night after months of ignoring my very existence? You expect me to believe your attentions sincere?"

His eyes grew wild, but his voice was controlled as he answered. "I couldn't compromise you in any way, Angeline—use your senses! If I'd paid you any kind of attentions there would have been talk and I'd have been forced to leave—or worse, you would have felt pressured to leave yourself. I knew how much it meant to you, staying at Lairdswood. It was really quite clear-cut, as I saw it: I could leave, or I could leave you alone."

"How thorough! Well, you did a good job, I assure you."

He covered the room in long strides and stood beside her. They were almost touching. "It's torture for me being near you, don't you know that?"

She felt his intensity, powerful as an embrace. Illogically she was angry, wanting to strike back at the pain and confusion within her.

"Oh, but suddenly now it's all right, is that it? A year—does a year mark some magical change? In an instant make everything permissible and proper?"

"No!" His voice was hoarse with emotion. "The difference is, I can't stand it any longer."

His eyes burned into hers; it was pain to meet them.

"I've never begged man or woman before. If I've wanted something, I've found my own way to get it." He stood back from her, shaking his head as though he were stunned. "Now you have it. As the old saying goes, my heart's in your keeping." He uttered a short, very bitter little laugh. "You know more about me than any living person—than I ever gave any person to know."

She stood, barely daring to breathe. "And you think I'll hurt you?" With sudden insight she knew what he too had suffered, sensed how vulnerable he was.

"You have no choice, my dear. You see, I love you. Oh, I want you, true, but I love you a thousand times more."

The corner of his mouth turned up, but the smile wouldn't serve him. His expression grew even more bitter and wry.

"Oh, yes, it's extremely ironical, I know. You see, from the first time I saw you, I knew it. I said to myself, 'Aubrey's got something here he can't handle.' I realized very soon that I loved you, Angeline. And then, of course, the pain set in. What is it they call it—poetic justice? That the dull, misused, maligned little brother should have the one thing I want most! That you should be his! The pathetic pity—the waste—the injustice!"

"I haven't seen any of this," she cried. "I don't see you fighting to have me!"

"That's the final irony." His voice had grown cold now, clinical, carefully free of emotion. "If it was only that I wanted you there'd be little problem." He cocked his head. "At least there'd be ways I could ply. But you see, I have no power to make you love me. How do I force that—demand it—" He made a small, hopeless gesture. "'Tis a fate you hold in your own hands, Angeline Stewart. Would to heaven—"

His voice had dropped lower, then stopped altogether. He crossed to the narrow French doors, past the laden table where the candles already guttered and spilled wax. He opened a door and the night air rushed in upon them, sweet with the musty fall fragrances, cool. He stood with his hand on the knob.

"I'm sorry, Angeline. As usual, I've made a mess interfering with your life."

She made a move as though to come closer. He held out his hand. "Have mercy, and allow me to escape with some shreds, at least, of past dignity. 'Adieu, Angeline, I have too grieved a heart to take a tedious leave.'" He turned. He disappeared into the darkness.

She stood watching after him, wanting him—loving him. What was she frightened of? Why had she driven him from her? The thought came to her then, *He won't come back.* She moved. She ran out into the darkness, calling.

"Hamilton! Hamilton!" In the still air her soft voice carried. But the night seemed to have swallowed him; there was no answer. She ran through Eliza's Garden, bathed in pale moonlight, then the arboretum where the trees choked the moon into slivers that pierced in weird splintered patterns of shadow and light. She was spent; she paused for a moment to catch breath, half expecting him to emerge from behind a dark tree.

"Hamilton, please don't leave me," she whispered. She thought of the stables and hurried there, sore-footed and limping. His horse was gone. She stared at the empty stall, then leaned against the

120

worn wood, weeping. She remained there for a long time not knowing what name to call on, or where she might turn for relief.

Fletcher had a reason of his own for remaining in Natchez. He was meeting with the Mormons now on a regular basis, studying with them, attending their Sabbath meetings. The missionary work had picked up and there was now a small gathering of converts. They sang hymns and read aloud from the Book of Mormon, the Bible, and the revelations of Joseph Smith. Elder Carlyle was surprised at Fletcher's quickness. He came to believe that no one had worked with the boy. It was his sister who had taught him to read and had read stories to him—everyone else seemed to assume that his speech impediment marked other, deeper impediments of the mind. He knew now that wasn't true. What Fletcher learned he retained and grasped with amazing understanding.

Elder Carlyle thought of all this and weighed it in his mind, trying to come to some sort of decision. Fletcher had asked to be baptized.

He pondered the question for a while, drew his own conclusions, and then, as he was wont to do, put the matter to prayer. Elder Logan did the same, getting much the same answer. Thus armed, they went forth to face Fletcher's father.

The man listened to them quite courteously. He was neither rude nor bigoted, but he was firm. They reasoned with him, contending that Fletcher understood baptism, that he was ready for it, that Mormonism could bless his life. He discussed the matter politely, asked a few questions. But in the end they made no headway; defeated, they left.

That evening, although the prospect was quite unpleasant, Edmund Gordon called his young son into his study and told him of his meeting with the two young Mormons.

"Did you give...permission?" Fletcher asked, stumbling over the last word.

Edmund coughed into his hand and shuffled some papers. "I don't think it would be wise, Fletcher," he said. "Do you understand?"

Fletcher shuffled closer. He had prepared for this and practiced long hours. Perspiration stood out in small beads along his upper lip. He had never approached his father this way before.

"Fletcher knows more than he can speak." He said the words slowly, enunciating as carefully as he could. "So hard to talk . . ." The sentence trailed and ended. He placed his hand on his father's arm. "Please. This is very important to me—father."

Edmund gazed into serious brown eyes, eyes he had never really looked into before—eyes amazingly like his Sarah's. He was moved by this encounter with his son. He touched the hand on his arm tentatively. "I didn't realize it meant so much to you, Fletcher."

The boy nodded, but other than that he didn't move. *What difference will it really make?* Edmund wondered. The boy would attend their meetings either way. He'd been impressed with the two young Mormons when he met them. And he couldn't deny how much they'd done for the boy—why, he'd bloomed this past year, hadn't he?

"All right, Fletcher. If it means that much—if you're serious about it." The fingers closed more tightly against his arm. "Yes, you can do it—yes, you have my permission."

Fletcher was beyond speech by now, but he reached over very quickly and hugged the man who had granted him this joy. It had been years—he could never remember having hugged his father. Quickly he kissed the rough cheek and withdrew, closing the door behind him.

Edmund sat there fighting the tears that gathered in his eyes, the tenderness that welled up inside him, suddenly very aware of his loss—the price he had inflicted upon himself these long, long years.

A week had passed and had proven her premonition: Hamilton didn't return to Lairdswood. He was at work still about the plantation; several servants had seen him. But he didn't come near the home buildings or the big house. Each day grew harder to live through, harder to face. Then one evening while searching through the office for some papers the overseer needed, she came on a letter, a letter from the law firm of Bailey & Johnson. It lay open inside the cover of one of the ledgers. It was addressed to Hamilton, but she spied her own name there and, in an instant, without really meaning to, she had read it.

...Pursuant to your request I have prepared the documents you requested, to wit deeds of conveyance to Lairdswood. It will be necessary for you to present yourself at the offices of the undersigned attorney and counselors to acknowledge the said instruments and set your hand and seal thereto. To complete the conveyance of Lairdswood to Mrs. Angeline Stewart it will be necessary to effectuate in-hand delivery. Inasmuch as I would find it cumbersome and perchance embarrassing to explain the circumstances under which the transfer is being made by you rather than Aubrey, I feel that it would be appropriate for you to deliver the same...

Whatever was this all about? First thing the next morning she had Woodrow bring round the buggy and drive her to town. She entered the large office and asked to see Mr. Phillip Johnson. She was immediately ushered in to another office, smaller but very elegantly appointed. She folded her hands in her lap. Mr. Johnson entered, came over to where she was seated, and took her hand.

"Mrs. Stewart, what a pleasure to make your acquaintance!"

His little eyes stared owllike from behind his round glasses. He walked back and sat down at his desk. It had long been his business to handle people, no matter how sticky the circumstances. But this one—

"Now, what may we do for you, Mrs. Stewart?"

"I've come to collect the deeds, Mr. Johnson."

"Deeds?" He rubbed one round cheek with a chubby finger.

"The deeds Hamilton instructed you to prepare." She paused for a moment, enjoying his discomfort. "They're quite in order, I hope."

"Yes, of course, Mrs. Stewart. It's just—well, Hamilton didn't inform me that you would be coming."

"No, he wouldn't have. Hamilton doesn't know."

The deuce! Just as I'd expected. Phillip rang for a clerk and instructed the young man to bring him the Stewart papers.

"He discussed the matter with you, I may assume?"

Angeline leaned slightly closer, fixing her eyes on the round face with the small, recessed eyes that held such a troubled expression.

"You may assume, my dear sir, that the game is over. Hamilton made the mistake of tutoring me somewhat in business and finance. Quite simply, I want to know what you two have been up to."

It worked. Phillip peered across at the lovely young woman. She looked cool and sure of herself. He made a decision. "You're quite right, my dear. I apologize. I shall be happy to disclose the matter to your satisfaction. Here's Timothy now."

So saying he took the materials his clerk had brought him, dismissed the boy, and turned his keenest attentions on the quiet young woman who sat beside him.

It required the better part of an hour; Phillip Johnson was painfully thorough if nothing else. But possessing a diplomatic strain he was proud of, he also fancied the lady needed some time. There were several difficult adjustments she must have been making.

Angeline had risen and walked several times to the window. Now she turned and thanked Phillip warmly and graciously. Perhaps after the strain he let down his defenses too quickly, for her next question took him totally by surprise.

"I must impose upon you, I fear, for one more small matter. If you would be so kind as to give me the address where Hamilton is staying?"

Phillip stammered a little before replying. "I don't believe I can be of much help there—I'm terribly sorry—"

"On the contrary, Mr. Johnson, consider again. Haven't we taken up enough of your time already this morning? Your son is in the next office, I believe. The information, I am sure, is at his disposal."

It was evident the lady again knew what she was doing. He arose with a little sigh. "Allow me, madam. I shall be back briefly." She inclined her head.

He walked heavily to the door and closed it behind him. He supposed, after all, it was really quite common knowledge that his Charles and Hamilton Stewart were drinking companions, had shared many a wild and dubious evening Down Under. Though neither young man was a bad sort, really. Just inclined to sow some wild oats—

"Well, hello there, father. You look a bit pale. Can I do something for you?" Charles sat back in his chair with his hands behind his head, welcoming the chance to be idle for a moment.

He was a pleasant variation of his father: round, boyish face with rosy cheeks—perfect for pinching, surprisingly irresistible to many women—eyes that seemed to be laughing to themselves and a smile that came quickly and gave the impression that mischief was about to break out any minute.

"Just write down for me the address where Hamilton's staying. Quickly—without any questions."

"I don't think I can do that." Charles didn't move a hair, but his eyes had grown interested. "I wondered if he might not be up to something. What is it?"

"Nothing of the sort you're thinking. Aubrey's widow is waiting in my office for that address."

Charles raised his eyebrows and gave a low whistle. Then he leaned forward slowly, took up a pen, and began scribbling. "He may string me up at dawn, but there—you have it."

Phillip took up the paper and placed it carefully inside his pocket. Charles chewed on the end of the long quill pen. "I'm willing to take a chance that this particular lady won't be an altogether unwelcome sight."

Phillip brought out a fine linen handkerchief and wiped his brow. "I pray heaven you're right this time, Charles. Or it's I who'll be strung up by the angry young scoundrel!"

Sixteen

A storm was trying to break. Though the wind was warm, still it blew strong enough to lift the arms of the trees, to scatter old leaves in a dozen hectic directions and whistle through the thin reeds that grew dense in the low river bottoms.

Far out on the river a few faint lights blinked, but in Natchez-Down-Under the windows were dark, or murky and smudged. Warm-tempered Mississippi boatmen crowded the gambling dens, barrooms, and dance halls for a good fling before their next stop in New Orleans. The hangers-on, crude and slippery-fingered, card sharks and brawlers stalked Silver Street, rubbing shoulders with plantation gentlemen in their lace-ruffled linen: Something for every mood, so the saying went.

Angeline left Nancy to wait for her at the top of the hill. "If I'm not back within a few minutes that means I've found him. Ride to my father's house; I'll come for you there."

Silver Street was steep, uneven and deeply rutted. Ginger stumbled a little, but Angeline urged her forward. The wind sucked the fine dust from the road, then swirled it about her. She could feel it in her teeth and hair. Horse and rider struggled until finally they reached the protected lip of the ledge where rows of dirty, leaning buildings squatted. Somewhere here was the one she wanted. She dismounted and tied Ginger securely to one of the posts; then, throwing her head back into the wind, she walked along the boardwalk.

There were no addresses posted here. Mr. Johnson had told her it would be the red brick building that sat between a yellow clapboard and a gray mud granite. But the buildings were jumbled and repetitive, with several red bricks and two beside yellow neighbors. She paused, and as she pushed back her hair a large hand closed on her shoulder, then slipped to encircle her waist. Her pulse started pounding. She wanted to run, but she couldn't move.

"I never forget a pretty face, Mrs. Stewart. What unholy purpose brings you here?"

She laughed; she couldn't help it. "Captain Leathers!"

"You're right to look relieved. You're mighty lucky it's me." He leaned close and though his breath smelled of whiskey it was mingled with a vague, masculine, pleasing scent. "There are few men here who would be concerned with a lady's honor."

She told him the name and description of the place she was seeking and sketchily explained her errand. He gave her his brawny arm and escorted her past five or six buildings to the one she wanted. When she began to thank him he protested.

"Oh no, m'darling. You're not safely delivered yet. I'm going with you."

The interior was much less shabby than she had expected. Garish by her standards, but passably clean. As they climbed a long flight of stairs Captain Leathers shouted, "Let's hope for his sake we find him alone."

Angeline smiled to herself. "And if not?"

"Why, if not, ma'am, I'll take an inch or two off his ornery hide."

They found the door and Leathers, with his large paw, pounded upon it. Angeline pressed her fingers into his arm.

"Now, don't you be nervous," he told her, winking broadly, "not a man with two eyes in his head could resist you, m'darling."

The knob turned, the door opened inward; Hamilton stood there, looking lean and tall and tawny. He drew in his breath. Captain Leathers grinned like a bushy, boyish giant.

"Mrs. Stewart to see you, Hamilton. Are you receiving?" His eyes twinkled, and he winked again.

"It would be my pleasure." Hamilton spoke very softly, stepping back from the door. Captain Leathers ushered her in.

"I'll leave you two then." He planted a kiss on her cheek.

"Thank you," she murmured.

He went down the staircase three steps at a time, sounding much like a clumsy bear trapped in a tunnel. They listened until he was gone, then turned to each other as though on cue.

"May I take your cape?"

She slid it from her shoulders and handed it to him, careful to avoid his touch. She sat, but he stood and looked at her in the old way: conjecture mixed with pain.

"Why have you come, Angeline? How did you find me?"

127

"Both weighty questions with weighty answers. How long have you—" she looked about her— "had this place?"

"Several years now. You don't approve." It was statement, not question.

She avoided his eyes. "It's not a matter of approval. Or really of what I think, is it?"

He walked to a sideboard, more cluttered and disordered than the ones at Lairdswood, and poured from a bottle that looked like wine, then turned, deliberately facing her again.

"Perhaps it's good that you've come, that you've seen this side of me, Angie. It's one of my natural settings, you know."

She nodded. She thought she knew what he was doing. "You asked how I found you. I went to see Phillip Johnson this morning and picked up the deeds you had so nicely prepared."

She had the pleasure of seeing him surprised, taken off his guard.

"And how in the world did you—"

"Never mind, Hamilton, that's not important. Though if you must know, I found the letter he wrote stuck in one of the ledgers. I want to know why you did it."

"That's my own business."

"I want to know!" She rose and walked over to where he was standing. "How is it that the deeds were transferred from *you* to me?"

"Phillip must have told you." He took a deep breath, then released it with a sigh. "When the place became Aubrey's legal possession Mother insisted he draw up a will and leave it to me. She was adamant—she'd seen too many fortunes flounder because the legal affairs were neglected."

"Did Aubrey want that?"

"He didn't mind. He wasn't married, had no prospects. It was always understood that as soon as he had a wife he would transfer things over—"

"And why didn't he?" Her voice was laced with strain.

He shrugged his shoulders, a rather helpless gesture. "I don't know. To be honest, I don't think he gave it a thought. He was so crazy in love with you, Angeline, so taken with being the master of Lairdswood, the fair-haired boy—"

"And, of course, he didn't expect to die." The strain was in her voice, but no sign of feeling.

She began pacing, her small hands clasped tightly behind her. "So all along Lairdswood was yours, and you knew it. You deceived me—did it please you to know I was at your mercy?"

There seemed no desire in him to fight back. He answered quietly, "I was sick and angry as blazes at Aubrey. Lairdswood was yours! Do you think I'd contest that, Angie? Do you think me little enough to wheedle it out from under you? Do you believe I could stoop that low? Angie!"

There were tears in her eyes. With a will she blinked them back. "You love Lairdswood as much as I do. I've always known that."

He was restored with that statement. His eyes grew beautiful. "Well, I love you more than I love Lairdswood." He would not turn away; he would not make it easy for her.

"Everyone thought you wanted to marry me to get Lairdswood."

He folded his arms. "What did you think, Angeline?"

So finally, suddenly, it had come to that. She stood before the gaze of the blue-gray eyes, the gaze that would allow her no deception, that could see so far inside her. She found she was ready.

"I thought—" she began very softly, "I thought that you loved me. More than any woman deserved to be loved. I thought you were exciting and fascinating. When Aubrey died I learned how unselfish you really were."

She paused. It wasn't coming out right. It was as though she were writing a treatise on his character. She ran a hand across her forehead and pushed her hair back. "Hamilton, I've been so afraid to love you!"

"All love is mingled portions of pain and fear. And courage to put your life in another's keeping."

"I know that! I know that at last. And at last I'm ready."

His hand on the edge of the sideboard tightened until the knuckles turned white, but he could not stop his trembling. He had suffered—and mastered—many emotions. But never before had he felt the wild power of joy.

"I love you!" The words were too much to be spoken, or the feelings so much deeper than the words. She went into his arms; he had never been so tender. She ran her fingers through the golden hair and kissed the sensitive mouth she had longed for.

"I give you courage for courage and gift for gift. I love you, Hamilton, more than Lairdswood."

The lips against her lips curled with pleasure. "You talk of my giving! You have given myself back to me," he cried. "There could never be any tomorrows for me without you."

At last the storm in fury swept over the river, whipping the water, tearing at the land. In Natchez-Down-Under-the-Hill, the mud-flat kingdom, ladies of the night and opportunists, dreamers and desperadoes all huddled together, drowning their fears in frenzied living, drinking, and brawling, pleasuring themselves into oblivion, until every emotion that hurt was smothered and even the wind was muted by their noise.

But alone, in an upstairs room, a man and a woman looked out with one face and one heart upon the storm, and past the tempest—unafraid of the future.

Book Two

Natchez, Mississippi
1861-1865

Seventeen

Angeline would always remember the day and the look in Hamilton's blue-gray eyes. He had ridden all the way from Jackson. His boots were muddied, his jacket stained with rain, his fine mouth drawn—and she knew the words he would say before he spoke them.

"Mississippi has seceded from the Union."

They stood looking at one another. She found herself remembering, with a tightness in her throat, Reuben Davis's words when he spoke to his Northern colleagues in the House:

> We will sacrifice our lives, burn our houses, and convert our sunny South . . . into a wilderness waste . . . at the hazard of bringing upon the world bankruptcy and ruin, famine and pestilence, lamentation and mourning. . . . Gentlemen of the Republican party, I warn you, Present your sectional candidate for 1860; elect him as the representative of your system of labor . . . and we of the South will tear this Constitution in pieces, and look to our guns for justice . . . against aggression and wrong.

Has it come to that? Has it come to that?

"Come tell me about it," she said. She led him into the library where a cheerful fire already burned in the grate. She poured him a drink while he removed his boots and stretched out his legs. He had been one of the delegates to the state convention, part of something that forever now would be part of him.

"They knew what they were going to do," he said, "before they did it."

"You feared as much before you went."

He turned the glass in his hands but didn't drink. "Did you read it in the papers?" he asked.

His question drew a reluctant smile. "Oh, yes. The *Free Trader* announced that in honor of the event bells would be rung and cannons fired and fireworks set off in the streets."

Hamilton knit his brow. "Well, they celebrated in Jackson. The ladies of the city presented the convention with a flag that bore a star—one single star. White on a field of blue."

"I'm not surprised," Angeline said, "but our celebration didn't come to much. In fact the *Courier* reported—here, let me read it—" She rose and picked up a paper from one of the tables and found the place she wanted. "The *Courier* wrote: 'Thank God, we have tears to shed; tears of bitter grief and indignant reproach—sadness and gloom, instead of rejoicing, marked both day and night.'"

He shook his head, "Well, in Jackson the following evening that crazy Irish comedian Henry McCarthy performed an original song entitled *The Bonnie Blue Flag.*"

"Already?" She set the newspaper down with a sigh. "Oh, Ham, how did it happen? How did it really happen?"

"There's no easy answer, Angeline, you know it. There's the old nightmare, of course, states' rights, and the pressures of increasing economic divergence between the industrial North and the agrarian South. Emotional issues both. But in the opening paragraph of the Declaration of Causes do you know what it says?"

She shook her head. He leaned forward, his eyes intense, almost fevered.

"I quote: 'Our position is thoroughly identified with the institution of slavery—the greatest material interest in the world.' It goes on then to list our complaints and causes—nearly all centered around the issue of slaves."

Angeline rose. She felt suddenly chill and rubbed her hands along her arms to warm them. There had already been the John Brown fiasco and the election of Abraham Lincoln, whom

Southerners referred to as that "wild man from nowhere." Those events were removed from her own world, however, and they had seemed dreamlike, ink-and-paper reality. This struck with a force, a grim personal power.

Wednesday, January 9, 1861: a day like any other day. She had been baking, Edmund supervising the trickling tail end of the cotton harvest, Afton out riding with Hugh, and Mississippi . . . cutting away her life with her own hands.

"Will there be war?"

He spread his hands. "How can we avoid it? More states will leave the Union every day. The ordinance drawn up at the convention not only separates Mississippi from the Union, but gives consent of the people of the state to the formation of a Confederacy—"

"A Confederacy of what?"

"Of such states as have or may hereafter secede from the Union."

Hamilton rose and walked to the window. Angeline followed and took the still-untouched drink from his hands.

"Vote was 84 to 14. There was prayer afterward petitioning heaven to protect and prosper the new republic. A brave, grand deed done by men trusting in God . . ."

They didn't join the children for dinner that evening. Angeline ordered something brought in and they ate together. And talked. There was nothing but talk left to resort to. The power rested in other men's hands. And the power would sweep them along like a leaf in the current.

Near midnight they went up to bed together. They had talked, but some things remained unsaid. She had not asked what might happen to Lairdswood. She had not said, *If it comes to war, will you fight?* He had not said, *I have no desire to die. I have no desire to ever leave you.*

But he held her in his arms and traced with his finger the pattern of silver moonlight across the bed and remembered very vividly what he had told her, years ago, before she had been his wife, when he had loved her with passion and confidence born of youth.

We'll be able to hold things here together, I promise. And no matter what else about me, I have never been known to go back on my word.

He caught her fine hair in his hand, let it run through his fingers. *I have no more hold on the future,* he thought, *than that.* Long he lay awake in the cold moonlight, full of painful remembering.

On February ninth Jefferson Davis was selected as president of the provisional government of the Confederate States. He was a stern and undemonstrative man, but one of unparalleled integrity and reputation. Three weeks earlier he had given his farewell address to the Senate.

"I am sure there is not one of you," he stated, "to whom I cannot say, in the presence of my God, I wish you well; . . . and hope for peaceful relations with you, though we must part. The reverse may bring disaster on every portion of the country; and if you will have it thus, we will invoke the God of our fathers, who delivered them from the power of the lion, to protect us from the ravages of the bear; and thus, putting our trust in God, and in our firm hearts and strong arms, we will vindicate the right as best we may."

So saying, he sat down with his head in his hands, and wept.

On March fourth Abraham Lincoln was inaugurated. The new dome of the federal capitol was in the midst of construction and marksmen were placed at the building's windows, prompted by fear for the President's life.

"I am loathe to close," the tall, sad man told the crowds assembled. "We are not enemies, but friends. We must not be enemies. Though passion may have strained, it must not break our bonds of affection. The mystic chords of memory, stretching from every battle-field, and patriot grave, to every living heart and hearthstone, all over this broad land, will yet swell the chorus of the Union, when again touched, as surely they will be, by the better angels of our nature."

On April twelfth Confederate batteries under General Pierre Beauregard opened fire on Union-held Fort Sumter. Three days later President Lincoln called for 75,000 volunteer militia to suppress the rebellion.

On April eighteenth Hamilton sold the last of his 1860 cotton crop. He was luckier than some; he had many connections and a little foresight. He prepared the cotton fields, but then took the advice of Thomas Hudson, president of the Southern Planters' Convention, and diverted large portions of field into other production, to supply them with the necessaries of life.

The following day, April nineteenth, a Friday, young Hugh McAlister rode over to visit. He and Afton walked out through the gardens, excitedly talking. Spring was in full bloom in the Natchez country; they were part of the youth and beauty of the spring.

Angeline could see them from her upstairs perch. She sat on the porch, in the rocker that had been Eliza's, watching her young daughter and her best friend's son. Dyanne had said years ago, cheeks flushed and happy, "You have a boy and I'll have a girl. When they're older we'll marry them off to one another and watch our grandchildren grow up together."

Angeline had given birth to a son, and a year later Dyanne had produced a son and heir. But by that time . . . by that time so much had happened. She and Hamilton had married and soon after Afton would come. Not a son of his own, but a daughter. She had feared a little—she smiled, remembering now. He had sat beside the bed where she was lying. Why did childbirth have to threaten her so? Take her down into such depths before it released her?

"There will be no more children, Angeline," he had said.

"I want to give you a son," she told him.

He laughed—an open, happy, confident sound. "You're a crazy woman, Angeline." Then he lowered his voice and bent closer to her. "I have a son already," he said.

She remembered the tears in her eyes and the joy in her heart at his statement.

"I made my decision concerning Edmund—" he paused— "the day when I knew you would live. I went up alone to the child and I faced it: one way or the other—hate or love."

A slight smile touched the sensitive mouth as he continued. "It wasn't really a difficult decision to make. So, you see, I have a son, and now a daughter. A little girl like you—" He stroked her hair.

She noticed that his fingers trembled. "I couldn't want more, Angeline."

He had bent to kiss her. "It's too hard for you. I won't let you go through this again. I won't let anything threaten to take you away from me, Angie."

And so it had been. And now suddenly Edmund and Afton were a young man and a young woman. Somehow the years had done this, but oh, so quickly. The trials of life had come, the low spots. But through it all she had known such happiness —

There was a hand on her shoulder. "What are you thinking? Of those two out there and what's happening to their world?"

Angeline smiled at the tall, fair man who looked down upon her. "You guessed wrong. I was thinking of us, Hamilton, and our world." She took the hand he held out and softly caressed it, running her fingers along the lean, hardened lines. "I feel young yet and fiercely happy — and fiercely protective —"

She stopped, suddenly finding it difficult to go on. They remained silent a moment, then he took both her hands in his one and raised her to stand beside him.

"Why do you insist on Eliza's old rocker still?"

She leaned against his shoulder. "You know why," she whispered.

They had never really talked about it much — once or twice when they had stood at night together, awakened by the rocker's rhythmical sound. She had always been convinced that it was Eliza. *But why?* It wasn't just Aubrey and Aubrey's child, for after Edmund was born the rocking continued. Until — until her wedding day, when she married the older son, Eliza's favorite — the handsome, cynical, sensitive renegade . . . and the lonely rocking at night had no longer disturbed them.

So she often sat there now, and felt close to Eliza. When she needed peace, when she needed a little strength . . .

Hugh stayed to eat and, of course, they talked of the conflict. Would it come to an all-out war? Hugh thought it would. He and Edmund bragged and boasted to each other, Afton watching them with a woman's unconscious humoring and pride. Hamilton spoke little and excused himself when the meal was over.

138

Two weeks later, on May fourth, the Congress of the Confederate States issued a declaration of war against the Federal Union.

And so yet another flag was destined to fly from the bluffs of Natchez—the brave banner of the young Confederacy. And the glory, the pride, the dreams of conquest stirred and whispered portentously as the winds of war blew over the river and awakened them from their uneasy sleep.

The fever to join up was in everyone's blood. Afton felt the difference in Hugh when he was with her. All he could think of was killing the Yankees and grabbing glory. She felt her own first flush of excitement ebb. Even when he bent to kiss her she had the feeling that his thoughts were still in the field of war.

"I'll come back in six months with a dozen Northern swords," he boasted, "captured from as many blue-bellied Yankee cowards. And with stories to tell our children and grandchildren, Afton."

She blushed slightly and dropped her eyes. Her mother would tell her she was too young to feel serious love for a man, even for Hugh, though Hugh was nearly family, and she knew both her mother and Aunt Dyanne wanted the match as much as she did. She was sixteen years old, just barely. Edmund had turned seventeen and Hugh soon would, too. Her mother had been only eighteen when she married . . .

But the age for joining the army was set at eighteen. Hugh felt that with some pull he could get in anyway. He was the eldest son and tall for his age. And somebody had to represent his family.

Afton liked the idea of waiting at home for Hugh: sewing flags and uniforms, pressing flowers, writing romantic letters to the front. Though at times she wished that somehow they could be married; she could send her husband off to war, she would be a wife, belonging to him—

"There's Edmund. What's he got?" Hugh broke into her reverie. Nowadays the two boys almost seemed to exclude her. After all, she wasn't a man going off to battle. For a moment a twinge of anger twisted inside. But it relaxed when they caught up to Edmund and he smiled down at her.

"Look at this: a new saddle. It just came in on the *Natchez*."

Hugh was eager. "We'll join the cavalry together, Edmund. Here, let me have it."

"Not so fast. Afton comes first. After all, Hugh, she's a better rider than the two of us put together."

Support of the war effort in Mississippi was overwhelming. Governor Pettus wrote to Jefferson Davis, frantic about the deluge of volunteers and what to do with them, where to put them. In June the Natchez Fencibles set out for battle. Two of Hugh's friends were in the group, which had been escorted by the Light Guard, the Troop, the Cadets, and the Quitman Guards. He watched the uniformed men take tearful farewell of their wives and sweethearts. The nobility of it, the pathos cut him deeply.

His own little brother had approached Captain Blackburn with a gift of twenty dollars from himself and five dollars from his little sister—something Hugh had not even known of—a gift from children to the noble corps. It had brought tears to the captain's eyes when he received it. Hugh felt humiliated. He went home determined to find some way.

That same evening at Lairdswood Edmund approached his father. Hamilton was alone in his favorite spot, the small card room. Edmund entered and closed the door behind him.

"May we talk a few moments, father?"

Hamilton nodded.

"I suppose you know what I want, but I hope you'll hear me out. I'm not eighteen yet, but in less than a year I will be."

Hamilton smiled to himself. Eleven months less than a year!

"I just want your permission to prepare myself, father, make application to some of the elite corps. I hear there are waiting lines for places in some of the choice ones. So if I move now—" He paused at the look in Hamilton's eyes.

"I'll be leaving Lairdswood within a month, Edmund. I'll need you to keep things going here."

"Have you told mother?"

Hamilton shook his head. "We haven't discussed it. But—your mother? I'm sure she knows."

Edmund rose from the chair where he'd perched, not sat; the movement was impatient. "I don't understand why you! It's I should be going!"

"You think I'm stealing the glory that rightfully ought to be yours?"

Edmund sputtered a little. His father was so direct, so outspoken.

"Edmund, you've always been easy for me to read." The boy winced at the words, though they were not unkindly spoken. "There'll be far less glory and romance to war than you think. Besides, your mother's the first person to consider."

Edmund glared a little. "She'd rather lose me than lose you."

Hamilton's smile was slow to come and it lent him an enigmatic expression. "I'd like to think you're right," he replied. "But there's more to it than that."

"Oh, she's just like all the other mothers. Not wanting their little boys to go off to war."

Edmund thought for a moment his father might strike him. Hamilton had risen and stood glowering over the boy. "Don't you speak in that way about your mother ever again. You young fool!" He seemed to spit the words at Edmund.

"You're not only the sole son she has," Hamilton continued, fixing the boy with a stern gaze, "but you're the last living link she has with Aubrey. If she were to lose you he would be gone from her forever."

It was as though a shock went through his system. Edmund seldom thought of the man who was really his father, who had died before he was even born. He had not spoken of him nor heard him referred to for years. He turned aside; Hamilton's gaze was too penetrating.

"You're man enough to face it, to think of it now."

The boy didn't reply. Hamilton sat and waited for him.

"When I was little I wouldn't let myself think about it." The words came very tentatively. "I wanted to believe you were really my father. I didn't want my father to be someone else—to be dead."

"That's natural, it's understandable, Edmund. I am your father in nearly every sense."

Edmund turned. Hamilton caught his breath. The boy looked very like Aubrey; young and vulnerable and a little defensive.

"Did you ever wish—well, did you really want me?"

Hamilton winced. He hadn't thought it would come to this. But then, perhaps it was time . . .

"Come over here, Edmund." He indicated a chair. Somewhat reluctantly Edmund crossed and sat. "Since you ask, I think you're man enough to hear this. Before Aubrey married your mother, I loved her."

Edmund drew in his breath.

"You didn't know that?" He shook his head.

"There's not much you know. Aubrey loved her too, don't mistake that. And she loved him, and she married him gladly. I know as long as he lived they were happy together. That's important for you to know."

Edmund nodded and swallowed.

"And this, too. There was nothing with us until long after. She nearly lost her life when you were born."

"I knew that."

"Yes, well, that brings us to the point of your question." Hamilton rubbed his hands along the arms of the chair. "For days we despaired of her life, and while I waited I did a lot of thinking about my life—put to rest many old ghosts that had plagued me. And I knew the last test I must face would be you."

He watched, attempting to catch Edmund's reaction. But the boy kept his face carefully blank, free of expression.

"When I was sure she would live I went up to the nursery. It was the first time I had seen you since you had been born. I knew I could either mistreat and resent you all my life, or—" he paused, not certain how to go on— "or I could decide to accept you as my own, and love you."

He stood; it was he who could not bear scrutiny now. "I picked you up and held you. You were beautiful, Edmund. As beautiful as Afton when she was born."

The boy looked down at his feet awkwardly, but Hamilton didn't see him.

"How do I say it? I started to love you from that moment. I've never looked back nor regretted, nor wished you were different or more my own—so you see, the loss would not be only your mother's."

What to say after such a revelation? Such an intimacy between man and man. Edmund cleared his throat. "I'm glad I asked you, if this was the outcome."

Hamilton smiled, content. "So am I. Try to buck up, Edmund. Be patient; see what tomorrow brings."

He walked over and put his arm around the boy's shoulder. "Whatever comes, it won't be easy. I thank God I have you, son."

That night Edmund lay wide awake in bed. War was very far away. He was thinking: *Funny. I was going to ask what he was like. My real father...my real father...* Alone in the darkness his thoughts were clear. It didn't matter what Aubrey was like; it would never matter. He would always know who his real father was.

_Eighteen

Hamilton had said he would leave within the month. Many men his age, oldtime friends, were already in uniform. Charles Johnson was in the unit he himself would be joining. It would be good to have such a staunch comrade beside him. But summer was over when at last he felt his preparations were ample, conditions at home in order, the timing right...no longer could he neglect his duty.

Angeline knew that Tom Ruskin had offered him the rank of captain, with a company to command and special duties. *Special duties*—she didn't like the sound; it conjured up frightening images in her head. *The less you know, the better,* Hamilton had told her. So she knew he wouldn't talk about it much. And she knew how hard it was for him. She had become adept at reading the blue-gray eyes.

In July at Bull Run, or what the Southerners called Manassas, their men under Generals Beauregard and Jackson routed the Union forces of General McDowell, and in the course of the battle a legend was born.

Jackson and his men, facing overwhelming odds, had formed a strong line and, incredibly, held their ground. General Bee, attempting to rally his own troops, pointed toward Jackson's line and shouted, "There is Jackson standing like a stone wall. Let us determine to die here, and we will conquer."

Thus the religious, quiet-natured man became known as "Stonewall," and his brigade as the Stonewall Brigade.

So who could triumph over the Southrons when they had such men to lead them? people were asking. The same month the Northern general George B. McClellan assumed command of the Army of the Potomac—no match beside the courageous Southern leaders. The spirit, the dashing confidence grew. They would win; they would whip the tails off those Yankees.

There were so many men who wanted to fight. What difference, more or less, could one man make? Angeline wondered as she sat in Eliza's Garden, surrounded by fragrant beauty on every side, what war would do to a man like Hamilton. He was brave, perhaps grandiose, but at the same time canny, calculated. Would that give him the edge he needed to live?

She shuddered deep down inside. Worse things than death could happen. He wasn't a man who could easily resign himself to a deficiency or handicap. She tried to reject the images on her brain, but she had no power over the pain that nibbled inside, gnawing the threads of her courage into ravels.

Hamilton found Afton alone in the stables. It was strange, he had often thought, that she should inherit this love of horses that ought to have gone to Aubrey's son.

"What a pleasant surprise," she said when she saw him. "It's not often I can cajole you here."

144

Her face shone so openly, so innocent of life. *How soon that will change,* Hamilton thought. "I wish to talk with you, Afton. I leave tomorrow."

She came up and laid her head on his shoulder. "Oh, papa, papa..." The term Angeline had taught her, the endearment. Her hair smelled like sunshine and new hay. He placed his hand very gently upon it.

"You must be brave for your mother," he said. "You may not see it, she won't complain, but she'll need you."

"I know. I understand how she is."

She lifted her head and smiled, her eyes clear and shining. *Beguiling,* he thought. *She's so nearly a woman.*

"I love her. I'll do all I can," she promised. "But how will any of us get along without you?"

Suddenly all the glory, the girlish romance, seemed vain and empty mockery. All she knew was that the father she loved was leaving. Perhaps to suffer, perhaps to die...perhaps he would never come back to Lairdswood again.

Hamilton stuffed Edmund's head with instructions. He could see the dismay on the young face grow. The slow grin spread into his eyes and over his features. Edmund thought with sudden insight, *He's a young man still. And handsome.* He knew women thought his father handsome.

There was certainly no excess weight on the lean, tall frame and few wrinkles in the firm, tanned skin. *He's got everything to lose to this war.* He had been thinking of only his own position, not what it would mean to a man like Hamilton.

For once his father misread his silence. "You know all this anyway, so now put it behind you. Follow your instincts, they'll lead you aright."

"I wasn't worrying about myself, father."

Hamilton nodded and flexed his fingers against each other, looking down at the cluttered surface of the desk. "Well, don't fret yourself worrying about me, either. It will weaken your judgment, Edmund. Give me your word."

"I'll try, father."

Hamilton ran long fingers through his thick, vermilion hair. "I can't promise what will happen, Edmund. But I believe I'll be back. I feel it in my blood."

The evening was dark for summer and the air warm and heavy. *There are too many sighs on the air,* Angeline thought. *Too many unshed tears to carry.*

She lay beside Hamilton with her head resting on his arm. He could see her face outlined: the small chin, the fine straight nose, the brow with dark hair tumbling over it. When he was a young man he had feared the confinement of marriage, believing a man needed freedom, variety. He had been terrified of waking up one morning bored with the face that sat across from his at the table, disappointed and tired of someone to whom he was tied.

He smiled to himself. The women who lay beside him had never grown boring, and his need for her had increased with each passing year. His need and this terrible, tender love.

"It's not right. It's not our war," Angeline said.

He sighed. He had thought all the talking was over between them. "As far as its making—no, you're right. But as for support, who better than you and I, Angie, Southerners to our fingertips. Bound up with Lairdswood, part of the land. We've profited more than most from the system. We'd better be prepared to defend it."

"I'd give it all away in a minute, Hamilton, rather than hazard losing you—"

"You won't. I'll come back, Angie. I promise."

How many men, Angeline thought with a shudder, *have made such a promise to women they love?* "I'll hold you to it," she said against his shoulder.

"You may do that," he whispered, his lips on her hair. "Have I ever broken my word to you yet?"

He could quiet her fears, but not his own. They lurched black— menacing, overgrown shadows along the walls of his mind. *I've always taken care of you, Angie. Heaven help me not to fail you now.*

146

On November first the Northern general Winfield Scott resigned as general-in-chief, and the full command of the Union armies fell into the eager hands of George B. McClellan. On November second the Natchez *Courier* printed one more propagandized appeal to the people. Under title of "Now's the Day and Now's the Hour," it pleaded:

> Our country needs the services of all its patriotic sons, and laggards should not be found. Will the few hundreds of patriotic young men in Natchez, Adams and the adjoining district, who have not yet gone into active service, still cling to home and its luxuries when their services are needed in the tented field? Such is not the spirit of Mississippians. Now's the day and now's the hour. Capt. Dougherty's company, now or soon to be in quarters, and Gen. Wood and associates, who will go into camp next week, offer the rare facilities of quarters, clothing and provisions! A roll is opened at the Courthouse. Let no man screen himself behind his wealth or his poverty.

Hugh McAlister clipped the article and stuck it inside one of the books on his desk. The following day he presented himself at the courthouse office, signed his name, and enlisted for active service.

That night he appeared beneath Afton's window. He threw small pebbles up at the glass and whistled a tune. It was quiet in the still house; she was quick to hear him. She dressed hastily and slipped down below. Without speaking she took his hand and led him to the quiet part of Eliza's Garden. Within the shadows of the summerhouse they talked.

When she learned he had really enlisted her face went pale. This was nothing to make light of; there was no turning back now.

"No one knows but you," he said. "It's better that way."

"What if they discover your age and send you back?"

He shook his head. "Turn away a soldier? They'd never do it. They'd pretend they didn't know first and look the other way."

"I wish you could say good-bye to your mother."

"Are you joking? That's one ordeal I'm glad to escape."

"Hugh!"

"Well, you know mother. She's so domineering. So *dramatic*. It's really best this way."

She turned from him and picked a long red rose, rubbing its silken smoothness against her cheek. "Are you frightened, Hugh?"

"I don't think about it. I guess everyone's scared a little, even grown men. Even men like your father."

Afton smiled through the darkness. He was trying so hard to convince himself.

"Edmund will be disappointed. I think you should tell him."

"Nope. That would be like rubbing it in. Besides, he can honestly say he knew nothing about it."

"And me? If they question me, Hugh, do you want me to lie?"

"Don't be silly!" He reached out and touched her hair. "It's different with a girl. What could you do to stop me? They'd have expected Edmund at least to try."

She nodded. She knew what he meant, so why argue? Why waste these last few moments...

"Besides—I *had* to see you." He spoke the words softly. Very gently he drew her close. His hand still in her loosened hair, he pulled her face to his and kissed her. He whispered, "I love you, Afton. I love you."

She could not get the words to come in her turn. But he was going off to war, so she kissed him and thrilled to the fierce demand of his lips, and at last promised to be his sweetheart.

He wove the deep red rose into her hair and vowed he would love her forever and ever. And she wept against his shoulder for many reasons, and when he left didn't want to let him go.

She wasn't so much afraid she would never see him, but afraid that the beautiful pain he'd awakened inside her, the new needs and feelings, would go unfed and die before they'd begun to blossom— like a rosebud, wilted and brown at the edges, that would never open into a full-blown rose.

The new year came, but they hardly marked its coming. Hamilton's letters were now the main thing they waited for. He wrote:

My command is well armed with brass muzzle-loading smoothbore Napoleons of what I consider a good class. Ammunition is more of a problem; I have enough for perhaps two-thirds of the men. We have petitioned tents from the government but none arrived. One week at home and I could work wonders, even if I were to purchase supplies from my personal funds. That would be much preferred to this continual frustration.

I have seen some fighting, skirmishes really, nothing major. But even then I will admit to a feeling of awed insignificance as I stood with the musket and cannon balls flying around me thick as spring hail, and men falling on every side, dead or wounded—horribly wounded. And the black smoke hanging above like a funeral pall—it is not easy to see such sights and forget. . . .

The new year was not going well for the Cause. Fort Henry and Fort Donelson both were taken by Northern forces. Then in March came the battle of Pea Ridge in northwestern Arkansas, which served to preserve Missouri for the Union.

Edmund followed most eagerly the naval battles. The old sunken ship the *Merrimac* was raised by the Confederates, plated with iron, and renamed the *Virginia*. At Hampton Roads on March eighth she attacked the Northern ships there, taking them by surprise and destroying two. But when she returned the next day she found a Northern ironclad waiting—the formidable *Monitor*. Built by the Swedish-American inventor John Ericsson, who called it his "cheese box on a raft," it was constructed of iron as well as being ironclad and it maneuvered entirely under steam power.

For four long hours the two ships battled, the *Monitor* moving more easily than the *Virginia*, but its shells having little effect on the Confederate ship. The *Monitor* withdrew, the *Virginia* returned to the James river, and not much was really proven either way. Except, as Edmund explained to them, they had prevented McClellan from using the route he wanted: the best route to Richmond, which was the James.

"That's the kind of battle I could enjoy," he told them, and Afton, who had just received a tattered, soiled letter from Hugh, turned white and left the room.

"I'm sorry, mother. Shall I go after her?"

Angeline shook her head.

What a fool I am! he berated himself angrily. *Both Hugh and father are out there fighting. And I make it sound like a game I can't wait to play.*

149

Nineteen

The battles were fought, but they were little more than names to Angeline, places on the map that Edmund marked to follow the war's progress. They had letters from Hugh or Hamilton now and again. But Hamilton told them very little. She realized that when after Shiloh and the long days of Corinth he wrote:

> I believe this to have been the severest battle in the war thus far. So many died or were permanently maimed. I do not fear, Angeline. What happens will happen. I take each thing as it happens—one day at a time—

Nothing of what he himself must have suffered. No complaints, no details such as the newspapers printed.

Summer was ending. They were faced with another winter and all that it would mean in terms of suffering and loss. Where had nearly two years of fighting brought them? Were they any closer to a solution, either way? Even with Robert E. Lee now commanding the Army of Northern Virginia they were not *winning*, though he had succeeded in the Seven Days' battles in driving McClellan back from Richmond. The capital was safe again and McClellan retreated to Harrison's Landing to lick his wounds.

At home, even on such self-contained islands as Lairdswood, the hand of war was beginning to take a hold. Afton and her friends kept busy sewing clothes for the soldiers and learning how to make homespun. Angeline had never considered herself much of a seamstress, so she was happy to allocate the task to the girls, providing them with materials and encouragement. Neither she nor Afton, nor any of the ladies of their acquaintance, had done spinning or weaving before. But between them grew a friendly spirit of contest to see who could make the prettiest homespun dress.

Many things became a point of pride: home tanning, home dying, home curing, home-brewed corn beer. "We must learn to live within ourselves," the *Courier* admonished. So Angeline made blue dye from the extract of logwood, red from red oak bark, and yellow from sassafras, swamp bay, and butterfly root boiled together. She produced homemade cornstarch, being careful that the corn pulp was properly mixed with water, that the water was cold enough, that the starch was thoroughly drained, and that the cake of starch was not allowed to sit too long and thus begin fermenting. She made economical candles mixing one pound of beeswax with three-quarters of a pound of resin to produce a candle that would burn six hours each night for six months at a cost of only fifty cents.

So they worked, and so they got by. But this was not living. This was a desperate biding of time until something or someone restored love and purpose and progress to life.

On September seventeenth Lee made his first invasion North. It was a good move backed by sound logic: remove the battle from already ravaged Virginia, rouse the increasing antiwar sentiment in the North, and restock depleted supplies by foraging the less devastated Northern countryside.

But, unfortunately, McClellan came into possession of Lee's orders. He pursued, but not quickly enough to repel the invasion. The armies met at Sharpsburg, Maryland, on Antietam Creek. Three separate battles were fought on September seventeenth, which came to be called the bloodiest day of the war. Over ten thousand Southern casualties, twelve thousand Northern. Lee's broken army recrossed the Potomac the following day. McClellan, from his own inexplicable point of reason, did not follow and pursue the enemy.

But the day had been counted a victory for the Union. Five days later Lincoln issued his preliminary Emancipation Proclamation, warning the South that if it did not return to the Union within one hundred days, all slaves in the rebellious states would be considered forever free.

This was almost impossible to believe. No one in his right mind could possibly think of turning loose thousands of these simple, uneducated people into society—especially a society crippled and bogged down by war. How would they care for themselves? It made Angeline shudder. How would Lairdswood function without slave labor? She longed for Hamilton with an intensity she remembered from her youthful days; it was not a welcome pain.

Christmas morning Angeline stood with Edmund and Afton passing out the holiday gifts for the slaves. Hester's son came forward with his wife and five little children. She handed out the handkerchiefs, pocketknives, and pipes for the adults, shoes and dresses for the little children, one by one, to smiling, grateful black faces. This was a ritual she had performed for nineteen years. *Can this really be the last time?* she wondered. Minerva's daughter, Dinah, came forward. She had nursed three of Dinah's children through diphtheria the summer before the war. The summer before the war ... would they always reckon life that way?

January 1, 1863, the Emancipation Proclamation became official.

Hamilton watched the reactions of his fellow soldiers in the camp. All were incredulous, many angry and disdainful. Others sank into a discouraged lethargy.

"No matter what happens, we've already lost," he heard one man complaining.

"I hope I don't live to see the day when the uniform of the United States army is placed on the backs of black men," Charles Johnson confided.

Hamilton had trouble sorting out his own feelings. He didn't think emancipation would work. Being a student of Jefferson's he had in some ways anticipated it. But reality was so very different from vague conjecture. If he were honest, there was much about it he found distasteful.

He wrote a long letter home to Angeline with instructions and suggestions. And encouragement—what encouragement he could muster. He found himself lying awake nights, longing to see her, to touch her once more, to hold her in his arms. How could he keep things at Lairdswood together without being there? He looked down at his ragged gray pants, at his boots lined with newspaper where holes had broken through, and thought of the days when life had been only a game, pleasure sold to the highest bidder: fine clothes, fine wines, fine foods, and good times Down Under.

Then Angeline had walked into his life and changed all that forever. He liked to think he'd grown up during those dark days of loss and suffering. And he was a lucky man; he was smart enough to know that. He had everything he wanted out of life. So how much more then did he have to lose?

"Captain Stewart?"

Hamilton looked up and smiled at the skinny young aide-de-camp. He wasn't any older than Edmund—perhaps younger—

"Major Douglas would like to see you, sir, at his tent."

He rose and brushed off his pants and followed the soldier. He knew what Douglas wanted; he had been waiting. It was one of those special assignments he had not spoken about to Angie, tailor-made for a cunning old rascal like himself.

The room, after all, held very few personal belongings: changes of clothing, a pocket watch, a few books. It didn't take Fletcher long to pack them together. There was a daguerreotype in a small frame on his bedside table. He removed it with great care and held it a moment, looking gently upon the young face that smiled back at his. She would miss him; she was the only one. He placed the picture inside one of the books. It was time to be going.

He had left a note for his father. His father was old; he would not grieve much. He had never grieved much over his son.

He walked to the courthouse and through the long hall to the recruiting office. His footsteps made sharp sounds along the polished wood floor. He didn't slow down. He must appear normal, like everyone else.

Old Chris Crippens saw Fletcher approaching. "Well, I'll be hornswoggled! Fletcher Gordon's come to enlist for his country. Won't Jeff Davis be delighted?"

Benjamin Bradley kicked him under the table. "Shut your trap!" Benjamin didn't like Chris Crippens. He smoked cheap cigars and his speech was as foul as his smell.

"Name, please," Benjamin asked, sounding very official.

Fletcher swallowed. His throat was dry and constricted. "Fletcher Gordon."

"No middle name?"

Fletcher shook his head.

"Your age, Fletcher."

"Thirty-four years last month, sir."

"He ain't no sir, Fletcher!" Crippens chewed on the dark, wet stump of a cigar. "You think cause the North is takin' niggers the South'll take morons?"

Fletcher colored. That was exactly what he'd been thinking. Perhaps now, with Negroes enlisting by thousands—perhaps now with the need so great, they would take him—

"Shut up, Chris," Benjamin growled. "You're the bloomin' moron." He turned back to the quiet man. "Pay him no mind, Fletcher. You'll have to fill out this form."

Fletcher took the paper. He could read and write as well as the next man. He bent over and started to write his name.

Hugh had been with Lee's forces for several months now. Like everyone else, he loved the man. He'd have followed him to the devil without thinking; fact is, that's about where he'd led them now and again.

It was spring in Virginia and Hugh couldn't help thinking of that spring two years ago when he'd walked with Afton and boasted like the green boy he'd been, painting the war in glowing colors and making a fool of himself talking glory and conquest. How different he would be if he saw her now. How different . . .

He chewed on his cold beans. He missed his mother. He wouldn't have admitted it out loud, but he missed her. *Serves you right!* he smiled to himself. That's what she would tell him. She would fuss and scold for a while, her dark eyes snapping. But in the end she'd be there with love and a gentle hand, good food, and a warm, clean bed to sleep in, her red, dimpled mouth curved into a smile. In the end . . .

He set down his plate. Darkness was falling. Here on the edge of the Wilderness forest it seemed to come fast. There would be battle tomorrow with "Fighting Joe Hooker," the Northern general who wanted to take the Rappahannock line. He had 120,000 men to Lee's 60,000. But that didn't mean he could budge Lee. Hugh lay down and pulled his blanket around him. Sleep was a soldier's best friend. He closed his eyes.

The Confederate attack cut the Northern army in two. While the Yankee soldiers sat eating their supper Jackson's men had spilled out of the forest, through the dense black oak, through the whispering pine, loosing their battle yells like an Indian war cry, driving the Union back. It was a bold, brilliant move. It was Jackson's old war trick, one he and Lee played well together.

But Jackson had hopes of enlarging the victory. Night was falling and the Union center still held. Another attack would change that. He rode ahead of his men on Little Sorrel—too far ahead. Turning back toward his own lines he was nothing but a shadow in the awkward darkness. Someone shot. Then there was a spatter of fire.

They stole him off the field so the men wouldn't know. But the men knew it. He had been shot three times in the arm, so the arm must go. He lay silent and grim. He had work to do. Death must not be the victor in this battle.

Lee, hearing that Jackson improved, wrote his old comrade: "You are better off than I am, for while you have only lost your *left*, I have lost my *right* arm." Then, hearing that he grew worse, Lee responded: "Tell him I am praying for him as I believe I have never prayed for myself."

Eight days after receiving his wound Jackson died from pneumonia and the effects of the amputation. "Better ten Jacksons should fall," he said before his death, "than one Lee."

So it mattered little that Hooker had retreated. If Jackson were lost, then what could be counted on? The star of the Confederacy trembled and dimmed.

Twenty

In Natchez all eyes were upon the Father of Waters, the wide bright river that fed the land, that sometimes flooded out the levees, but carried away the cotton and brought back gold—the river that sang the dreamer's dream and churned the tall silver wheels of commerce. Now the river carried a new and deadly danger: squat, mean, ironclad gunboats that spewed fire at the shorelines, mined the levees, sank the graceful white steamboats, and rocked the legend with tons of dirty Mississippi mud.

Grant was growing impatient; he wanted Vicksburg. New Orleans was already held by Union forces. But the stretch of river from Port Hudson to Vicksburg remained firm in Confederate hands. This summer of 1863 Grant planned to change that.

Afton rode to their own narrow bluff above the river and looked down on the silvery serpent below. How many times since childhood had she sat here, singing songs to herself and dreaming her own long dreams? Or skipping down the bluff to Wheezy Willie's hut by the river with a question to ask or a cut to be healed, running along the clean white sand with Willie's son, Buster, with the gulls' sharp crying above and the water's soft murmur. A melody came to her now, unwanted, unbidden:

> Weep for the mighty dead,
> The nation's joy and pride,
> Send forth the mournful tidings
> On hill and mountainside.

The words spoke of Stonewall, one of the many songs written for Jackson. But didn't the words speak for all of the South as well? "Send forth the mournful tidings . . ." There was nothing to life for them but mournful tidings. The Negroes had nearly all deserted. There were a few old faithful hands, but what could they do? And those who stayed, or promised to stay, wanted wages. Where would the money come from without a crop?

156

It seemed to Afton one endless round of ruin, with nothing to halt the process that had begun. Hugh was somewhere with Lee's army, moving northward. And her father? No one knew where Hamilton was. He had become rather strange and secretive in his letters. They had suspicions of their own, she and her mother. She wondered if Edmund knew anything. But he'd never talk. He'd grown up these past years without father. She wondered how the war had changed Hugh.

Didn't it change them all? She looked down at her fingers. They were stained with dirt and the nails were broken and cracked. It was she who had the care of Eliza's Garden and the other bordering, manicured flower plots. Her mother criticized it as a lost cause, told her she ought to concentrate on the vegetable gardens and the herbs they needed for medicine and food. But her mother was not seventeen, she thought hotly, and in need of something to cling to. Her youth had been lived. She had had the romance and beauty, the magical courtship, the making of Lairdswood, the love of two men. She felt tears well up in her eyes and she fought against them. What right did these strangers have to destroy her future? Turn all she loved to ashes before her eyes?

She wiped the tears on her sleeve and turned her horse homeward. Her mother would be awaiting her coming, with half a dozen tasks for her to do. Edmund would ride in tired, wanting some supper. She leaned low over the gray horse and urged him into a run—faster, until the ground became blurred and dizzied, faster, until the wind wove knots in her hair. Faster, until the speed matched her anger and cooled the passions that tore so cruelly inside.

Angeline picked up the latest issue of the *Courier*, not so thick now, and many-colored. Newsprint had long since disappeared and what publications persisted had resorted to any color and quality of paper they could find. It was front-page news, the destruction of the *Natchez*, burned during the latest naval campaign. Tom Leathers's gaunt face stared out from the column at her: the long, beaked nose, bright eyes, still cunning and young, under a shelf of forehead and a bristly brow. His beard had turned gray but his hair was thick still. She trembled slightly. Just seeing him there unleashed a whirlwind of carefully guarded emotions, old memories—how could they be painful still? She replaced the paper and walked to the mirror at the end of the settee. Cautiously, but coldly, she gazed at the image reflected there.

Her own brown locks had no gray in them. There were only a few slight wrinkles around her eyes. Her skin was as soft and clear as Afton's. And her lips—how she longed to have Hamilton kiss them. How she longed for the sound of his voice, the curl of his smile, the look in his eyes that could pierce right through her. She clutched at the back of the couch. She felt weak inside, weak and more than a little frightened.

The siege of Vicksburg had been in process since early May. Vicksburg was the real stronghold, with giant batteries high on the bluffs of the eastern shore, commanding a large stretch of the river and effectively repulsing gunboat assaults. Natchez did not occupy a strategic position and was not fortified by Confederate arms. There were only two cannon existing in the city, one of these an old gun captured from Burgoyne at the battle of Saratoga, and kept more as a curiosity than a viable weapon. If Vicksburg fell, Natchez would fall with her.

The state capital, Jackson, had already been taken. The Union generals had feasted in the governor's mansion, then proceeded to destroy the railroad depots, the bridges, the cotton factories, the newspaper presses, the homes people lived in, the churches. She couldn't conceive of such destruction occurring here.

Almost she was glad that Hamilton was absent. She couldn't see him standing aside before such things. She had visions of him protesting, resisting, then being hurt and crushed, his beautiful body broken— She would wake up with such visions at night and sleep would desert her, and she would sit in Eliza's rocker and wait out the dark—pray and rock and remember until morning.

Vicksburg was a city beset, surrounded. The armies had struggled, losing thousands of men, Pemberton never having numbers sufficient for victory. Grant finally gained possession of what he most wanted: Haynes' Bluff overlooking the Yazoo River. Whole fleets of steamboats could crawl up the Yazoo now with reinforcements, food, and ammunition. Pemberton could do little more than prolong the agony. His lines were so long and his numbers so few that his soldiers were forced to stay awake in the trenches, day and night, week after week, in all kinds of weather—drenched by the rain and blistered by the sun, virtually locked up in their own fortress.

So, too, with the civilians under siege. Wrote one: "We are utterly cut off from the world, surrounded by a circle of fire." There was no way into or out of the city, except for the hidden holes like rabbit warrens, like foxes' dens, where some slipped through—some few who thought the Cause worth the effort.

Edmund Stewart considered himself one of the few. He had steady nerves and an uncanny sense of direction. He could go anywhere in the Natchez country blindfolded. He had learned the tunnels and byways of Vicksburg like the back of his hand. He figured he'd done little enough to support the war effort; this was one thing he was equipped to do. Several times in May he'd slipped into the city, bringing money and medicines and light supplies. If his mother knew, she did not reveal it, did not strain the truth by facing it eye to eye. It was June, and he figured this trip would be his last one—if he could get his mother to agree to his plan.

He made his way toward the caves by the uncertain moonlight, a bag of supplies on his back and a gun in his hand. But the streets, though littered and cratered by the cannon, were silent and empty as he passed through. The labyrinth of caves didn't slow him; he avoided the grasping hands, the curt question or two. He knew exactly where he was headed.

Sally Fielding heard the tentative knocking. It was a pattern she instantly recognized. She rose in the predawn dark and unlatched the low door. A familiar shadow glided through. She raised her hand to touch his face; he took it and kissed it. She pulled him over near the fire and stirred the red coals. His eyes were as warm as the glowing embers.

"I worry about you," she said, her voice low.

"You never know when I'll come, so you don't know when to worry."

"I worry always." She smiled. "I suppose that's a woman's way."

He opened his bag and pulled out the items he'd brought them. She watched him, very aware that his presence beside her was a wonder worked by Grant and his siege. She had not known that Edmund Stewart existed until that morning when, hungry and dirty, she had walked the Vicksburg streets clutching a few dollars of Confederate money, her instructions from home to find something—anything—to eat.

She had walked with tears in her eyes. The previous evening, just as darkness fell, a shell had torn through their roof, breaking up the room where it burst, sending pieces and fragments through both floors down into the cellar where they had run. For safety. There was no safety, even there. As they hurried downstairs a large fragment had struck her mother. Sally had watched her tumble and fall, then lie still—watched Melinda, the black girl, try to lift her and seen the crushed hip with white bone sticking through.

Even now she closed her eyes against the vision and the patient pain in her mother's face. Her father was somewhere with Pemberton in the trenches. There was no one close to turn to that she knew. And no one, if asked, had means to help them. They had found a doctor to treat her mother. He stayed five minutes, dressed the wound, and gave them instructions. But he took no pay. When he left he advised them to move, find a place in one of the caves in the cliffside. She dreaded the thought of the dank, cramped caves. She would rather die than huddle in fear. And yet, there was her mother.

The streets were noisy and crowded. Somehow in the jostling she had stumbled against the tall young man. He had righted her with his hands on her shoulders, pushed back her tangled hair, seen the tears in her eyes.

"I've been looking for someone who needs help," he told her. And she had thought she would cry at the tenderness in his smile.

He followed her home and somehow took over—in a quiet, unassuming way. By nightfall they were settled at one of the cave sites with medicine and food stashed away, with clean bandages and clean water for drinking. He had moved in her mother's bed, so she rested in comfort. There were so many kindly details he had thought of.

That was four weeks ago. Four times she had seen him. Four times he had safely slipped through, with help for others—she knew—besides her own family. They had learned so much about each other during those visits—in long discussions, in things unsaid. Laura Grover was considered one of the beauties of Vicksburg. Edmund had taken supplies to her family twice. She had tossed her head and blinked her pretty blue eyes to attract him. But he had not stayed to visit at Laura's. It was here he came, to sit beside Sally. It was here he talked, it was she who listened, she who felt the deep gaze of the warm brown eyes . . .

"I won't be seeing you for a while."

She knew it. A tight hand gripped her inside. "You won't be coming again? I know the risk grows greater."

"That it does. But then, so do the rewards." He was watching her. Her heart fluttered, like a bird that was caged and could not be still.

"I won't be far away, Sally." She felt cold fear grip inside her again. "Pemberton cries for soldiers to man his trenches. This is child's play, toting supplies. I'm more needed there."

You're more needed here, her heart cried, but she couldn't speak it. She nodded. She could find nothing to say. What right did she have to stop or stay him, to demand, to request, to implore him to stay?

He dropped to his knees on the cold packed earth before her. "Sally, look at me. Sally, please."

Bravely she lifted her eyes to face him. But already they were moist with tears.

"Go ahead and cry," he told her softly. "There's beauty in your face even when you cry."

She shook her head.

"Oh, yes. The first time I saw you, you were crying. Ever since I've been bewitched by your tears."

She reached out a hand and touched his face. "Be careful, Edmund. If you didn't—if anything happened—"

"Oh, I'll be back. We Stewart men are stubborn. When there's something we want, we don't let go."

He kissed her before he left: one sweet, chaste promise. There wasn't much of a moon to watch him by. She stood by the low cave door and gazed into the darkness. He was a shadow shape; he was darkness now. She heard Porter's mortar shells boom into the silence. They were part of the darkness, too. The shells and the cave and the ugliness and the dying. And the love that had no hope, no place to go. She stooped and walked back into the cold shelter, feeling chilled and empty inside.

The young man had chosen a position close to the fire. It was too hot to sit inside the tents, and not dark enough to use the lanterns. But here the fire gave light to read. He opened the small, worn volume he always carried. How many times had he read it through? There were even parts he had learned by memory—a verse here and there, whole pages sometimes. He had really become very good at reading. He practiced on newspapers his father brought home, even tried the poetry Angeline used to read aloud to him. But this was the book that had been his life, given him understanding, purpose, and hope.

He turned to Mormon near the end of the book and thumbed through the pages. The destruction of the Nephite people meant more to him now. He was seeing the destruction of his own people. He had been in battle and tasted the fear and pain. He had seen the terrible suffering and destruction.

The men in the company liked Fletcher. In the beginning he had been the butt of every joke. But when that wore off they came to accept him. And slowly the acceptance turned into respect. He was always the first to go into fire, the first to obey an order, no matter how hard. The first to stoop and pick up a fallen comrade, no matter what danger it posed for himself. He didn't complain and he didn't shirk his duty, and many a man had known kindness at his hands. So they came to feel rather protective of him, screening him from embarrassment and unpleasantries. He was company mascot, a good omen, a lucky piece for every man's pocket. That was what most of the men believed.

Fletcher believed that the Lord had placed him on purpose with the best group of soldiers to fight in the war. He felt humble and inadequate and grateful. He had never been treated as an equal before, except perhaps with the slave boy, Moses. But man to man—this was sweet and new. He held sacred the role of friend and comrade, and would gladly have given his life for any one of the men.

He bent over, immersed in his reading, and no one disturbed him. In fact, several of the men, when no one was looking, had picked up Fletcher's peculiar book and looked through it, even read some of the passages he had marked. Mormon scriptures—Joseph Smith's gold Bible. Some had never heard of it before, others knew only the tales that had circulated. But they all knew that Fletcher took it quite seriously. And some of them, holding it, reading it, formed their own impressions, and feelings that would stay with them the rest of their lives.

Fletcher was reading of the last great war of the Nephites:

And it came to pass that they came to battle against us, and every soul was filled with terror because of the greatness of their numbers.

Well did Fletcher know that feeling: a sickness in his stomach that lasted for days, a burning terror that flamed at sight of the endless lines of blue-clad soldiers. A particular passage had caught his eye. He read it over and over, thinking upon it.

But, behold, the judgments of God will overtake the wicked; and it is by the wicked that the wicked are punished; for it is the wicked that stir up the hearts of the children of men unto bloodshed.

So everyone paid the price for the wicked. Fletcher thought of these men he had grown to love. He thought of Angeline, though the thinking was painful. His understanding was like a fire that burned within him, a wound that no mortal power could heal, a loneliness of spirit he must live with. Slowly he read and slowly the soft night settled upon him.

163

Hamilton slipped into the jacket and settled it over his shoulders. It felt good; it was a near-perfect fit. Major Douglas handed him the papers: the Union pass, the credentials, the letters of introduction—all forged. A false identity, a new shell, but the same familiar man inside. The man who had traveled North many times before the war on his private business, who knew the Northern cities, the Northern mind, the Northern factories where he held an interest. The old wry smile played at his mouth and eyes. Poetic justice, this. Betray his own interests. Send information to Morgan that Morgan would need: what railroads carried what shipments and where they were headed, what stops they would make, and where they would be least guarded.

The Northern factories produced 5,000 rifles a day to the South's 300. They turned out boots for men's feet and food for their stomachs. It was shortage that put a stranglehold on the South: shortage of fighting men, shortage of weapons, shortage of tents and blankets and clothes. What they could not produce they must somehow capture—appropriate—divert—grasp!

Hamilton turned his horse to the dark road that headed northward. He wore a different uniform and a different name. No one knew who he was or where he was going. Angeline lay behind him, part of an old dream. He knew he had only one weapon now that could serve or save him: his mind, his keen concentration on the task. As he rode, the miles and the dream fell behind him and were lost in the indiscriminate dark.

Twenty-one

The guns barked into the city day and night, regular as clock-work, broken by intervals of silence when the tension was almost worse than during the noise. The citizens in their caves ate rats and mule meat. Pets such as dogs and cats had long since disappeared. Even small songbirds were sometimes served up for supper.

Niles, with Grant and his men, waited out the city. Knew, as the rebels knew, that the end was near. He wasn't as exultant as some at the prospect of the city's downfall. He felt an inbred sympathy for the South. Even here in the trenches he loved the Southern air. It had a certain quality, soft and fragrant, more dense than the thin, cold Northern air.

This morning five more Confederate soldiers had slipped through to the Northern lines. The saying went that the rebels could die here, well-fed cowards, not starving martyrs. He wondered how many soldiers had deserted. The civilians had no such option, no such escape. To them the lines were closed as well as the river. He had seen couples and even whole families attempt to get through. Turned back politely at the lines, they would try the river, be forced back from the shore by gunfire, forced to return to their pitiful shelters with the shells flying thick around them.

Edmund lay on his back and stared at the high white sky above him. His mother had granted permission for this three-month enlist-ment. At last he wore on his back the Southern gray. But this wasn't his idea of being a soldier. He could taste defeat in his mouth like acrid rust. He'd begun to feel very bitter against the Yankees. Cramped here like some trapped animal, helpless and mocked. There had never been time to think as there was here. He'd always been too busy before. Now things preyed on his mind that he'd never thought of.

Edmund didn't like being part of a losing cause. He knew what was going on this morning. The night before, Pemberton had conferred with his major generals. Grant's engineers were bringing the Federal trenches closer and closer to the Confederate works. They had dug tunnels and planted mines to blow up the strong points. None of the generals believed that the men had strength left to fight their way out of the trap. General Bowen had said they might as well get it over with. So now, while the guns still roared, still spewed forth destruction, Pemberton negotiated surrender of the city.

It was one of the longest days Edmund would ever live. At five in the afternoon the river batteries rang forth with one last shot, then all was still. Darkness fell. Across the night sky rockets arched and exploded over the city. A myriad of holiday colors stained the air. Pemberton had obtained one advantage, one small advantage. His soldiers were to be released on parole, not shipped North to prison camps. Grant thought it was wisdom—31,000 soldiers would tie up a lot of shipping. He believed, anyway, that the men were disheartened, would probably ignore their paroles and go home. Edmund would be going home, but he found no joy in it, except perhaps to see the relief in his mother's eyes.

The morning was calm, too calm, and the air was heavy. Niles watched as the rebels pulled down their flag. He saw the white banner rise, the flag of surrender. He checked the watch he carried; it was four o'clock in the morning of the Fourth of July. Independence Day in Vicksburg—how about that? He watched the gray-clad soldiers walk out of the breastworks, stack their arms, and then fall back. His own men pushed forward, took possession, pulled down the limp white flag. He watched as the stars and stripes rose proudly, thirty-six bright feet of flag floating upon the Southern air. *Why*, he wondered, *does this have to happen? It's crazy, what I'm doing here.*

He marched with the other soldiers through the city. Some of the men expressed surprise at how little damage was done. Looking around the rubble-strewn streets he decided that the city had suffered more than enough. The civilians lining the streets did not look friendly. He had heard how some had reacted to the surrender, howling their anger, calling Pemberton a traitor. He couldn't help respecting that kind of defiant pride.

He was very hot. His tunic stuck to his body; his blue trousers rubbed against his saddle. They had marched all the way from the Tennessee border and hammered for months to get into this place. He ought to feel some sense of elatioṅ. But he only felt dusty and tired and hot.

Sally, watching the soldiers, thought they looked well-fed and polished, their horses sleek, their arms and uniforms bright. She hated the sight, she hated the surrender, yet behind it all a hidden relief seeped through. It was over. No matter what else, it was over. She had to find out if her father was alive, she told herself as she worked her way past the soldiers, through the pressing crowds in the glutted streets. She knew the place where the men would be gathered, the worn men in gray who had dashed themselves against the bright blue power and lost. Would her father be among them? Would Edmund—would Edmund . . . ?

From a long way off in the distance he saw her. He had wondered if he could find her in the crowds—wondered if she would want him at such a moment. . . . It was strange what happened inside him when he saw her. It was as though some part of himself fit back into place, her features loved and known and familiar. Not familiar with two months' knowing—but back past memory, past time and place.

He began to walk toward her. She hadn't seen him, but it seemed as though she could feel him near. She lifted her eyes and found the brown eyes upon her. Edmund knew that his heart was reflected, laid bare. She looked and saw what he wanted her to see there, and her own heart answered him, joy for joy.

While Grant clung with bulldog tenacity to Vicksburg, Lee made another bold move into the North. Believing that the Northern army remained south of the Potomac, he let his own men roam in a long, loose line, collecting the food and supplies so abundant in Pennsylvania.

Then he learned that things had gone terribly wrong. The Yankees had somehow stolen a long march and were close by at Frederick, Maryland. The Army of Northern Virginia must concentrate. He sent orders to his generals to reunite near Gettysburg.

Meade, meanwhile, chose a strong defensive position behind Pipe Creek, fifteen miles south of Gettysburg. His battle plans were vague, as Lee's were. So three pugnacious men helped make their decision.

A. P. Hill was trying to get his Confederates into Gettysburg. He saw no reason why the Yankee cavalry should try to keep him out. But Buford, the Northern cavalryman who opposed him, liked a good fight as much as Hill. So did his superior, Reynolds. And Meade had given Reynolds a free hand. So Reynolds made his own decision, sent a message to Meade for more men, and determined to fight for Gettysburg inch by inch. He rode out in front of his lines, urging his men to strike a good blow. A bullet hit him and he fell from his saddle, dead—and the Battle of Gettysburg surged forward.

Lee was not ready for a large general engagement. He had less than half of his army on the field. But what was shaping into place was a Confederate victory, so he seized the moment of opportunity.

Hugh was part of Lee's victory. He watched the right half of the Federal line collapse, bore down on the flank of Howard's Dutchmen until they finally broke and ran helter-skelter through Gettysburg until Howard and a brigade of infantry stopped them. It was good, but now they must finish what they'd begun. And, as usual, it was Lee who labored under a handicap. The Northern army was larger in numbers and it stood for once in the defensive, on its own soil. And there was not room here for Lee's kind of battle, the brilliant shifts and feints he knew so well. It was down to a slugging match, nothing better—the one kind of fight Lee wanted to avoid.

July second dawned. Hugh saw the sun rise; he had been unable to sleep, feeling nervous and tight. He marched with the men and watched them assemble, some in the craggy ravines of Devil's Den, others in a long wheat field and a dusky peach orchard where the quiet fruit ripened above their heads. There was the moment of spellbound silence before the battle when men wondered what they were doing here, pinned bits of white cloth to their shirts for identification: name, company, division, home address. Where to send the paltry contents of the gray pockets when the man inside the uniform ceased to be, when his flesh became part of the waste and carnage and his face a number on a casualty list.

Then the sudden press of bodies forward, the bark of the cannon, the bright red flame. The bodies falling; ignore the bodies, throw yourself against the solid line of blue steel, blurred by the settling fog of gunsmoke. After hours of fog in his eyes and nostrils, after hours of wearing his body out, he found himself in a littered farmyard. Crazily he smelled the farm smells: fresh milk, molasses feed, warm manure. They were within an inch of success, but the canister fire was murderous at this close range. They stopped; they moved slowly back. Hugh felt himself stumble and looked down at a hideous litter of human fragments: hands, the stump of an arm, a section of leg, a part of someone's face with one eye showing. With strength that came from horror he ran.

Fletcher was one who lived through the day's battle. He had clambered up the steep slopes of Culp's Hill, thick with young trees and fallen timber, hanging on while the day passed into darkness. In the gray woods the flickering lights from the sputter of musketry fire glowed on and off, like innocent fireflies.

Fletcher laid his head on the cool, damp earth with no blanket beneath him. He was exhausted; he didn't attempt to read. He closed his eyes and let his mind run over certain passages he knew by heart . . .

> And my soul was rent with anguish, because of the slain of my people, and I cried: O ye fair ones, how could ye have departed from the ways of the Lord! . . . Behold, if ye had not done this, ye would not have fallen. But behold, ye are fallen, and I mourn your loss . . . and my sorrows cannot bring your return . . .

Someone kicked his boot; he raised one eyelid.

"There's a spring out past the Federal's right. We're goin' for water. You comin', Fletch?"

Fletcher groaned. His throat was dry with hours of dust and gunpowder. But he was more tired than he was thirsty; he shook his head.

"Not this time. Thanks." He turned on his side. The men going out together passed and were gone. In the stillness he heard a cry that was stifled. He moved; he raised his head, he listened again. The cry came stronger now and a voice followed. "Water? Has someone got water out there?"

It came from a few yards away, where the wounded were gathered. Men with lips as parched as his, who could not rise and go for water. Fletcher pulled himself to his feet and stumbled forward, grabbing two extra canteens as he went, hurrying to catch up to the shadow men who had gone before him.

At the spring the shadow figures were even darker. Fletcher thought he recognized one or two. He bent over and felt cool water on his fingers, heard it gurgle into the neck of the canteen. Then someone shouted, "Hey, those are Yankees! What in thunder are they doin' here?"

A shot rang out. Folds of cloud closed over the moonlight. No one could tell what was gray or blue. Men grunted and swore and slumped, and the shots kept coming. What hit him Fletcher never knew. He slumped like the others slumped, his face in the water, the canteen emptying silver at his feet.

Morning came slowly, as though to soften her intrusion. Men shook their tired bodies awake. Lee had only one card left to play: a center attack on Meade's line at Cemetery Ridge. He was putting nearly 15,000 men into this attack. But Hancock, Meade's best general, had 9,000 veterans, protected by stone walls, fences, and breastworks, and backed by an abundance of reserves close at hand. Longstreet, pointing to the Federal position, warned Lee that "no fifteen thousand men ever arrayed for battle can take that position." But what choice did Lee have but to try, with that desperate faith based on the assumption that when the Army of Northern Virginia gave its all, no one and nothing could stand in its way?

Lee's bombardment began, went relentlessly forward, on and on. The sound was like a weight that obliterated: two hundred guns in action in one square mile, each getting off two or three rounds per minute. And there was more to fear than even the guns. Deadly fragments from the rocky ground, torn loose by the fire, drove jaggedly into soft bodies that froze still, destroyed as surely as by the enemy's fire.

170

Hugh was part of Lee's assaulting column that watched for hours, waiting, poised. At three o'clock the bombardment ceased of a sudden, and an ugly silence spread over the smoking field. Men paused and turned, aware of the drama, and sucked in their breaths as out of the woods marched column after gray column. A mile long from flank to flank the line moved forward, battle pennants snapping overhead, generals gliding like silk on tall, dark stallions.

It was a sight that no one could see and forget. Out into the open field they halted and dressed their ranks as though on parade. Hugh, standing straight and unblinking, felt the pride, the raw emotion, and for a moment was part of the exultation that could never be destroyed by a thing like death. Then the line began to roll forward, beautifully, irresistibly.

Up on the ridge the Federal gunners waited. Their fire tore frightful gaps in the moving line, so vulnerable, so unprotected. Pickett, heading the charge, urged the brave men on. He had handed Longstreet a letter before the battle to give to a girl in Richmond if he should die. "If Old Peter's nod means death," he wrote her, "good-bye, and God bless you, little one."

The cloud of dust and smoke settled over Pickett. Hugh felt the familiar taste in his throat. The Northern gunners fired into the rolling cloud. Hundreds of soldiers gave way, shot down. Hugh saw nothing but his own private nightmare, knew nothing beyond the need to push on.

Armistead, by some clumsy miracle, crossed the wall, he and a very few men who stumbled with him. Hugh saw him place his hand on a Federal cannon. Saw the hand jerk and tremble and slide. Saw red, heard red in his ears, against his temples. Cried out, and didn't know he cried. Fell into swirling red circles of darkness.

It was over. Lee told a disheartened Pickett, "This has been my fight and upon my shoulders rests the blame."

Hugh wasn't there to hear his statement. He was moving with a long line of prisoners, moving North. And mercifully he and Lee knew nothing of the flag of truce on the Vicksburg hill, of the terms Pemberton was making for surrender, for the loss of all they had hoped for in the Mississippi Valley.

Twenty-two

Angeline stood and watched the boats steam up the river. Farragut's fleet. They brought the end. She knew they brought the end, but she could not believe it, could not picture what the end would mean in terms of how she would live her tomorrows.

On July thirteenth the city of Natchez surrendered without a struggle, without bloodshed, with only an unheard sigh. On the sixteenth of July a St. Louis steamer sailed the river to New Orleans. As Lincoln desired, in his own language, "the father of waters rolled unvexed to the sea."

Edmund was home, but he was different—more quiet after his taste of war, more drawn into himself. Angeline watched from a distance, shut out and helpless. She knew little of the Vicksburg girl. But she was a woman; she could guess very well what she didn't know. So everything shifted and changed and went forward. Perhaps even the war could not cripple love. She hoped not. She watched her son's eyes, and she hoped not.

Though there was no bloodshed in taking the city, very little destruction, the presence of the enemy brought change. Change, and in many ways chaos. They had captured ten thousand bales of cotton—some of the cotton Angeline's. They had set up camps; they had made conditions. One of these was the oath of loyalty.

"I'll never take such an oath," Edmund told her. And he said it in the new, quiet way.

She thought to herself, *We're not in Natchez. We'll mind our own business out here. We'll be safe.*

But the countryside crawled with bands of marauding soldiers, men who had killed and plundered in Jackson and Port Gibson, who had torn up railroads and bridges and homes. Such men, she knew, fed on hatred and vengeance. Edmund began sending them to their beds each night armed. Sometimes, coming back from a ride alone in the moonlight, he would sit in Hamilton's office, his gun on his knee. Sleepless, watching, cold-eyed and silent.

Sometimes he would hear her rocking—his mother upstairs on the porch, alone. Through the square of open window he heard her, regular as a clock, steady as a heartbeat. He knew she was strong, that she hugged her own pain to her. He knew she would help if he'd only ask. But he didn't know just exactly what he needed, and he sensed that she could not fill his need. It was too late; he had turned his own corner and left her. Some other woman must fill the need. He knew and he thought, and he wondered, and he doubted. But it always helped to lean back and close his eyes and listen to the steady rocking, the rhythmical, creaking lullaby.

Niles was one of the Union soldiers that ravaged the country; he was part of the enemy, both feared and hated. He rode with the men, he blew up the bridges, tore up miles of railroad track, destroyed cars and engines, burned thousands of bales of cotton and bushels of corn. But the waste appalled his heart, and the lost profit his head. And he thrust no bayonets through family heirlooms, demolished no pianos or libraries. He stood back from all that, an uneasy intruder, his human nature too sympathetic, his childhood memories of the South too vivid and warm.

He rode this mild November morning from Port Gibson along the old Trace Trail with a few of his comrades back to their own lines. The road was secluded and dark; they passed along slowly, in no hurry, with no particular place to go. They swapped stories that grew into tall tales that got them all laughing, looking more like young boys than they had in a long, long time. They approached an old rickety wagon laden with cotton and half a dozen ill-clad, unwashed females who were doubtless on their way to trade at Fort Gibson. Though cotton trade was illegal, that bothered no one. Even the state and Confederate governments traded cotton for the supplies the army so badly needed.

"Let's have some fun," one of the soldiers said, placing his horse sideways on the narrow trail, blocking the passage of the wagon. The girl who was driving pulled up with a colorful curse.

"Git outta my way, you blue-bellied weasel," she shouted.

By now all six soldiers had gathered in the road. Niles, drawing closer to the wagon, caught the strong, warm smell of whiskey. One of the girls held a dirty baby on her lap. They all stared out from eyes that were smouldering and disdainful.

"We just want to save you ladies a little trouble. Show us your passes to trade and you're free to go."

A grim and stubborn silence was his answer. One of the girls loosed a long brown stream of tobacco spittle. It hit the neck of the soldier's horse. Her mouth was streaked with tobacco stains, Niles noticed.

"You shouldn't have done that, honey," the soldier said.

"I think we should go," Niles told his companion.

"Come on, Frank, leave 'em alone. It's no good."

Frank moved a few feet closer to the wagon.

"It's not worth it, Frank," the soldier urged.

"I think these ladies need a friendly little reminder—" Frank moved closer, determined now— "of how conquered women should treat a gentleman."

Frank moved, and one of the girls moved with him, and the cotton bales parted and moved. Niles saw it too late. The shot rang out before he saw the weapon, before he saw the heads with the rebel caps. Frank swore as he slid off his horse. More shots were coming. Niles turned; he was in the back, somewhat protected. He was nearly past. He made himself small in the saddle, low on the horse's back. Then he felt the burn all along his side, up into his shoulder. He clutched the saddle; he must not slip or fall. He kept going, and nothing else came to stop him. How long he rode desperately forward he didn't know. But his head felt dizzy and light and his limbs were shaking. The pain had become a consuming thing, like thirst after hours of black smoke and battle; like thirst it rode him and gave him no peace.

He was a soldier in uniform and, no matter what, this was enemy country. A wounded Yankee, alone—he refused to think about it, to allow fear to rear into a monster like the pain. But he knew he needed help and night was falling. He pulled up in a shady ravine to gather his thoughts.

He was probably twenty miles from Port Gibson, a tedious journey back over the dark Trace Trail. He shuddered. If there were closer camps than that he didn't know them, wouldn't know where to locate them alone. But he was probably less than ten miles from Natchez. He had been to Natchez before as a boy. And to the plantation where his father visited. He would head there. Perhaps — perhaps they would take him in.

He rode, he hoped in the right direction. He saw things he believed to be landmarks, but he couldn't be sure. He *wanted* them to be landmarks; perhaps that was all. Evening came, and he saw his own shadow, long and wavery. He didn't notice when full darkness crowded out the light. He was shaking now. He felt himself slipping. He dreamed he was slipping down and down. He shook his head against the dream and clung on tighter.

At a little fork in the road his horse caught a tree root and stumbled. This time he fell, but it wasn't a slip and a glide. It was a thump, a hard crack that shot pain up his forehead, licking white tongues of flame behind his eyes. He groped across the ground like a blind man. His hand sunk in a mound of wet leaves, then touched something firmer. Something that sent a shiver along his spine.

He drew back. What his hand had touched was a body, thinly covered with dirt and a scattering of leaves. He sat back on his heels and rocked and shivered and his tired brain imagined the dead eyes glowing out at him through the papery leaves.

I have to get out of here! he mumbled. He crawled a few feet. Where was his horse? He called. He called again, but the silence echoed. What if someone else was out there to listen? He rose to his feet, supporting himself with his hand on a tree. How could he walk? How far might it be? He couldn't just lie here and die. He started forward, head down, pain jolting through him at every step.

Edmund sat in Hamilton's office watching. He had seen signs of raiding parties nearby. He would stay here all night just in case, just to be certain. About two o'clock he heard the noise. He rose and walked to the window, his gun ready. At first he saw nothing. He walked to the side door that led into his father's office from outside.

Then he saw the man. He was reeling wildly. At first Edmund thought he was drunk, but then he knew. He put down his weapon and started forward. The man who collapsed in his arms wore a coat of blue. But his face was young and pale. While Edmund decided, trying to weigh in his mind what was right against what was loyal in wartime, his mother appeared like a shadow at his side.

"Bring him inside," she instructed, as though telling him, *you know better!*

"He's a Yankee," he said as they carried him together.

She ignored him. "He needs our help," was her reply.

They laid him out on a blanket on the floor. He was unconscious still, but he moaned and muttered. Edmund lifted a lantern to see his face. Angeline gasped and reached for his arm, her fingers clutching. "This boy is Warren Ellis's son."

"No, mother, he couldn't be."

"Yes, yes, I know him. Niles Ellis—Niles Hamilton Ellis is his name."

Edmund remembered how the Northern boy had been named for his father. A feeling ran through him he didn't like.

"Bring him up to the small south bedroom," Angeline instructed. "Quickly!" she urged when he hesitated. There was no way to countermand his mother. He bent over the motionless form of the boy.

Hamilton walked through the narrow Philadelphia side street. He was on his way to factory number four. Major Stanley, substantial stockholder, patriotic citizen, checking shipments of beef and weapons and shoes. Supplies to be sent to the Northern soldiers. Vital supplies that would win the war. A soldier can't fight on an empty stomach—must take care of the boys—it had been too easy, almost too smooth, too natural. So far.

But here he was within blocks of Warren Ellis's place. Before the war that house would have been his first stop. He chafed at the fact that this was denied him. He would go to Warren's factory, drop his name—little personal things that only friends of Warren's would know. It was over two years since they'd corresponded. Warren had become quite powerful in the North. It wouldn't do to reveal his Southern connections; that wouldn't serve anyone's purpose, either way. The war had destroyed their value to one another. At least for a while—temporarily. But he missed the old, warm association. To drop in now for a drink and a chat...

He walked up and down the aisles of the textile factory, between rows of army blue trousers neatly stacked. He expressed interest, asked a few curious questions, listened and looked. He knew how to please, how to build confidence, a subtle relaxing, so that men said things they might not normally say, showed him forms, invoices, shipment records.

Ray Jones, plant manager since '52, was one of Warren Ellis's oldest friends. He swapped stories with the handsome stranger. It was evident he knew Warren well. Why then didn't he mention Warren's illness? Wouldn't he know that Warren lay dying a few blocks away?

Casually, with his back turned, he asked the question. "Have you been to see Warren yet?" He pulled out file after file and waited.

Hamilton took a deep breath. He could smell the trouble, almost see the muscles tighten along the man's neck. What pit was Ray Jones trying to dig? He groped along the blind ground cautiously.

"I tried, but no one—" He paused. He was going to say, "no one was home," but he thought it through quickly and said, "no one answered."

"Oh, really." Mr. Jones wasn't good at being casual. He turned back to Hamilton but he dropped his eyes, fidgeted with the consignments he'd been signing.

There was a reason behind the question. *What reason? What reason? What direction should I take?* "Frankly, I'm concerned."

Mr. Jones raised an involuntary eyebrow.

"It's not right. Someone should have answered the door."

Hamilton was good at this; he half enjoyed it, even now when the danger was spread like thick syrup to slip on. He put his elbow on the desk, placed his chin in his hand, and gazed across at Mr. Jones candidly, forcing the man to meet his eyes. "I'm concerned. Aren't you?"

"Well, yes, it's a nasty business." Ray Jones chose to believe the directness he saw in the piercing blue eyes. He had meant to make this man squirm a little. He was very aware that his plan had back-fired somehow. "Struck down by this cancer somewhere inside him, when he'd never been sick a day in his life." He lowered his voice, becoming confiding, clandestine. "I swear, he's wasted to nothing. It's wretched to see."

The pain in Hamilton's eyes was real; he couldn't have hidden it if he'd tried. "That bad? Well, I'll get in to see him before I leave here."

He pushed back his chair and rose. What was in his eyes now he didn't want any man to read. "His son? Does Niles know?"

Mr. Jones walked with him, comfortable with the new camaraderie. "The boy's fighting somewhere in Virginia and Warren won't write him." He paused, as though savoring something. "What I want to know is does Warren believe he'll get better? Heaven knows he couldn't. I don't believe Warren would lie to himself—or does he mean to save young Niles the suffering?" He shook his head in exaggerated solicitude. "Either way it's a nasty business."

Hamilton held his control though the man made his insides shudder. When he left he went directly to Warren's house. There were times beyond time when oneself didn't matter, when tomorrow couldn't be measured against the moment: the man who might be waiting inside to take him, the unintentional betrayal Warren might hold in his hands—he had no luxury to consider such matters. He walked up the familiar steps and rang the bell.

The old Oriental servant answered. He stood aside and Hamilton strode in, and was swallowed by silence.

"I'm here to see Mr. Ellis," he said, in his own old tone.

"Mister Stewart." The servant bowed low. "I shall announce you."

"No, please. I'll announce myself." He moved quickly forward. He knew which door led to Warren's room. He turned the knob and let himself in.

Here there was no silence. Two men, attorneys, he figured, were arguing softly. A doctor was growling orders to a nurse who pulled at the arm of her unwilling patient, urging him to answer the doctor's questions.

Warren, propped up against pillows, not looking like Warren, a ghost of Warren with Warren's eyes, saw him at once and froze, his mouth open, the annoyances around him forgotten instantly. For a moment they simply stared at each other.

"Out! Out of here," he cried, his voice a shadow, lacking the old resonance and too kind. "An old friend of mine has come. We have much to talk of. Come back tomorrow, next week—some other time."

He shooed them out with his arms; his merry eyes sparkled. Hamilton graciously held the door and closed it behind them, waited a moment, then checked to be sure they were gone. He heard a mischievous chuckle from the bed. He turned. Warren cocked his head and watched him.

"You scoundrel, what are you up to now? I thought you'd look handsome in uniform, Hamilton, officer's *gray*—I never pictured you all decked out in *blue*."

He'd forgotten! He'd really forgotten. His grin was sheepish.

"Well, Warren, why didn't you blow the whistle? Let those two gnawing lawyers have at me?"

The smile froze; the sick man shook his head. "Six months ago I just might have done that. All's fair in love and war—you know the adage. I have a little different perspective now."

"Bosh! Perspective has nothing to do with it, Warren. It's a weakness you've always had. Too soft a heart. You wouldn't turn in a fox that was eating your own chickens, would you? You might sit up and sing to the chickens half the night, but you wouldn't blow off the fox's mangy head when he came round the corner!"

"Hamilton, thank heaven you're here."

They talked. They caught up on four years of talking, things that mattered, things that had nothing to do with the war. When it came it fit in, it felt only natural.

"Niles doesn't know about me. There's no way of *telling*. I'll be hanged if I'll send poison letters to the boy."

Hamilton nodded. "I'll find him and tell him." It wasn't an offer. It was a statement that required no promises and no thanks.

"I hadn't thought this was how it would be. I don't want to leave him. His mother's been gone so long—he's got only me." There was no self-pity in his voice, no sense of the maudlin. "I'd like to ask you to watch out for him, help him now and then, Ham."

"You don't need to ask me, Warren."

"Yes, I do. He's not me. He's been fighting the South—he might not take too kindly. You need to be able to say, 'Your father wants this.' That's all. It will make a difference with Niles."

Hamilton nodded. That was all that was needed. They talked for a while longer. When he rose to go, Hamilton stepped closer, intending to stick out his hand to Warren. One last warm clasp for old times. Instead he bent lower, threw his arms around the frail form on the bed.

"Good-bye, dear friend. Heaven knows I'll miss you. But you'll never be gone to me, Warren. Not while Niles lives."

There was nothing Warren could say. They clung to each other, as men cling, with a man's fears and a man's strengths. Hamilton left with tears in his eyes and the certain knowledge that a human heart can break a dozen times, never really heal, never be immune to the breaking, never fully dissolve the burden of pain.

_Twenty-three

He was hurt more badly than they had expected. He had walked too long through the damp night air with a hole in his side, with no protection. He was delirious with fever. They called in the doctor. Someone must sit with him, he instructed, day and night. Afton paced, hands on her hips, her eyes flashing.

"It's disgraceful, mother. How could you do it? He's an enemy soldier, can't you see that? He'd shoot Hugh or Father on sight and think nothing of it. He'd come here tomorrow and loot the place—he's the enemy, mother."

Angeline's lips went white but she didn't answer. She and Nancy took turns sitting with the boy. She had nothing to say to Afton or Edmund. There was distance between them now, a depressive mood. The third night Edmund came into the room and looked down on his mother, sitting quiet and self-contained in her low armchair.

"You're punishing us," he said bluntly. "You've always been very reticent with your feelings—private to a fault, mother."

She looked back at him, smiling gently. "I know that, Edmund." *Except with your father,* she thought. He thought it, too, but neither of them tried to say it.

"You're going to bed." He lifted her to her feet. "I'll take over here." She blinked calm eyes at him.

"I don't trust you," she told him candidly. "I know how you feel. I don't want you doing something you don't believe in."

She had always been too much for him. He shook his head. "Listen, mother. I've thought about it. This is different. I don't feel the same way you do, but I understand. I'll do all I can to help him—for your sake. I give you my word on it, mother."

She looked into his eyes. She saw very deep. She leaned up and kissed his cheek. "All right, Edmund."

"Good night, mother. Go to sleep. Do you promise?"

"I promise, Edmund. And—thank you."

She went to her room. He sat, for the first time in months feeling peaceful and happy.

It was good she had gotten that night's rest. The following morning a courier came from Natchez. A courier meant only one thing: bad news.

At first she felt only relief to learn that it was Fletcher. She could live with the loss of Fletcher—she could live with that pain. Not Hamilton—never Hamilton—

Up in her rocker she unwrapped the little package the boy had brought. Instructions on the body, he said, to deliver it here. Such pathetically few remainders of a person: his watch, the glass face shattered and ruined, a copy of *Pilgrim's Progress* he'd had as a boy, and another book printed with the title *Book of Mormon.* She held it, she traced the lettering, she remembered... such painful and confused and warm rememberings...

The book was worn. Fletcher must have read it often. She turned the cover. Her own face stared back at her, but younger, untouched by life and suffering. Young and innocent and untried— the daguerreotype taken on her eighteenth birthday. She felt hot tears burn into her eyes. *Oh Fletcher, Fletcher, I hardly knew you!* She couldn't bear to think of him dying, lonely and afraid, with no one to really care, no woman to love him. She cried for his death; she cried for his pain. She cried for a gentle life wasted, and no way to make time go back or change.

Afton avoided the room where the Northern boy mended. Stubbornly she would not give way, feeling some awful need inside to be cruel and angry, nurturing the feeling that gave her back strength for strength. When the courier came with the news of her uncle's death a hard hand had gripped with pain inside her. *Hugh!* He had fought at Gettysburg, too. But days passed and no word came and she felt certain that anything bad would have reached them by now...

She came in from riding. She saw Dyanne's horse and she knew it. She flew into the parlor—the library—the music room. She saw Dyanne's pale face and froze with horror. "Is he dead?" she cried. "Is he dead?"

Her mother came to her, led her to a chair. "No, darling, no. He's in prison. Hugh's in a Northern prison."

"Where?" she demanded.

"It's a place called Point Lookout. We found it on Edmund's war map. It's along Maryland's Chesapeake Bay. He's well—" She stopped. Afton's eyes burned holes through her. She was startled to see the hatred reflected there.

"Your mother was about to say that he's well cared for—"

"Well, he is," Angeline interjected. "The North feeds its prisoners. We don't have food enough for our own men down here."

"And whose fault is that?" Dyanne's eyes flashed anger. "They've no right! The impudent rubbish. They're trash, Angie honey, worthless trash."

Angeline didn't reply. She saw the same determination in both sets of eyes. They would hate. They needed their hate to sustain them. Her daughter whirled at her suddenly.

"Mother, how are we to bear it? And you with your—"

Angeline caught her arm. Roughly she pulled her away from Dyanne's line of vision and fixed her with a look that sent fear to her heart. "This is my house, Afton. That's something you need to remember. Go to your room until you have calmed yourself."

She obeyed, but she trembled with anger and indignation. Angeline knew she would still have to deal wth her daughter later. For now she turned back to comfort her friend.

He woke with the same peaceful feeling; he loved waking up here. There was so much here that revealed a woman's touch: the soft blended colors, the lace curtains with matching coverlet of pale lace over the bed. Flowers placed so they caught the sunlight, fine linen that held the fragrance of cologne—or a woman's skin . . .

He had only faraway memories of his mother. He had not lived so close to a woman for many years. He liked this Southern woman; he'd always liked her. He remembered her from his visits here as a boy. She was delicate, porcelain-beautiful, porcelain-perfect. He smiled to himself, recalling the innocent, boyish outlook of those days.

Hamilton Stewart had been the hero he looked up to. To think of being named for such a man! Hamilton was obviously like his own father, successful and wealthy. But he was wealthy with so much more polish, so much more flair! He admired the cavalier air the man wore that fit him as well as his tailor-made clothes. He was gallant and cultured, but at the same time high-strung and impulsive. *A man to be reckoned with*, Niles had decided. *Mysterious. Cunning.* He built castles around his idol that never toppled. And in every castle *she* reigned as queen. The woman with the beautiful face and the kind brown eyes.

This morning she had brought him breakfast and seen to his comfort. He must have drifted back to sleep after she left. He lifted himself to a sitting position. He must exercise to gain back his strength. No further than the porch, she had made him promise. He swung his feet to touch the soft rug, then pulled on slippers and robe. He would walk by himself. It would please her to know it.

It took more steps than he thought to reach his doorway. He leaned there, pausing for breath, then went cautiously on. A few steps at a time, very carefully—

She hit him like a whirlwind, all flutter and motion. He swayed; he would have fallen without her help.

"I'm sorry! What are you doing here?" Afton demanded.

She led him to a chair; he sat shakily down. She was uncomfortable and embarrassed, and therefore angry. He smiled. She looked very beautiful that way.

"It's amazing how much you have changed and how much you haven't. You're not the same little girl. Your nose is quite different. But you have the same wonderful darkness in your eyes—"

"What are you talking about?"

"I remember you," he said softly, "from the times I used to come here as a boy."

"You must have been all of ten then." Her voice was disdainful. He smiled. She hadn't known he could smile that way, hadn't known he would be so handsome to look at.

"I was nearly twelve the last time I came. Old enough to never forget—"

"Well, I don't remember."

He inclined his head; he refused to be insulted. "Well, I do, and it's amazing to me."

She looked up, interested, still not wanting to show it. "What amazes you?" she asked, like a challenge.

"That the vision is not dimmed by reality. You're even more lovely than my dreams have kept you."

She blushed. She was taken too much by surprise. An awkward moment passed, then she rallied. "Were you planning to come to Lairdswood as the mighty conquerer? Before you got hurt and crawled here for assistance? How convenient that Lairdswood was not yet destroyed!"

184

He didn't seem to feel her venom, but took the question quite seriously. "I've wondered that myself for weeks now. I fell in love with the South when I was a boy. And Lairdswood was at the center of that adoration. I've wanted to come back desperately. But I didn't want to cause trouble by coming—"

"Well, you've certainly done that now," she flung at him, then was sorry, because she saw the look that came into his eyes.

He stared at her. "Yes, I know that, Afton."

She felt little and mean underneath his gaze. He rose and began to walk back to his bedroom. She moved as if to offer him help, but he waved her aside. She had gone too far in being unkind; she realized that. Her mother would be most unhappy if she knew. She watched the tall, handsome boy move painfully forward, feeling torn and confused in her heart and her mind.

Angeline had the meal for Niles set out on a tray. She meant to ask Nancy to carry it up to him, but Afton appeared at her elbow.

"I'll take it, mother."

Before she could think to stop herself she looked sharply up. Afton met her eyes, but her young cheeks colored.

"It's a penance I owe him, mother. Never mind."

Niles saw her enter the room and his sadness fell from him, the gloomy, hopeless guilt he had nurtured all day. A single white rose lay across the tray above the food dishes. He touched its petals.

"Did your mother send this?"

"No, the rose is from me. A way of saying I'm sorry." She turned to leave him, then hesitated and smiled. "Eat your food. I'll be back."

There had been a long spell when he couldn't break away from Lairdswood. Work in the daytime, watching for danger at night. And the Yankee soldier's coming hadn't helped any. At last he just turned his back on it all and left. He knew the back roads still, the wooded pathways where even the Northern soldiers didn't ride. Once or twice he saw parties off in the distance. But no one noticed him; no trouble came galloping by.

As the first stars like bright jewels lit the sky he pulled up before Sally's. He walked eagerly up the brick walkway and rapped on the door. Sally opened it herself; she had seen him coming. He knew things were all right still—he saw it in her eyes. He stood and held her right there on the doorstep.

"I'm glad you've signed the oath, Edmund. That means you can come here safely now."

The oath of allegiance to the Washington government! Edmund went stiff. "I haven't signed the oath, Sally," he said. "I will never sign it." She moved in his arms and looked into his face.

"You must find some way to come to terms with it, Edmund. You can't go on like this, risking your life." *Risking all that is life to me,* her heart added.

"Would you have me perjure myself just to stay alive? I can't do that, Sally. You know I can't."

"Am I destined to live my life worrying over you?" She smiled bravely, but he knew she was suffering. He didn't want to cause her any pain. Yet how could he rearrange his own conscience, change the sum of all that he was inside? He hugged her to him, soothed by her warmth, her fragrance, content with what he saw before his eyes—what the moment held and no more. How wonderfully simple. To be able to live life a moment at a time, not always gazing at the past with sorrow nor peering off into the future with fear.

Angeline knew Edmund had gone to see the girl in Vicksburg, the girl she did not know, had not even seen. She knew he had not signed the oath of allegiance, knew from Moses that the soldiers were tightening their control, letting no one move who refused to sign it, enforcing strict and unpleasant penalties.

She sat in Eliza's rocker with Fletcher's book beside her. She often picked up the book, reading here and there, passages he had marked. She was coming to know him better than she had when he was a child, when she had been mother and father and everything to him. She could read in these pages the heart of the man. She found comfort in the book, and a closeness to Fletcher. There was much here to give her comfort, to give her strength. She could see why Fletcher had read and reread it. . . . She turned to the worn pages of King Benjamin's sermon and started to read.

And now, if God, who has created you, on whom you are dependent for your lives and for all that ye have and are, doth grant unto you whatsoever ye ask that is right, in faith, believing that ye shall receive,

O then, how ye ought to impart of the substance that ye have one to another—

She asked for much, but what she asked for was right, she knew it. Yet could she ask, as Benjamin said, in faith?

And if ye judge the man who putteth up his petition to you for your substance that he perish not, and condemn him, how much more just will be your condemnation for withholding your substance, which doth not belong to you but to God, to whom also your life belongeth.

She thought of Niles. It pleased her to know she had given freely, without withholding of herself, without fear. But the rest. She smiled to herself. When she had first read it, that passage had offended her, "your substance, which doth not belong to you but to God . . ." Lairdswood belonged to her, not to some great power that claimed all she had purchased at such a terrible price! She was bound up with Lairdswood, heart, blood and sinew—there was no way to unmingle the two.

". . . God, to whom also your life belongeth . . ." Strange how that line should comfort her now. If her life belonged to God, then God must know her, listen to her, love her, perhaps. This God of the Book of Mormon that Fletcher worshipped was not like any god she had ever known. She was drawn to him with a compulsion, a fascination. She was beginning to know why Fletcher had loved him. She was beginning to give him a place in her heart.

There were little things Niles could do while his body mended. One of these was to work on the grounds. He learned very quickly which gardens were Afton's dominion, and for a long time he didn't dare venture there. Then one day he came upon a weed-choked border where thistles outnumbered the roses, and he set to work. He was down on his knees when he heard the voices: feminine voices, angry and strained. He hesitated. He rose. He could see them walking—Afton and an older woman who was in tears. Then Angeline came up and the voices dropped some and she and the other woman went inside.

But Afton turned down the path where he was working. She came with her usual spirited stride. But she didn't look up; she was carrying something. He saw as she approached that it was a letter. Her cheeks were flushed, her color high, but there were no tears in her eyes. She looked up and saw him, slowed her pace, and tucked the letter behind her wide skirt.

"News from Hamilton?"

"No." Her eyes were veiled now. "We don't hear from father often. This letter's from Hugh."

"And that was Hugh's mother I saw with you, crying?"

She glared at him. "Really, it's none of your business," she said. "It's good Dyanne went inside and didn't see you. She'd have torn you to bits without blinking an eye."

"As you'd like to do?"

His gaze disturbed her. She brushed past him to where the walk widened to enclose a small bench and sat down with her back very purposefully toward him.

"Why do you hate me, Afton? Or do you fear me?"

"Fear you?" She whirled to face him, her dark eyes stormy.

"Yes. I represent insecurity, shaded ground. I disturb you by not quite fitting the jaded image: All Northerners are evil, all Southerners good."

He paused. He walked very close and bent down to face her, so his questioning gaze was level with her brown eyes.

"Do you believe that, Afton? Do you condemn me?"

"How can I do anything else?" she cried. "You're the enemy; you've come to destroy us! The boy who loves me is shut in a Northern prison. If you were off in the field you'd be killing Southern boys—"

He caught what she said, the sentence giving him hope, the arrangement of the words "the boy who loves me." She hadn't said "the boy I love." It took his breath away and he struggled to answer. "There are Northern boys in Southern prisons. There are brothers fighting brothers on both sides. It happens, Afton. It's people thrown together, with nothing totally black or totally white."

"And what does that have to do—"

"With us?" he finished. His voice was very gentle and so were his eyes. "Do you believe certain things can be destined to happen?"

188

"Like war?" she snapped.

"No. Like some people meeting each other, in spite of all circumstances, against all odds."

"Niles!" She couldn't let him go on. "I must read Hugh's letter. Dyanne will be leaving; I must read the letter now."

He sat silent a moment. She didn't like the pain in his sensitive eyes. Slowly he rose to his feet. "All right, I shall leave you." He started to go, then hesitated. "I'll be nearby in case—in case you might need me."

He turned, he gave her no chance to reply. She sat for long moments and didn't open the letter, seeing too clearly before her the pain-filled eyes, trying to quiet her heart's wild beating and the trembling tenderness she was feeling inside.

Twenty-four

The food was edible, though the portions were scanty. Coffee and a loaf of bread for breakfast, a tin cup of soup and a small piece of meat for dinner. They poured vinegar over the meat to prevent scurvy; the vinegar killed everything, including the taste. Hugh was hungry, though. He was always hungry. The short rations, a guard informed him when he asked, were given in retaliation for the starving of Northern prisoners in Southern camps.

He had never been so confined before in his life. That was what swallowed up most of his patience—having nothing to make the hours move. He would sit in a corner and think, but his thoughts were worse torment than anything imposed from outside. Memories came like little red demons to mock and torment him. He saw his own despair gaze back at him from the other men's eyes. There was no way to escape himself, to get lost in action. He stared out at the glaring white stretch before him: white tents, white sand, the reflection off white water —

"What's the matter with you, rebel? You look so glum I just might keep this-here letter for myself." The guard dangled an envelope back and forth, just out of reach. "You got no call feelin' sorry for yourself, buster. I got a brother at Andersonville. You think this is rough? We give you coffee here. They ain't even got water. There's a stream runs through the camp ankle deep. They drink from it, wash in it. They don't eat like you do, reb. Bread and water. Sometimes crackers. Sometimes a piece of bacon rind. Over one hundred deaths a day from disease and starvation."

He flung the letter at Hugh and Hugh caught it.

"You're just lucky, rebel, you're here and alive."

He walked on. Hugh turned from the glare at the window and opened the envelope carefully.

Christmas 1863. Afton hadn't heard from her father in months. Hugh was in prison. Only a handful of Negroes was left on the plantation. There had been no cotton harvest to drag on into December, no seed to sow in the coming spring. There would still be roast mutton with biscuits for dinner, chokeberry wine, and molasses gingerbread. There would be no presents this year and no new dresses. But there would be holly for decorating, a yule log and games and candles — and Niles.

How did it happen? How had it grown, this mutual attraction. She had avoided it, ignored it, fought against it. Yet it seemed to have life of its own accord, seemed to draw her irresistibly toward him, in spite of the logical reasons she knew in her mind, seemed to live on its own urgent need, its own secret beauty.

Niles was conscientiously trying to get better. He was a soldier; he must remember that. He was mending, but the doctor had ordered him not to ride yet. His commander had been informed, his permission granted. There was nothing very pressing going right now. He was one less man for the army to care for. A week more, maybe two — they stretched on like forever. *Who knows what might happen*, he told himself, *in that much time?*

190

Two days before Christmas a letter from Point Lookout Prison arrived. Afton read it alone in her room. She was in there for hours. When she came out her face was pale and her eyes were red. She headed, of course, to the stables and the horses and rode out the rest of the afternoon.

When she didn't appear for dinner her mother was worried.

"Her mare is back in the stables," Edmund said. "She's somewhere about the place, mother."

After dinner Niles went out for a walk. He wandered aimlessly, but his eyes searched sharply. He had always been good at games of hide and seek. But he walked until he was exhausted and didn't find her, and was forced to come in shaken and disappointed.

The horse in the stable was only a ruse; they should have known that. Where the bluff jutted over the river, dark with old trees, she sat alone with her tears and longings.

"There is an affliction peculiar to Point Lookout," Hugh had written, "caused by the glare of the water and sand. It seems the eyes for a while go blind. Last night as the sun set, a red ball sitting on the water spitting long tongues of flame, my eyes became balls of red flame, and then white—and then nothing. Nothing but black that was blacker than night. Someone led me to my bed. It's a common thing here. This morning my eyes were better. But I dread the nightfall. Dread the nightmare of never seeing you, Afton, again . . ."

She cried tears of love and guilt and pity and anger. When she was all cried out, the pain was the same. So she hiked down the bluff to the shack that hugged the shoreline where Wheezy Willie the fisherman lived. His son, Buster, had lost both an arm and a leg and was home now. They asked no questions, showed no surprise when she came. She sat on the cold dirt floor and drank Willie's whiskey and sang war songs with Buster until she was hoarse.

> Oh! yes, I am a Southern girl,
>   And glory in the name,
> And boast it with far greater pride
>   Then glittering wealth or fame . . .

It helped to sing, to shout out the ugly emotions.

> The homespun dress is plain, I know,
>   My hat's palmetto, too;
> But then it shows what Southern girls
>   For Southern rights will do.
> We send the bravest of our land
>   To battle with the foe,
> And we will lend a helping hand—
>   We love the South, you know.

The words were sung to the tune of "The Bonnie Blue Flag." She cried as she sang, and Buster thought nothing of it, though Willie refused to fill up her mug again. She sang out all the impurities and the pain, telling herself what she wanted to know:

> The Southern land's a glorious land,
>   And has a glorious cause;
> Then cheer, three cheers for Southern rights,
>   And for the Southern boys!

When he thought she'd had enough Willie saddled his pony. She had come here as a small girl with her troubles and questions. He had helped her then. But he couldn't help her now—not really. Not any longer. He left Buster with tears in his eyes and he took the girl home. Angeline met him outside the house.

"Thank you, Willie. I figured at last that she might be with you."

When Willie was out of earshot Afton turned to her mother. "I'm sorry, mother. I really am. I hadn't meant for any of this to happen." She ran pathetic, little-girl fingers through her hair. Angeline controlled an impulse to reach out and hold her.

"You've been drinking Willie's whiskey."

"Only the weak stuff. Only a cup or two. I'm all right—that way, mother." She looked suddenly very tired and very young.

"It's too much to sort out tonight. Let's sleep on it, Afton." She led her daughter into the darkened house, more silent than the outdoors. "Remember, Afton, I'm here and I love you. I may not be able to help much, but I'm here. I never had a mother to turn to."

192

"I hadn't thought of that. Was it hard for you, mother?"

"Very hard, very painful at times. When I married Aubrey I had your grandmother, Eliza."

"Was she like a mother?"

Angeline smiled into the darkness. They climbed the long stairs, known and familiar, not needing a lamp to light them. "Not really. More like a spirit sister, an older friend. Someone I could both trust and look up to."

"But wasn't she rather—well, you know, rather—strange? I've heard so many stories—"

"Aren't we all rather strange in our own ways, Afton?"

They had reached Afton's door; Angeline entered and lit a small candle. She gazed at her daughter's face in the pale, pulsing light.

"You're so like her, Afton. You would have loved her—you would have understood."

She kissed her daughter lightly on the cheek and left her. Passing the room where Niles slept she saw that the door was ajar, that a low light burned. She paused at the doorway.

"She's all right, Niles. She's home. You can go to sleep now."

She could feel him grin into the darkness, feel him relax.

"Thank you. It's a confounded business. Loving a Southern girl with a Southern heart and a Southern mind."

She walked into the room. "I'll put out the light for you, Niles." She waited till they were in darkness, then asked, "Where is your mind, Niles, and where is your heart?"

"Right here. I'm afraid they'll always be right here."

There were so many different emotions in his voice: pain and quiet resignation, wonder and challenge and even joy. She bent over and kissed him lightly on the forehead. "As long as it stands, Niles, Lairdswood will be your home." Then quietly, very quickly, she left him to think his own thoughts and dream his own dreams.

When the moon rode high behind clouds that trailed long inky fingers Moses woke with a start. He had sensed something, rather than heard. Now he heard it: a scratching sound, a movement, a muffled scuffling. He gathered his limbs from the bed and rose noiselessly, reaching for the gun hidden under his mattress, silently praising Edmund for insisting he place it there. He dressed, keeping his eyes on the pistol that sat like a small black smudge on the shadowy floor.

At the big house no one had stirred in the uncertain moonlight. No one heard the small, introductory sounds: the pouring of gunpowder, laying of fuses, men dropping behind tree and bush, weapons trained on the house. When it broke, it broke like all fury around them, a flood-tide of noise in the rifled night.

It took long minutes to pull on pants and shoes, reach for rifles and load them. Edmund met Niles at the bottom of the stairs. For a moment they both checked, staring at one another.

"There are soldiers out there," Edmund said. "I heard one of them shouting."

"I wouldn't doubt it. What difference does that make?"

"I don't know. You tell me."

"You think I'd let anyone lay a hand on Lairdswood?"

Edmund's expression didn't change. It was hard, unrelenting.

"You've got to trust me!" Niles met his gaze, unflinching. "If you won't trust me now you'll never be able to trust anyone, Edmund."

It was slow to come. At last the eyes changed, Edmund nodded.

"You take the south door. I'm going to check on the women, give them instructions. I'll meet you back there in five minutes."

Niles set up a steady fire, one gun at the window, one through the porthole Edmund had cut in the door. He could see the bodies out there moving, shadowy figures, firing profusely, but so far doing little harm.

The intruders had not expected to meet such resistance. The man shooting that gun had a powerful aim. They staged an awkward conference. Their greatest damage could be done without risking well-loved hides. The leader gave the signal to light the fuses. He then began to lead his men away in search of a more vulnerable plantation.

Moses was in the barn. He saw what was coming. Cursing and creeping closer, he took trembling aim. One man went down, but another bent over the powder and the darkness exploded in gaudy orange flame. Moses ran and dived. The explosion racked him, rattled his bones like gambler's dice. He scrambled back to his feet, though his legs felt like water. He could save the horses. At least he had to try.

Afton saw the glow against the sky and knew what had happened. She took a small pistol and ammunition and slipped down the stairs and out the back way, an inconsequential shadow.

Niles saw the shadow flicker, then melt into nothing. Something clicked inside his brain and his flesh went cold. He called through the dark to Edmund. "Your sister's out there. You'll have to cover things here. I'm going to find her."

"You can't," Edmund shouted back. "It's suicide."

"Where would she head to?" Niles was already moving.

"The stable to save her horses. Heaven help her now."

Niles bolted. He figured the best thing to do was keep moving. A ball whizzed past his cheek. His repeating rifle could fire eight rounds in succession; he fired a spatter now in both directions, and on legs that had only invalid-walked for weeks he ran across the dark, uneven ground.

The stables were almost gone. He held his hand up before his face, the heat from the blaze hitting him with waves of red-hot weight. He skirted the crumbling building, and then he saw her, pulling a blindfolded horse by a rope. The animal, terrified, reared and snorted, moving half a dozen steps back for each inch won forward.

He moved toward her and then he saw the figure, knee on the ground, elbow on knee, taking aim. He whirled, the figure convulsed, the gun rolled harmless. In an instant he was beside her, his hand at her waist, leading her and the animal to protection.

"You fool," he hissed, drawing her roughly forward. She tugged and pulled as roughly away. They reached an enclosure where half a dozen horses were gathered and a Negro man with a rifle blocked the way. He moved to let them pass. She whirled round to face Niles.

"You've no right to interfere here. Leave me alone."

"Do you know how close you came out there to dying?"

"What difference does it make? It's my own business—"

195

He grabbed her wrist. "You little fool. All this isn't worth a plugged nickel without you in it! Don't you know how important you are? You can't die!"

She stopped. She couldn't pretend any longer. She wiped her tears away with a blackened hand. "Niles—Niles—"

He found her lips and kissed them. Roughly, gently, possessively. He felt her quick response, her return of emotion. She felt what she had feared, a love that tore through her with a woman's passion, a woman's joy, filling every dark corner with beauty, flooding the hollows of pain with light.

All things end. All good things end. Several days after the attack, Niles left them. His company was being transferred back to the front. Only skeleton forces were needed for occupation. The work of devastation had already been done. They needed more men to kill, to be killed in battle.

He came back briefly to say good-bye. Stood in the parlor, handsome in uniform. Talked small talk for a few moments, suddenly awkward. When he thanked Angeline one last time he kissed her fingers and said in low tones, "I beg your permission, madam, to return when the war is over. Heaven willing."

"Do you remember what I told you?"

He swallowed and nodded. "Yes, thank you. I shan't forget it." He had had to make sure.

How do you say good-bye to an enemy who is half brother? The two young men clasped arms and the awkwardness left them.

"I'll never forget what you did," Edmund said.

"It was my privilege to be of service, believe me." His eyes strayed and sought the brown eyes that watched him.

One moment alone, walking out to where the others waited.

"Miss Afton, may I write?"

"Yes, of course. And I'll answer."

He thought of the Southern boy in the Northern prison, looked into her eyes and saw that she thought of him, too.

"Godspeed."

He kissed her lightly on the lips. "I'll be back." It was a most solemn promise.

She smiled a sad little smile. Her eyes asked the question: *What then? What then? What tomorrow will there be?*

He rode away without looking behind him. He said to himself, as he'd said a thousand times: *I'll do everything I can to win you. To hang onto all that is beautiful here.* He said it to himself and it gave him some comfort. But he wished, as he rode, that he'd said it to her, out loud.

_____ *Twenty-five*

The law office of Bailey & Johnson had not changed much. Less, Angeline thought, than most things through the years. Strange. She felt much as she had the first time she came here. Tense. A little uncertain, a little afraid.

Phillip Johnson had died years ago, but his son would be here. Charles, newly returned from the war. Given honorable discharge with one leg missing. He was spirited; he had spunk. She heard he'd adjusted. She had given him time to adjust before she came.

It was summer now—another long winter lived through. She didn't travel much when the roads were bad. But her father was failing fast, so she came more often to talk with him, keep him company, cajole him out of his anger at the pettiness of the soldiers whose presence he had to live with day in and day out. Every now and then he would mention Fletcher, sometimes giving her glimpses of his pain, but closing the doors before she could enter to help him. Once or twice she almost mentioned Fletcher's book, but always thought better of it. It was her secret, something untouched, unsullied by the world.

Summer 1864. They talked of Jeb Stuart mortally wounded in May at Yellow Tavern. As they carried him off the field and his men

retreated he had shouted, "Go back! Go back! and do your duty—
Go back! I had rather die than be whipped!"

He had died—to the strains of "Rock of Ages." And the South
bowed under the whipping and went on.

Grant still held Petersburg under seige—U.S. "Unconditional
Surrender" Grant, with his old bulldog tenacity. And Sherman was
moving relentlessly on to Atlanta. Sherman, the one most-hated
name in the South.

Talk of the war naturally led into personal channels. What was
Hamilton up to, anyway? Why did she never hear from the man? It
was good she had that boy to look after matters. Fine boy,
Edmund, sensible head on his shoulders— So Angeline figured
today was the day to see Charles Johnson.

Timothy, the young boy-clerk, now in his thirties, now a
partner, led her into Phillip's old room, the same room where she
had sat as Aubrey's new widow and shaken the stout, kind man's
complacency.

Charles sat waiting for her behind the desk now. He wouldn't be
like his father after all. The war had seemed to slim and stretch him.

"I won't presume to rise. Have a seat, Mrs. Stewart." Incredible.
The mischievous sparkle was still in his eyes.

"You look well," she told him honestly.

"Misfortune agrees with some people, so I've been told. I know,
the lean, hungry look appeals to most women." He paused. He
didn't want to take this vein with her. "You look beautiful,
Angeline. I wish Ham could see you. Forgive me if I look once for
his pleasure, too."

She smiled. He still was too boyish to be offensive.

"Where is Ham? What is he doing?"

"Hanged if I know." He shook his head in dismay. "I'm sorry.
That's not a good answer. Not proper—but very accurate, I'm
afraid."

"You were with him—you've been his confidant since
boyhood—"

"I know, I know, but this is a deadly game. You don't go
handing out information. Men's lives—his life—might hang on
such expediencies."

"He's a spy. He's a government agent, isn't he, Charles?"

He put out his hand as in protest. "I won't answer that question. It's important that you never hear that statement made. Truth is, anyway, I don't really know."

She rose. She felt more limp than angry.

"I'm sorry. I'm truly sorry."

She tried to smile.

"You know Hamilton, Angeline. Don't worry. I'd bet my other leg on his pulling through."

She did smile then and took the hand he offered.

"Oh, one more thing. And it isn't good news. Warren Ellis died last month. Eaten up by cancer." He watched her face go pale. "I was afraid you might not know. His solicitors wrote me. We've done business with Warren for years."

She didn't hear; he could see that. She was thinking of a boyish face, eyes that were Warren's eyes, honest and gentle. She was thinking—she groped for her chair and sat back down, overcome with pain both old and new.

A man in this end of the business had only a limited value. To be effective he must learn how to strike and move on. Cut his losses, leave no trails behind him, keep clean and concise and emotion-free.

Hamilton was one of the best and he knew it. He had performed his Northern assignments brilliantly. He would move now to other fields of action. At his own request these were to be nearer the front. He had known for the past several days that Warren was dead. But he hadn't been able to find his son. He needed to find the boy and tell him. Put the matter to rest, fulfill the trust.

He rode alone through the gathering Virginia twilight. Lonely. He had grown used to loneliness now, used to draining his thoughts and priming his senses. No visions of home rose up in his head. It was months now since he had conjured up Angeline's features. He couldn't afford the luxury. He rode with his senses alert, finely tuned to each other, doing all he knew how to ensure that he stayed alive.

Twenty-six

Hamilton folded the papers and tucked them inside his breast pocket. "Thank you, sir." He saluted the Northern general.

"Major Stanley." The man returned the salute.

Hamilton turned with ease, with no apparent hurry. Lifted the flap on the general's tent and stepped outside. Called for his horse and while he waited exchanged a joke with the sentry on guard. Then he mounted and rode through the tented campground, excited at what he carried inside his pocket, but glad to be out from under the general's eye. A few more yards and the camp would be behind him. A few more yards of this steady pace.

Niles rode back toward camp with his Southern prisoners. Three of them, officers every one. One had spied Niles down by the spring, but Niles got the drop on him, then discovered that there were two more—miles from their lines and unescorted. So he took the chance, surprised them as they were watering their horses, gathered their weapons and made one man tie the others while he watched, then tied the remaining prisoner, hands behind him, legs secured under the belly of his horse. A nice plum to ride into camp with rebel brass!

A few hundred yards from camp he saw the lone rider in blue approach him. He squinted his eyes: Who was the rider? An officer, he could see, as the man drew closer. He sat tall in the saddle, face lean and handsome, hair like the mingled shades of campfire color. He looked familiar . . . Niles drew rein.

Hamilton had assessed the situation in a moment: the young officer bringing his loot back to camp. But even from this distance the boy looked familiar. He slowed, he watched the young face carefully, wondering what capricious fate had arranged this moment.

The officer sat his horse in an easy manner. "What have we here?" Niles didn't like his tone. He stared incredulously as the officer drew out his pistol and aimed it squarely at his own chest.

200

"Your weapons, please," he said as he grabbed the lead rein and pulled the boy's mount close to his own. Deftly he removed Niles's knife and his hidden pistol. "Don't try anything rash." He glanced at the prisoners. "I'd be happy to pick you off one by one."

He smiled, but the smile was whimsical, lopsided. "We've something important to see to here. If you boys could just behave yourselves for a few moments." He winked at the foremost man and the man's eyes smiled. Something about the voice betrayed him. His accents weren't precise and clipped, but languid and honeyed and lazy—and Southern.

And suddenly Niles knew the man. And suddenly he was sick, and then angry. Hamilton saw the anger darken the boy's features.

"So you've finally figured out who I am." He was leading the horses back around the curve in the road, down a little gully, away from eyes that might stray by, might happen to see.

"What do you want of me?" Niles demanded.

"Patience, lad."

They left the prisoners in a group and rode a few rods further, but where Hamilton could watch both the prisoners and the road. Niles could contain himself no longer.

"You've no right to defile that uniform, rebel spy!" He spit out the words with indignant venom. Hamilton leaned back in the saddle and folded his arms. Calm, so blasted self-contained. Niles remembered that now. What had he called that quality? *Cavalier.* It disgusted him.

"We're not here to discuss my merits. Nor yours, for that matter." The man's gaze was too clear and demanding. Niles glanced away.

"Look at me, Niles. I've something to tell you. And I've no time to ease you into it as I'd like."

"There's nothing I'd like to discuss with you," Niles replied.

"Well, you're a prickly pear. Warren didn't warn me."

At the sound of his father's name Niles went stiff all over. Hamilton marked it as he continued. "You don't listen well, boy. I didn't say discuss. I have something to tell you. I was with your father last winter in Philadelphia—"

"The devil you were! In that uniform? You mean to tell me my father saw you, knew you for what you were and didn't—"

"Be quiet, Niles. For heaven's sake, let me say it." Something in Hamilton's voice stopped him cold. "He's a much smarter man than you are, Niles, believe me." The blue eyes wavered and couldn't hold. Niles watched, sure that what he saw in the eyes now was pain.

"Besides, as he said himself, his perspective was altered. When I saw him he was dying, Niles."

"I don't believe you! Why should I believe you?"

Hamilton reached into his pocket and drew out an envelope, wrinkled and worn. He held it out to Niles. "He asked me to give this to you." Niles made no move.

"Why you? He had friends, loyal friends he could have chosen."

Hamilton drew back his arm, placed the letter across his saddle. Disgust was in his blue eyes, thick in his voice. "You don't know beans about friendship, do you, boy? Or loyalty—or integrity, for that matter. Or love." The word seemed to ripple along his bones. "How dare you judge your father and his decisions! The letter's for you. Do you want it, boy?"

"Please." Niles held out his hand. Hamilton moved and placed the letter against his palm.

"Is he dead now?" Niles asked the question without moving.

"Yes, he died three months ago."

"Painful? Was his dying painful?"

Hamilton hesitated, made the boy meet his eyes. "Yes, as painful as anything you've seen here. More than a man should be asked to endure."

Hamilton turned, rode a few yards away. Niles felt his departure. His eyes were closed. He was drowning in pain. He wanted to curse, pound his fists against something! But he was aware that the quiet man waited and watched. He wanted to cry. Like a child, he craved comfort. Craved...the voice, the gentle hands, the beautiful face. It was Angeline's face he saw, her comfort he cried for. How twisted! That he should hate this man, and desire his daughter, and love his wife.

202

By the time Hamilton rode back Niles was able to face him. Ham had been doing his own thinking. He couldn't exactly say to the boy: "I don't know what that letter says, but I know one thing. You're bound to me, Niles, by a·promise made to a dead man." That wouldn't work right now. The boy thought him so much vermin. There would be other places for that, other times. This was more than enough to throw at him in one sitting.

"If you don't object, I believe I'll take my leave now." Niles blinked at the man with the slow, enigmatic grin.

"I'll have to report you, Mr. Stewart. I think you know that."

"Of course I know that. And I think you know that these prisoners will have to come along with me."

Niles struggled not to show his frustration. They rode to where the three prisoners waited. Hamilton cut their ropes and returned their weapons, then turned back to Niles, who was watching.

"I hate to do this. But I'm going to hit you as hard as I can. Anything less I'm afraid would be suspect. We'll roll you down into the gully—right there. Send your horse back into camp. They'll come out and find you." The caustic grin tugged at the corners of his mouth. "Who knows? With some luck you'll end up a hero."

Niles had no time to protest, to prepare for the blow. One moment he blinked his eyes, the next moment was blackness, with red firecrackers exploding against his brain.

_____Twenty-seven

Afton had not heard from Niles, though he'd promised to write. Her letters from Hugh came less frequently. There was work, always work enough to be doing. But days she was hungry and nights she couldn't sleep. It was Niles's face that disturbed her slumber—Niles's lips and Niles's eyes. She had been little more than a child when Hugh left her. She was nearly nineteen years old now, nearly a woman. Didn't a woman have a right to follow her heart?

Edmund rode through the gathering shadows toward Vicksburg. His thoughts, in the gloomy silence, were of the war. Everyone said the end was near now. He agreed. He didn't see how they'd kept going this far.

Richmond—ruined, evacuated—had fallen. Richmond, the center of everything real and symbolic in the South. He had heard that when Lincoln walked the streets of Richmond, Negroes fell to their knees in the streets before him. "Kneel only before God," he was reported to have told them.

President Davis was in Danville trying to hold things together. It was any man's guess what he felt now. In November the North had reelected Lincoln. Lincoln was better by far than McClellan would be! Actually, he didn't mind Lincoln. There was something about the man's gaunt face, or maybe what Edmund could read in his eyes. Over a year ago, after Gettysburg, his mother had made him sit down and read what Lincoln had said there. He found a gentle pathos in it, an eloquence of expression and thought. If somebody in the North had to hold the power, he'd rather it be Lincoln than most other men. He'd learned enough about human nature to know that.

Vicksburg was a city of laughter and pleasure. Gaslights spilled their glow on the crowded streets. Tied up at the wharf a showboat glittered, calliope music bubbling over the air. Edmund was told that Sally was out for the evening, attending one of the balls in town. That didn't sound like Sally. He hesitated. Should he turn around and go back or try to find her?

He walked till he found the address, a fine, stately mansion owned by a Northern gentleman and his wife. He walked past. The crowds spilled out through the open side doors: men in blue uniforms, ladies flirting and laughing. Sally couldn't be part of that crowd! He vaulted the hedge and skirted the gardens. When the moment was right he slipped inside, through the patio doors to the sparkling ballroom.

The sight before him dazzled his eyes. There was a fairy-tale world of beautiful women around him. He had never seen women dressed that way. He had been too young before the war to remember, to have been in such awesome company. Dress after marvelous dress floated past him: pale, delicate satins, golden brocades, velvets stained as bright as a peacock's plumage. Fair skin against the deep velvet, beautiful eyes, hair that brushed smooth white shoulders like silken rose petals—it was Sally he watched dancing by! A man in a long blue coat held her, arm at her waist, fingers against the white skin. It took his breath away to see her beauty, strangled his breath to see the man's pleasure and pride.

When the dance ended he strode out on the floor and found her and confronted her bluntly. "What are you doing here?"

She recoiled. This wasn't like Edmund. He seemed determined to be discourteous and unkind.

"Edmund, come over here, sit down, and I'll tell you."

"Tell me here and now," he demanded. "I'll not be waylaid."

"All right." She knew how he felt about Yankees. He would know, of course, whose house this was. It was a Yankee he'd seen her with, dancing.

"My aunt and my cousin are staying with us," she explained. "They are old friends of Major Hinckley and his wife. It was one of those invitations that can't be refused. My mother insisted. Edmund—please."

He glared at her, hurt and unrelenting.

"Did she insist that you dance with the Northern soldier and look up into his eyes that way?"

"Excuse me; I believe you are bothering the lady."

Edmund didn't deign to look up or turn his head. "Excuse *me*, I believe the lady is with me, sir."

"Oh, no, on that count you are sadly mistaken. This is my home, sir, and the lady is my guest."

Edmund turned to slowly face the blue-coated Yankee, at the same time placing his arm around Sally's waist.

"Miss Fielding is coming with me." It was a statement, a challenge, the glove thrown down.

"You're a rebel, aren't you?" He looked Edmund over with cold disdain. "Let me see your pass. Your signed oath of allegiance."

Edmund glared at the Yankee, not moving a muscle.

"I demand it, sir," he pressed. "It's my right to demand it."

Sally thought she would faint from the fear inside. With the most casual disregard Edmund turned, took the arm that Sally offered, and walked off the floor. He was used to walking unscathed through the jaws of danger. He was used to going his own way. Alexander Hinckley blinked his eyes and watched him. Another young man who'd been watching moved up beside him.

"Are you going to let him disgrace you? Let's get 'im, Alex."

His mother would never stand for trouble right here on the grounds. Half a block away they caught up with the girl and the rebel.

"Halt!" they demanded.

Edmund kept walking. Hinckley drew out his pistol and fired once, over their heads. Edmund pushed Sally against the fence they were passing, protecting her with his body. "Go home," he demanded.

"I won't leave you."

"For the love of heaven, Sally, go home!" He turned back to the men.

Hinckley still held the gun. "You got one more chance, rebel. Be a good boy and show us your pass."

Edmund didn't move.

"Let me soften him up a bit," his friend whispered.

Hinckley nodded and held the gun against Edmund's temple. The man hit Edmund once very hard in the stomach. Then again. Edmund moved to fight back. Hinckley clicked back the hammer.

"I wouldn't do that, rebel." His eyes glistened. "It's a sure way to get a bullet inside your skull."

The man who was hitting Edmund enjoyed it. He kept hitting until he was down, then he started kicking. Sally dug her fingernails into her palm to keep from screaming, and ran as fast as she could for help.

There was a knife in Edmund's boot if he only could reach it. He rolled onto his stomach, then up on his knees. But the blows kept coming, the blows were vicious. He slipped beneath them, then suddenly reared, swept his body and arm around in one murderous swing. The other man grunted and stumbled back. Edmund struck him. Square in the middle, once more in the face. The man cried out and fell to his knees.

Edmund lunged for Hinckley. He never even heard the shot. It shattered his lungs, splintered his shoulder, and snuffed out the raging pain at last.

Coming back with a friend she had fortunately happened to meet, Sally heard the shot and went wild inside. She had almost made it! She threw herself against Hinckley, pounding his chest, crying and calling him names like a mad woman. He threw her off with horror and distaste. A crowd had gathered to watch. Hinckley moved closer.

"Listen, Sally, you'd better not think about causing trouble." His voice was cold and ugly. Sally moved back. "He's illegal. He's got no right to be walking the streets here. I could have him thrown into jail—let him die there. You want that?"

He continued as Sally began to moan. "You know I can do it. I have the power." He kicked at the motionless body, more confident now. "Get him out of here. Out of Vicksburg. You understand me? Now! You get him out 'fore I change my mind."

She bent over the poor bruised body to hide her tears. He moved to the edge of the circle that had gathered. "Just a rebel trouble maker. You know the type, folks. Everything's under control. You can go on home..." His voice droned on, his voice became echo as they lifted Edmund and carried him away.

They made a bed in the back of a wagon. Sally held his head while her father drove. After a while she lost track of the towns, of the hours. After a long while she felt the wagon shudder and stop. She lifted her head. The stars glimmered like bits of ice in a pewter sky. By the dim light she could see the tall square front of the house. White with six columns, long porches upstairs and down. A brick walk bordered by trimmed hedges. An air of peace and serenity. Lairdswood.

There was no warning. Someone banged at the big front door. Angeline lit a candle and went down the stairs. When she saw him—when she opened the door, when they carried him in—it was like a scene of Dante's making, a horror re-created, relived. She indicated the card room. "In here," she told them. They had to bend up his legs; he was tall for the couch. The man didn't want to let her see him. She stared him down. "I've been through this once before," she said.

It was Sally who fetched the basin of water and held it while Angeline washed his face, cleaned the cuts and bruises with deft, sure fingers. Her father went out to the cabins to rouse a black man, a black man named Moses, to ride for the doctor. Then he returned, but Angeline shooed him away. *There are a few differences this time,* she thought grimly. *This time I am the mistress and in command.*

Sally felt it. Sally watched her, drawn by her gentle eyes, by the strength in her face. *She's very beautiful. Stately—more young than I had imagined...*

Angeline, wringing out the cloth over the basin, looked into Sally's sweet young face. *So this is the girl. She's very lovely. I like the way she will meet my eyes. Her skin's very pretty...*

"Tell me what happened," she said. Sally shuddered. She knew she would need to be honest with this woman. She took a deep breath and began to speak.

It took the doctor a long time to get there. When he came in he asked them kindly to leave.

"I'll do all I can for him, Angeline," William Humphreys promised. "I had trouble enough getting him here; I don't plan to let go."

They walked out together. The older woman's eyes were large and haunted. She stood and stared at the blank, closed door.

"That's the room where his father died," she said softly. Sally felt a tremor run through her like ice. "I was pregnant with Edmund. I'd planned to tell him when he came home that evening from hunting." She shuddered, rubbed her hands along her arms.

"But they carried him in. Hamilton carried him in like a baby. He never opened his eyes. He never knew."

"I had no idea—"

"Of course you wouldn't."

They waited a long time. Angeline walked in the gardens. She didn't want to repeat the scene, to be standing outside the door when it opened. She prayed, as well as she knew how to pray, to the only god she had any feeling for, Fletcher's God. She prayed that this cup would be lifted from her, that she wouldn't have to live through the nightmare again. She prayed for Hamilton. How could he take it? How could she tell him and watch his face?

And at last she prayed for the girl, young and frightened, who, if Edmund lived, would be part of Lairdswood, she knew. Another woman to take up quiet possession, bear children here, work her way into the house, begin to think and feel and breathe Lairdswood.

When she came back inside, the doctor was in the hallway. He walked over to where she stood and took her hands.

"He's young and strong," he said, "and the wound was clean. I've dug out the ball—heaven knows I've had enough practice. He'll live, Angeline. Your son will live."

Sally, listening, turned to the quiet woman, who looked suddenly vulnerable and young. She saw behind the beautiful eyes that met hers all the qualities that had made her love the son. And she went to the arms that opened for her, laid her head against the soft shoulder, and cried.

Twenty-eight

It was over. It was done with and ended. How could four-and-a-half years of hell and inhuman suffering end so briefly, so quietly?

On Palm Sunday, Lee met with Grant near Appomattox Courthouse, in the front room of Wilmer McClean's farmhouse. Lee's men had been living for days on parched corn for rations. He discussed terms with the Union general—magnanimous terms. On April ninth Lee made formal surrender; the Army of Northern Virginia was no more.

Grant authorized trainloads of provisions for Lee's twenty-five thousand hungry boys. Ordered his men to stop the victory salute they fired. It wasn't his way to rub salt into the wound.

Lee appeared and a shout of welcome rose up from his army. Then silence, sudden silence, as a sign of respect, with every hat raised and tears running down grim faces. He rode slowly through his lines. Hamilton was there. He watched the men reach out to touch him, to press their fingers against his horse. Lee and Traveller had covered the dark road together. Now there were no roads stretching to distance; there was no place to go.

It was over. Hamilton stood and listened as Lee gave his farewell address to his troops:

> I need not tell the survivors of so many hard-fought battles, who have remained steadfast to the last, that I have consented to this result from no distrust of them;—I have determined to avoid the useless sacrifice of those whose past services have endeared them to their countrymen . . .

Seventy-eight thousand Mississippi men had served in the forces. Thirty-six percent didn't live to return. Fifteen thousand died of disease, twelve thousand in battle.

> I earnestly pray that a merciful God will extend to you His blessing and protection. With an increasing admiration of your constancy and devotion . . . of your kind and generous consideration of myself, I bid you an affectionate farewell.

It was over. Lee rode head bare, tears flowing freely. Officers and men, by the terms of agreement, could return to their homes. The veteran soldiers gently retired the Confederate flag for the final time and, with Lee's admonition in their ears—restore the country and reestablish peace—they began to retrace their steps back home.

It was over. It was only just beginning.

Could New Orleans be anything but excitement and madness? The streets were strewn with returning soldiers and greedy civilians. Hamilton walked Bourbon Street. He had seen to his business, tied up what loose ends he could find to tie. It was time to turn his back on it all. It was time to go home.

He found the boat on which he'd booked passage and went aboard. There still was nothing more wildly romantic than a steamboat, sitting low in the water, all glitter and lights, head reared into the stars, gently dozing and dreaming, water lapping against her sides like a lullaby. The saloon, he noticed, still boasted a garish gilt ceiling and rows of dazzling chandeliers. There would be better fare here than hardtack and cornbread.

A light-footed colored waiter brought him a drink. He smiled at the man and took a look around. Even wars as bad as this one didn't kill off the card sharks, he noticed. And riverboat gamblers reigned supreme. Hamilton, watching a group of men playing, thought he had one pegged. He ambled across the saloon for a different view. One of the young men at the table looked very familiar.

He circled and walked up behind him, stood a moment, then placed his fingers lightly along the lad's arm. "I wouldn't play that hand, son. The odds are against you."

The other players looked up; the gambler snarled. "Keep your nose out. This game isn't your affair."

Hamilton's eyes were flint hard, more gray than blue. "This young man is my affair." The gambler didn't answer. Motioning toward him, Hamilton continued. "I would suggest, gentlemen, that you check this man's cards. I believe they might not be quite in order . . ."

That was all that was needed; the men would take care of the rest. No reason to stay for the fireworks. Hamilton turned. He felt someone at his elbow.

"You turn up in unlikely places," the young man said.

"Unlikely places! This boat is headed for Natchez. What about you?"

Niles returned his steady gaze. "I'm heading to Natchez. Or, more precisely, to Lairdswood. How about you?"

Hamilton smiled. His smile could be so compelling.

"If you recall the last time we met," Niles went on, "you left in quite a hurry."

"I recall that. I see you survived our little encounter." Hamilton, curious, cocked his head. The young man, he could see, was enjoying something.

"As it happened, you weren't the only one with news. If you'd stuck around I might have told you about your family—"

"What! You have a poor memory. As I remember, you wouldn't have given me the time of day."

"You're right," Niles smiled.

"So, where's the difference? The war's over and everyone's friends? I don't think that's it."

"You don't give a man an inch, do you?" Niles walked to the deck. There was moon on the water. He leaned over and watched the line of the shore slide past. "You gave me a letter from my father, remember? He has a way of putting things—or he had. I've had plenty of time to think—"

"That's not all."

"No, it isn't." He turned, and his eyes were so guileless that Hamilton started. "If I'm going to marry your daughter, I figured I'd first better come to terms with you."

Hamilton raised an eyebrow. "So cut and dried? And the terms?"

"The terms are simple. You did what you had to. You were loyal to what you believed was right. If a man does that, another's got no right to judge him."

"Why, thank you for explaining it for me so well." Hamilton's smile had turned lopsided, but his sarcasm was gentle.

"Drat you! All right. I sound a pompous young fool!"

He stared at the older man and his eyes became gentle, gentle and tired and touched by pain. "My father loved you," he said. "That's enough for me."

They watched the river for a while in silence.

"Marry my daughter? Has that been settled?"

"She hasn't said yes—but I haven't asked her." There was tenderness in his voice that he couldn't hide.

"A bit confident, aren't you? Some would say cocky?" There was laughter in Hamilton's voice.

Niles tilted his head. His eyes met the sparkling challenge in Hamilton's eyes. "How could anyone named after you, sir, be anything less?"

They rode the oak-lined path to Lairdswood together. One in a faded gray jacket, the other in blue. One with his old dreams tattered and desecrated, one with his new dreams shining behind his eyes. The trees leaned over the path, arms meeting, trailing the long fairy moss above their heads. Surrounded by beauty they rode, surrounded by memory, crushing the dust of yesterday under their feet, growing tomorrow's secrets inside their hearts.

Afton had been out riding. She sat and watched them, aching with recognition and delight. It was as though she had already seen it happen: the man in gray taller and older, well-loved, woven with childhood content and pleasure; the man in blue younger, exciting, unknown, woven with shades of promise and desire. Both of them part of her; something she couldn't deny.

She rode like a rush of fresh air to meet them, stirring the moss into tangles as she passed. Hamilton drew in his breath. For a moment it had been Angeline riding to meet him, young again! Then he held in his arms his woman-daughter and he could see in her face that her beauty was her own—drawn from Angeline, from himself, from Eliza, but wonderfully fashioned and rearranged.

"I think I'll ride on ahead and find your mother. I believe Niles has a few things he'd like to say."

She turned to the boy. He reached out and touched her, wiping the tears from her cheek with a gentle hand.

Angeline was alone in the arboretum. The arboretum had always been overgrown. Perhaps some of the trees needed pruning, but trees are patient. The war hadn't done any damage here. The past rested undisturbed, unchallenged, moving surely, painlessly, noiselessly into the present. Nature survived by such natural process; why couldn't men?

"Angeline."

She had not heard nor seen him. She turned at the sound of his voice. He sought her eyes. Gray-blue eyes that were laughing and hungry, brown eyes that were wide with wonder and joy.

It was as though there had been no yesterdays, no pain. It was as though there had been no time, no distance between them.

He kissed her hair, her throat, her lips—at last he held her. There was so much to say, and no words to use.

"How can it be so good between us?" he asked. "Better than when we were young?"

"All good things get better. Truth doesn't tarnish with time. Neither does love."

"Nor beauty."

She was more beautiful today than when he had left her. Beauty could grow from inside, he knew that, and slow the hands of time and change.

There would be long days ahead for her to work beside him, to memorize again the lines of his face, to gaze into his blue-gray eyes—to get lost in the gazing. There would be long nights ahead to lie in his arms and listen, to say all the things she wanted to say—Angeline knew that. But there was one thing that needed saying right now, one thing he needed to hear.

"You kept your promise. You held us together, Hamilton."

"Not alone. It was a young man's boast. You did it, Angie."

She threw back her head and smiled, though her eyes were misted. "Only because I'm part of you, then. Through the depths of despair, with everything falling around us, it was you who kept me going. And you came home."

"Yes, I came home. But there's still tomorrow." He felt empty, knowing how great was his need to give, how much he could no longer offer.

"Yes, there's tomorrow." She shook her head. "We've never run away from tomorrow, have we? I love you, Hamilton. What are we waiting for?"

He lifted her into his arms, though she protested, and carried her through the gardens toward the house. The tears ran down his cheeks but he didn't stop them. He had never felt so alive and so clean before.

She touched his burnished hair with tender fingers, and pressed her cool lips against his cheek.

"Welcome to Lairdswood, Hamilton. Welcome home."

Epilogue

Jamie Ellis stood on the bluff above the river. He held in his hand the book his father had given him. The book and the faded picture of Angeline Gordon. It made him feel warm inside to remember the moment, that afternoon in his father's study when his father had talked to him man to man and revealed to his son his deepest feelings. Jamie regarded the time as sacred between them. Maybe some boys wouldn't. But he and his father had never been much for talking things out together, for putting words to what they were feeling inside. That afternoon something had happened between them. Both felt it, both knew it was rare and good. He walked out of the room knowing more about his father than he'd learned in the past nineteen years—knowing that he would never do anything to defile that moment, to destroy the faith and joy in his father's eyes.

It was as though he somehow carried it all inside him. Because of his father's conversion to the gospel he was here. And this book he held was part of his father's conversion. These people whose dust could not speak from the grave, but whose spirits could speak to his listening spirit, had part in what he was, and his sons to follow— and *their* sons, on and on. He was here today, as full of his yester-days as of his tomorrows . . .

He drew out the old, dim daguerreotype. Angeline Gordon. Some of his sisters, his father had told him, had Angeline's nose. Rebeccah had her eyes, he could see that. Was it Angeline who had marked the Book of Mormon? He had read and reread, even memorized, some of the sections. He felt he knew something about the person who'd marked them. But it was Fletcher's name written inside the cover. Was it he who had read the book? Jamie wished he knew.

He turned, with the picture in his hand, and faced the river. The grand old Mississippi still rolled to the sea, deep and sure, its bright surface sparkling. Angeline Gordon Stewart — what had she been like? Had she ever stood on this very bluff by the river, where Silver Street wound down to the flats below, and gazed across the beautiful sweep of water? How had the river looked to the deep brown eyes? What feelings had stirred behind the beautiful face?

"Well, I'm here," he said out loud, "if you want me. If you've anything to say, you can say it now. I'm here, and I'm doing my best to listen."

His companion waved to him from down below. There were three sets of Elders waiting; he'd better be going. He took one last, long look. A steamship sat in the water, tall and graceful: the *Delta Queen*. Her stern wheel churned a stream of frothy white bubbles; her whistle shivered across the clear air.

He walked the steep, rutted path to Natchez-Down-Under. As he walked he slipped the picture back inside the book. But the face stayed with him — the face and the beautiful eyes. He knew there was more here than what he was seeing, a few dusty old buildings that hugged the river's edge. He could *feel* it.

He smiled to himself. He was glad to be living. He was where he should be, doing what he ought to be doing. He couldn't wait to see what tomorrow would bring.